# Haunting The Scavenger

Arlo Blackthorn

Cover: Arlo Blackthorn & Z.F. © 2025
Editor: Morgan Cunningham



First Printing March 24th, 2026
ISBN: 979-8-218-81502-8

This book is dedicated to
Morgan & Maxine

*Please see the very back of the book for a list of content warnings. This novel contains content some readers may find upsetting or disturbing.*


☽ ✧ ☾


You can learn more about Arlo and his work at:
**www.arloblackthorn.com**

# PROLOGUE

DECEMBER 5th, 2002 - Upstate New York

Snowflakes collected in the pale eyelashes that ringed the woman's empty amber eyes. Her expression was still blown wide with shock. Short blond hair slipped from her headband as her head lolled back, staring out into nothingness. Her body had been impaled upon the wing of a stone cherub that sat atop the gaudy fountain. Her organs had begun to slip out into the basin of the fountain, the water dyed an awful shade of rust from her blood. Flashes of crime scene photography illuminated her bluing flesh.

The muffled stillness of the night air was punctuated by the shrill sound of police sirens, their red and blue lights illuminating the banks of fresh white snow. Several cop cars were crowded around the fountain that sat in the center of the roundabout in front of the dilapidated Victorian mansion. The structure was a dark looming void in the night, a forgotten set piece amidst the action. Sitting on the crumbling porch was a tall shivering figure draped in a blanket. Their head was hung in their hands, face obscured by a curtain of frizzy strawberry blond curls. They were being consoled with little effect by one of the many disgruntled EMTs.

A gorgeous woman with long black tresses and wrapped tightly in a fur coat was speaking furiously with the police detective in charge. The investigator looked far more disgusted by the corpse behind her than she did.

"His mother, *my sister*, just jumped off the third-story balcony in front of him, and you want to take him in for questioning!?" The dark-haired woman spat at the officer. Her tone was sharp and accusatory.

"Ma'am, with all due respect, he is the only direct witness. The kid needs to give a witness report at the least. As you said, he was alone here with her before calling you to the scene," the investigator tried to explain to her.

"You and I both know he's in shock. What could you possibly

expect him to tell you?" She snapped. Her expression grew mournful, her emotion changing in a flash. Tears welled up in her mesmerizing lavender eyes.

"My sister struggled with her morbid demeanor since childhood," the woman began to cry. "She's been quite unwell for some time, no matter how hard I tried to help. The cutting of her department's funding must have been the last straw, oh, the poor girl!" The dark-haired woman pulled a handkerchief from her coat and dabbed at her running mascara. "Her work has been the only thing keeping her going in these past years!" She showered sorrowful tears at the investigator, who was growing increasingly uncomfortable. The detective hesitantly reached out to console her before retracting his gesture and standing up a bit straighter. The crying woman sighed and rummaged in the pocket of her fur coat. She produced a large snakeskin pocketbook and shuffled through it until she'd pulled out a thick white envelope.

"Perhaps this could convince you to expedite your inspection? So our family can properly morn?" She sniffed, offering the envelope to the police investigator. He swallowed hard as she brandished it in his direction.

"Ma'am, I couldn't possibly... take this." His eyes glazed over as the dark-haired woman walked closer to him, the very essence of night gathering around her. Her voice was now only audible between the two of them.

"You are going to take this bribe, and you are going to take all your little underlings and leave my property untouched. You won't question my nephew. You won't question me. You will take my sister's body directly to the morgue where she can be transported to the funeral home without delay. Let us call this a *donation* from the Giovanni family, yes?" She said with a venomously cool tone. The man's face went blank as he took the envelope.

"Yes, of course... we won't be giving you any trouble, madam. I... apologies for my... rudeness. My condolences," he said in a slow drawl, as if the words were being pulled from his mouth. She gave him a pat on the cheek with a gloved hand.

"That's a good *porcellino*," she said with a vicious grin that revealed her razor-sharp canines.

# CHAPTER ONE

JULY 20th, 2003 - Upstate New York

The broiling summer air was as asphyxiating as a wet blanket stretched over Montague's face. He stared absentmindedly at the morning light pouring over him through the skylights overhead. He brushed lingering nightmare sweat from his brow. Slowly his foggy mind woke, causing him to become acutely aware of the deflating air mattress underneath him. He was far too large for the cheap thing, and his back ached. Despite his best efforts, he always woke up halfway sunk to the floor in a too-soft plastic cocoon. His little pseudo-bedroom setup was horribly out of place in the meticulously decorated living room, clashing with the matching sage furniture set.

With a soft grunt, he rolled up and out of bed, reluctant to face the day. He pulled on the pair of baggy bluejeans that were crumpled in the "not so dirty" pile on the floor, not bothering to change the tank top he'd been sleeping in. Despite the best efforts of the house's stale air conditioning, it was still oppressively humid. The summer heat was already starting to seep into the large ranch-style house, making his bare feet stick to the floor as he walked into the kitchen.

The "Tuscan" aesthetic kitchen was a bit claustrophobic, likely from the unnecessary quantity of ceramic roosters and bottles of mystery peppers in oil strewn around as "decoration." His best friend and host, Mina, was already sitting at the kitchen island on one of the bar stools. She was a short woman with heavily tattooed arms, a pretty soft face, and dark monolid eyes. She was texting away on her pink Sidekick, its plastic charms rattling in time with her furious thumbs. The sweet cereal in front of her was dyeing the milk blue as it went soggy.

"Good morning, sleepyhead," she greeted him, not looking up from her texting. "Coffee's still hot." She nodded her head towards the percolator on the counter.

"Morn'in," he replied with a grunt. "Don't you work today?" He asked, pouring himself burnt coffee and getting his own bowl of tooth rotting off brand cereal. He grabbed the newspapers that were sitting on the edge of the kitchen island and started flipping through them as he sat down to eat.

"Not till noon," Mina replied, absentmindedly running her hand over the fly-aways in her sleek black hair. "How did you sleep?" she asked.

"About as good as you can expect," he shrugged with a mouthful of processed grains.

"So not great? Maybe I can ask the 'rents to see about getting a fold-out?" She asked, looking up from her phone finally. She closed the keypad and slipped it into the front pocket of her grease-stained pastel pink overalls.

"Don't worry about it. I don't plan on leeching off your parents for much longer," he said, pulling open the classified section, scanning over for any new listings he might have missed.

"You're not a leech, Monty! You know you're always welcome here. You're as welcome now as when you were seventeen," she added.

He grumbled a "sure," which came out far more sarcastic than he'd intended. "This just isn't the same as high school. Being disowned for being outed to my parents is, like, fundamentally different from being a dropout loser."

"Dude, it's only been a few months. Cut yourself some damn slack. It's not your fault your professor took a long walk off a short pier."

"Mina, that sounds worse than just saying she killed herself," he cringed. As by some strange twist of fate, at that same moment his eyes scanned over a job listing that made his heart skip.

"I'm sorry. I'm just saying that Dr. Giovanni's death was super sudden, and you two were pretty close. I don't think anyone is surprised that the stress of that whole thing led to you flunking out. They honestly should have let you take a leave of absence," she clarified. The mention of his professor's name made his stomach squirm. His eyes flicked back to the same surname printed in the papers in his hand. He shook his head, folding them shut.

"But they didn't, and now I'm here. If I could have swung it without the scholarship, they probably would have let me. Either way, it doesn't matter. I don't have a degree, and I don't think any labs would hire me with a 'trust me, bro, I did three years of biochem at SUNY,'" he said with lingering bitter bile in his throat. He pushed his cereal away, beginning to feel nauseated. Mina let out a short, frustrated breath.

"My point is, don't beat yourself up for things that are clearly out of your control," she said, visibly fed up with Monty's self-deprecation. "Speaking of, how is the job search going?"

"I wish I'd hear anything back from that ski resort," he sighed.

"I'm sure something will pan out eventually. I can see if Kev would change his mind if you need me to?" She suggested, mentioning the man who owned the body shop she worked at.

"I will think about it, but," he brandished the newspapers now clenched in his fist, "I have a lead I'm gonna check out today."

Mina raised her brows into her blunt fringe and gave him a thumbs up. "Well, good luck!"

)  ✧  (

Montague proceeded to spend most of the day wasting gas in his 1992 Dodge Caravan that Mina had revived for him. It was not until the afternoon college radio show came on over the stereo that he realized he'd spent most of his day procrastinating. He turned the tinny rock music down and parked along one of the many disused side roads that connected the more rural properties in town.

The whole town had a positively abandoned feeling in the off season. It was one of those ski resort spots in upstate New York that only saw action between fall and winter. Soon the quiet downtown would be packed with tourists, all ready to pick apples or break their ankles on the bunny hill. That being said, most of the entry-level, low-skilled, local jobs were seasonal, so finding work in late summer was not impossible.

He straightened out the slightly crushed morning papers across his front dash. His eyes scanned over the classifieds again in an attempt to find the advertisement that had leapt out at him over breakfast. Just as he was ready to assume he'd imagined it, he found it again. It was a simple manual labor position that promised decent pay and room and board. That fact alone was not what had caught Monty's eye, although it was an attractive job offer. No, it was the name of the person who had placed the ad in the classifieds.

*Cameron Giovanni.*

It was reported that Dr. Giovanni had jumped from the third story of her family's estate. However, many, including Monty himself, had suspected that there was foul play involved in her death. He couldn't remember who Cameron was, but he was almost positive that they were Dr. Giovanni's child. He wondered if there was enough money in the family estate to warrant matricide. He shook the thought from his head.

Just the chance to get close to that place sent electricity through his fingertips. He stared down at the phone number in the ad, speculating that, even if it was a scam, he'd have very little to lose. Worst-case scenario, no one would pick up. Without even realizing his fingers were moving, he dialed the number on his dying flip phone. He eagerly waited as it rang, for what felt like an abnormally long time.

"H-hello?" a quiet voice cautiously answered the phone. He could feel his heart racing with anticipation. He was genuinely surprised anyone had answered.

"Hello, is this the Giovanni estate? My name is Monty–I mean Montague Varon, and I'm calling about your ad in the paper for a groundskeeper," he began in the most professional voice he could muster. He absentmindedly slipped a finger through the silver chain around his neck that sported a small hamsa amulet.

"Oh… You're the first person to call about that," they paused.

"Are you still offering the position?" He asked.

"Yes! Yes, it's still very open… Sorry this is short notice, but would you be available to come to the estate for an interview today?" They asked. "Let's say around five o'clock this evening?"

Monty was taken aback at how soon they wanted him to come. He glanced at his watch.

*3:52 PM.*

"I would be more than happy to," he replied and then shuffled around in his center console looking for a pen, "can you give me the address?"

"Certainly, it's 67 Blackberry Place. It's a hidden driveway, easy to miss. If you are coming from downtown and see a horse ranch, you've gone too far down the road," they explained. He scribbled the directions down on the side of the newspaper.

"Great, got it!"

"I have to ask, before you come all this way, do you feel confident you can manage the workload? I will provide all the tools necessary for the job. However, this position will be fairly grueling."

"Oh, yeah, I'm expecting a load of manual labor," Monty replied.

He was not thinking about the actual logistics of the job. His mind had become preoccupied with the prospect of finding out what had actually happened to Dr. Giovanni.

"Good, then I look forward to meeting you. When you get up to the gate, just hit the buzzer and I'll let you in."

"Okay, I'll be there soon, thank you," he said and looked over his notes again. Without another word, the person on the other end hung up.

For a moment he pondered if this was a bad idea. He had so many unanswered questions. There was no guarantee that those answers would be found on that property. His mind wandered to the person he'd just spoken with. Their voice sounded thin and sharp with misery. What sort of life did Dr. Giovanni live to leave behind such an heir?

Montague peeked at himself in the rearview mirror. Two exhausted brown eyes blinked back at him. His goatee was a bit unkempt and his thick black hair was in a perpetual state of messy. All of this, mixed with his slightly crooked aquiline nose, made him look older than he truly was. He let out a sigh of discontent, realizing how disheveled he looked.

*Oh well, no time to fix this mess.*

He had no issues finding the previously mentioned hidden driveway. It had a weathered postbox at the end of the drive with a golden '67' emblazoned on the side. Just a little way up the drive was a huge wrought-iron gate that looked as if it had not been touched in thirty years. The bars were entangled with dried summer weeds, rusted beyond recognition in some spots. The gate appeared to go all the way around the property, swallowed into the acres of woods that sprawled on either side of the drive.

He hesitantly leaned out his window to press the archaic-looking call button. It let out a horrific buzzing sound. After a long pause, the gates swung open with an earsplitting squeak. The actual driveway itself was a horribly maintained dirt road leading up a hill through heavy tree cover. Every inch felt unpleasant to drive on, as if he himself were rolling bare on the gravel. As the house came into view, he felt a souring sensation in his stomach.

Sitting coiled upon itself on creaking boards was an oppressive, looming Victorian with a tower to the east spiraling up into the trees. There was a balcony on the third floor that hung heavy over the center of the house, almost threatening to come crashing down on anyone unfortunate enough to be standing below. The wraparound porch was warped in a way that made it look like an unwelcome smile. It too was engulfed by what once was likely a beautiful garden, now rendered to withering wisteria and writhing weeds. The columns holding up the balcony's support looked ready to give way at any moment, soft and rotting.

Along the ivy-plagued western half was a glinting glass room that looked like it might have once been an atrium. Now plants spilled from its broken glass roof like the guts of a slaughtered animal. In front of the manor, there was a decaying paver stone roundabout with a magnificent sculpted fountain sat in its center. The tear-streaked cherub atop the fountain had its wings outstretched to the heavens, and a mouth agape in warning.

*Oh, fuck this.*

It was hard for him to wrap his mind around the fact that this was where Dr. Giovanni had lived. The place looked virtually abandoned. Did she truly live in such decay? He had a nagging sensation that someone was playing a prank on him.

He parked his minivan in the roundabout and steeled himself to walk past the forebodingly dry fountain. He found himself holding his breath as though he were passing a grave. The porch did not do any work to ease his nerves as it creaked violently under his heavy feet. He gave a firm knock on one of the huge double oak doors to the mansion. He examined the rounded stained glass over the doors as he waited. They were shaped like spiderwebs, and through them he could see nothing but pitch. This place might have been beautiful once, an opulent display of wealth, but it had long been left to rot. Despite being no more than a few minutes, it felt like he had been waiting at the door for an eternity.

Finally, one of the large wooden doors opened to reveal a tall wisp of a person. They were a bony structure with broad shoulders, sharp hips and a slender waist, all accentuated by a clinging black dress. They had long, delicate features with downturned lavender-blue eyes. Framing their dour face was a wild head of curly strawberry blond hair that cascaded past their shoulders. They patiently hung in the doorway like a spider on a thread.

"You must be Cameron?" Montague tried his very best not to stare at the beautiful stranger before him.

"Yes, Montague, correct?" They asked in a cool, mid-toned voice.

"Yeah, I'm here for the groundskeeping—" he paused to look up at the decaying porch, "um, the job you posted in the papers." He nervously straightened his gray plaid flannel, pushing his sleeves up over his elbow a little further. He was too hot, and yet he felt uncomfortably underdressed. He should have gone back to Mina's and changed.

"Please come inside." Cameron waved him into the mansion. He followed automatically.

Montague's jaw dropped at the size of the entrance alone. In front of him was the largest staircase he had ever seen, covered with a rich, albeit dusty, burgundy carpet that lolled over the entrance like a fat tongue. The railings were of carved wood, twisting up to the two other stories as though they were snakes slithering up the steps.

At the top of the entrance on the third story was a grandiose stained-glass window. It sported a huge golden serpentine family crest that cascaded dim light in hues of red and gold into the mostly dark entrance. High above them was a heavy, cobweb-encrusted chandelier. The crystals hanging from it were so deeply caked in burnt dust that they looked like pale obsidian.

"I'm afraid that the estate is in far worse condition than you may have expected," Cameron continued as they led Montague down a dark, dusty hallway to the main living space. Every inch of paint and ancient floral wallpaper he could see was cracked or peeling. The home itself was also horrifically dark. Oddly, light struggled to penetrate the old walls, likely lending to the musty smell of the place. He felt a lack of traction under his work boots from the amount of dust that was caked to the old-growth oak floors.

The drawing room was not much better. Not only was it covered in soot, but there was also a strong lingering smell of cigarette smoke. Dust stuck more aggressively to the nicotine-coated walls. Two opulent and faded couches sat across from each other with a glass coffee table in the middle of them. The furniture sat on a defaced rug in front of a fireplace that had a low fire crackling away, casting a gloomy glow over the room, and making the room swelteringly hot.

Above the fireplace hung three portraits. Directly over the mantle was a huge 'family portrait' type painting. In the oil there was the figure of a rather harsh woman with short bleached hair dressed in a modest golden gown. Her face was narrow with a long sharp nose and sad amber eyes that gave her a perpetually severe cast. Montague instantly recognized her as Dr. Giovanni.

Sat in front of her was a young person with almost the exact same face as her, but with an impressive head of curly strawberry blond hair. They looked like a gangly teenaged sort, dressed in a dark, blousy dress that was far too juvenile for them. He assumed this strawberry-headed adolescent was a younger Cameron.

On the left, there was a single rococo-style portrait of a woman he did not recognize. She had a softer face than the other two Giovannis, but her eyes were unsettlingly similar. Her appearance was more sultry than sour. She was depicted in beautiful jewels with a head of dark wavy hair. On the right was another portrait of the doctor. She looked a tad younger in this one, with longer bleached hair and a classy yellow dress. She was adorned with only a simple golden locket with a script G on it.

Cameron waved a hand for Montague to sit on the couch

opposite them, bringing him back to the task at hand. A plume of dust met him as he sat down on the couch. Now sitting in this spot, he realized the room was absolutely littered with empty wine bottles. Cameron produced a gold cigarette case and pulled out a black clove cigarette for themself, before holding the case out to him.

"Oh, no thank you, I don't smoke," he said with a raised hand.

They raised a slender eyebrow. "No worries. If you change your mind, all you have to do is ask." They snapped the case shut and lit their cigarette with the elaborate serpent-shaped table lighter in front of them. With a twist of guilt, he realized then that they spoke exactly like their mother.

Cameron took a long drag and sat quietly for a moment. They then opened the folder that was on the table and pulled the papers from it onto their lap. They brushed their hair from their gaunt face.

"So, I put the job title down as groundskeeper, but in all honesty, I-I am not sure exactly what you'd call this job," they stuttered. "I need someone to fix up both the land as well as the mansion. I would like to restore it to at least a state that makes it appear that *someone* lives here. I know it's a fairly tall order. The first few months of the job would just be repairing everything as much as possible before the winter. The long-term portion of the job would then become routine maintenance."

"That's a lot of work for one person," Montague remarked. Cameron nodded in agreement.

"I don't have a time limit for when it needs to be presentable. There are just a few things that must get done before the fall sets in. The pay is five hundred a week, *cash*. You will also receive lodging accommodations with utilities paid. I'll obviously pay for all the materials and equipment needed for repairs as well," Cameron outlined their contract. Montague nodded along. It was slowly dawning on him that this *was* real and not some kind of prank.

"What are these lodging amenities included in the job?" He asked, curious, but ultimately knowing he was not likely going to turn down the opportunity.

"There is a servant cabin near the back of the property. It's not nearly as old as the manor, it has a fireplace, electricity, and water. No internet unfortunately, but there is a landline connected to the rest of the property. It's a one-bed, one-bath, little thing really," they explained.

"I mean, that would be fine by my standards," he replied, shifting uncomfortably, attempting to hide his eagerness.

"Did you bring your resume?" They extended a bony hand. He nodded, pulled the slightly crumpled copy of his resume from his jeans' back pocket, and placed it in the outstretched hand in front of him. Cameron unfolded the paper and imbued it with a large plume of clove smoke. They scanned over the paper with a blank expression.

"I see you attend Syracuse," they remarked.

"Yes."

"Ah, but you did not complete your degree?" They noted with a raised eyebrow.

"I took a leave of absence. I still hope to finish my biochem degree at some point," he lied. A sour expression sat unwavering on Cameron's face. Their features were hard for him to read.

"I see," Cameron sighed and flipped the paper over, only to find the other side blank. "Don't look so nervous. I don't care if you finished. I was merely curious." They paused and wrapped one long, spindly arm around their body before looking up from the papers.

"Do you feel confident you could handle this job?" They asked.

"Yes, I think I could fix up this estate and make it look habitable," Montague replied, continuing to lie through his teeth.

"Lovely, well, all things considered, would you be open to starting soon?" Cameron inquired.

"How soon?"

"I could have you move in as soon as you're ready."

"Does that mean I'm hired? Could I start tomorrow?" Cameron paused for a moment, causing Montague to regret his eagerness.

"I suppose you could get situated tomorrow, yes. I can meet you out front in the morning, let's say nine?" they suggest.

"Works for me," he nodded emphatically, suddenly very excited and additionally confused as to what just happened.

"Fantastic!" Cameron tried to give a polite smile, but it just contorted their face to look as if they were in great pain. They extended their thin, heavily ringed hand. Montague gave it a firm shake. He was taken aback by how cold and clammy their handshake was.

"Cool, I look forward to working with you," he said through his own forced polite smile.

"I look forward to working with you as well." Cameron pulled their hand away. "I will see you tomorrow. I will show you your accommodations then, as well as give you some paperwork to fill out," they instructed as they put out the clove cigarette. They got off the couch. "I'll give you the rest of the weekend to get settled. Your first official day will be Monday." Montague nodded in understanding.

He tried his best to contain his feelings as he walked back to his minivan. A mixture of anxiety and genuine giddiness twisted in his stomach like angry butterflies. His curiosity began to bloom again. His mind was already trying to fill in the gaps of the parts of the estate he had not yet seen. He wondered what was in there, and why the place looked abandoned despite the doctor being dead for less than a year. There was also something bothering him about the fact that it appeared that Cameron lived there completely alone.

Sticky spider silk on his hand took him out of his head for a moment. A little arachnid had already managed to build a web in the handle of the driver's side door. He had interrupted it in the middle of fighting a juicy fly twice its size.

"Get out of here, little dude," he mumbled as he brushed the creature onto a nearby leaf. He wiped some of the leftover web residue that stuck to his hands on his dirty jeans.

# CHAPTER TWO

MONTAGUE pulled up the horrible dirt drive just a few minutes before nine the next morning. He had not told Mina the whole truth, worrying she'd disapprove. He had purposefully left things vague, hoping she would assume he was actually talking about securing a job at one of the many ski resorts. Some of them did often offer staff lodging, so it was not a huge stretch of the imagination. He assumed she might have some foreboding words for him if she knew he was now parked in front of the Giovanni estate.

He slung his duffel bag over one shoulder. As he looked up from locking his car door, he saw that Cameron was already standing in front of the fountain waiting for him, somehow managing to arrive there silently.

"I hope I didn't keep you waiting," Montague remarked, unsure of how long they had been there, watching him. He could have sworn he'd not seen them outside when he pulled up. Maybe he just needed more coffee?

"Don't worry, it was not long," Cameron said flatly. "Come with me. I'll show you your accommodations." They motioned for him to follow.

The groundskeeper's cabin was behind the manor itself, a good acre or so away. At the back of the mansion, there was an overgrown field that had the potential to be an impressive lawn. Near the house was a disgustingly neglected inground pool. The stone sculptures that decorated the pool area were all decaying and overrun with moss. The area that should have been a pleasant spot for recreation looked far more like an abandoned cemetery. The slimy green swamp that sat engulfing that half of the property buzzed like the mosquito paradise it was. The few ugly cherubs still with their heads appeared to watch the two of them as they walked along the stone footpath that led to the back end of the property.

Most of the land surrounding the house was woodland that, Cameron explained, was technically their property.

"I strongly suggest you do not go into the woods. We have a bit of a coyote situation out here," they warned Montague, who just nodded.

At the very back of the developed land, two buildings stood, just beginning to be engulfed by the tree line. The groundskeeper's cabin sat next to a large barn shed that was shut tight with a rusty padlock. The cabin itself was far less unwelcoming than the mansion, though it too had an uncomfortable amount of vegetation attempting to claim it back into Mother Nature. It was far more modern in its build. He guessed it was from the seventies or so.

"You have quite a lot of property," Montague mentioned. "Do you plan on hiring more staff?"

"Eventually, I don't want more people here until it is more hospitable. For now, it will just be you," they explained, now standing in front of the cabin. "Here are your keys. Two for your home, top and bottom lock, both the front and back are the same. One for the tool shed. There's a lot of things in there from the previous groundskeeper, but I'm not sure if any of what he left behind is in working order. We will have to sort that out."

"Lastly, these are the ones to the manor itself. These are for all the doors to the outside, the coach house for you to park your vehicle in, and the one for the cellar. The rest of the doors inside are locked by only me. If you find a locked door that none of your keys go to, it's meant to stay locked," Cameron explained, handing over the large key ring to Montague. "Does that all make sense?"

"Yes. You mentioned a previous groundskeeper?" he inquired.

"He was employed by my mother before I inherited the estate. He was quite old, so we both decided it was best for him to *retire*," they explained. Montague looked over the ring of keys again, trying to memorize their order. Everything about this situation rang a little alarm bell somewhere in the back of his mind that he was either too stubborn or too stupid to heed.

As soon as he looked up, Cameron had vanished like a ghost, which only added to his mounting unease. Nonetheless, he let himself into his new home. It was not in as much disrepair as he had expected. It was dusty, but otherwise everything was clean and neat, as if it had not been touched since the previous tenant left it. The kitchen and living space were an open floor plan with the small fireplace across from the little gas stove.

*Fire hazard*, he noted to himself, looking back from the stove to the fireplace.

Across the way were two gnarled wooden doors. One led to a small bedroom with a humble bed, little dresser, and a grand window that had an, at the moment unpleasant, view of the swamp at the back of the manor. The other door led to a tiny but clean bathroom with a shower stall almost too small for him to use. He began testing the lights and water and looking inside dusty cabinets. Satisfied with his accommodations, he walked back to his van to get the rest of his things.

Cameron did not return until after he had carted all of his things into his new lodging. They arrived carrying a stack of bleach-white linens and towels. Montague gratefully grabbed the stack from them.

"Is that all of your possessions?" They asked, looking around at the mess in the living space. He had only a few bags of things and was largely missing most home essentials.

"Yes," he admitted with a tinge of embarrassment. Cameron appeared to realize the rudeness of their comment.

"Well…" they clapped their hands together in an attempt to diffuse their misstep, "if there is anything you need right away, please don't hesitate to ask. I've also brought some paperwork I need you to fill out. I will come and pick it up Monday. For now, just get settled," they instructed, "oh, and here is the number too the house if you need me. The landline is over there on the wall… cell service out here is quite spotty."

"Thank you very much." He took the stack of linens and paperwork. "If I go into town for food, is there anything you need me to pick up for you?"

"No, *grazie*, I appreciate the offer but I have everything I need at the moment," Cameron gave another pained smile. With that, they turned and left, closing the front door softly before Montague could ask any more questions.

☽ ✧ ☾

Monday rolled around uneventfully. The majority of Monty's weekend was spent crafting an elaborate lie for his best friend that he knew he'd soon forget the finer points of. Depending on how long he stayed here, he knew he'd eventually have to tell her, but not yet, not while she could still talk sense into him.

He relished how nice it was to finally have an actual bed and shower to himself. Not to mention having his own kitchen, which was a pleasure and luxury he'd never really had before. Privacy, plumbing, hot food. He nearly had forgot why he was here in the first place after a few full night's sleep in a clean bed.

Getting ready for the task ahead of him that morning, he found himself staring in the mirror a little too long. His face felt unfamiliar. He still felt like a teenager inside, but there was this grown man staring back at him. A man who looked just like his father, only somehow even rougher around the edges. He was far older, and sadder, than he remembered being. His dark olive skin had taken on a bit of an ashy hue from a summer spent sheltered in air conditioning. He tugged at the heavy bags around his eyes.

*Some sun will surely do me good.*

As he checked himself, flannel, jeans, boots, keys, and so on, he heard a soft knock on his front door. He hastily tucked his shirt in before opening the door. Cameron loomed in the doorway, a parasol over one shoulder blocking the morning sun from touching their pale skin.

"I hope it's not too early for you?" They asked.

"Not at all!"

"Good, could I have that paperwork I gave you?"

"Certainly," he stumbled over his own feet a bit as he handed over a manila envelope with his full name, *Montague L. Varon,* scrawled across it.

"I wanted to go over the tools in the shed with you this morning, so I can make note of what might need to be replaced or added," they said, flicking through the papers. They appeared to be keen on avoiding eye contact.

"Cool, yeah, that sounds like a good move," Montague nodded. Cameron was already walking away as he closed the door to his cabin.

"Well, for starters, a new lock for this would probably be good," he noted as he wrenched the rusted padlock open. It would have been easier to just rip the locked hardware from the old wood. The shed itself was absolutely filled with gardening and lawn-keeping supplies. Everything he could possibly need, and then some, lawn mowers, leaf blowers, pool cleaning equipment, assorted knives and scythes, some things in far more disrepair than others.

The two of them took inventory. Montague attempted to start the machines to see which ones worked. The few that did whine to life were thirsty for gasoline. When he tried to rev the weedwacker, it began sputtering dark foul smoke that made them both choke. After a few hours, Cameron had written an extensive list of tools they would need to get and left Montague to begin his work.

The first thing that needed to go was the wheat field that had overtaken the lawn so he could even make his way to and from the manor. Despite the mower being in better condition than other tools, it was not happy cutting through several acres of grassland. It threw a fit of protest as he tried to mow over the too-tall vegetation.

After several stops and starts, he resigned himself to sharpening the scythe and cutting most of the grass by hand. Analog would suffice as an alternative to risking a mower blade snapping off and slicing through his flesh. He tried not to give it much thought, choosing to slip on his headphones to listen to his beat-up portable CD player. He hacked away at the grass rhythmically, humming to his nu metal, and praying he didn't get bitten by ticks or fall into poison ivy.

By the time midday had rolled around, he was drenched in sweat and reconsidering taking this job. It was the sort of late summer day where the sun was punishing, and the cries of cicadas rang in his ears unendingly. Their cries being header even through his headphones. His white tank top was transparent from the amount of sweat that had drenched him.

He examined the blisters forming on his broad hands, noting how dirt settled deep into the lines in the pales of his palms. He was just about done with cutting back half of the yard when he saw a black-clad figure floating to him across the lawn. In the midday sun, Cameron looked out of place, appearing not to cast a shadow along the lawn. He assumed it was an optical illusion from the high noon sun. They were carrying a tall glass of water.

"You look exhausted. Here, you really should not overwork yourself. I can't have you fainting from heat exhaustion on the first day," they remarked, handing him the glass. Montague gratefully downed the water before saying a word, ice pooling in his stomach in contrast to the heat.

"I can handle a little heat, but thank you. I needed that," he replied with a smile, sweat still dripping into his eyes.

"You do know you can take breaks if you need to?" Cameron mentioned, tilting their head slightly so their hair fell into their eyes. They looked straight through him as they spoke. "It's quite hot," they added, squinting up at the sky.

"I appreciate the reminder," he said with a smile. He noticed they seemed unbothered by the heat despite being fully covered in black cloth.

"Jeez, how are you not cooking dressed like that?"

"Oh... I guess I'm just not a very warm person," they shrugged, grabbing the empty glass from Montague's rough hand.

"Even then, you have to be sweating a little? Isn't it hot inside? I don't see any air conditioning units or fans?" He leaned on the scythe, studying the strange person in front of him.

"You would be surprised how well old plaster buildings stay cool," Cameron remarked to the glass in their hand. There was something about them that felt alien; their movements were too fluid, like they were composed of lingering smoke in a skin suit. Montague realized suddenly how long he had just been sitting, staring, saying nothing.

"I will be back in a bit when you're done," they paused, before turning and sauntering back up to the manor, leaving him to stew in his awkwardness.

# CHAPTER THREE

THE sky was streaked with bright orange blood as the sun crawled behind the tree line. Frogs began their deafening songs as the cicadas turned in for the night. Montague had already had a break and something to eat after he realized how long "a bit" was to Cameron. It was nearly nine now, he was still working, and his employer had yet to reappear. He had rigged up a string of light bulbs in the shed so he could continue to clean and organize the mess of tools still left inside.

"You've done a fabulous job so far," Cameron said from just behind him, causing all the hair to stand on the back of his neck.

*How the hell did they manage to get behind me without me noticing?*

"Thank you, ma'am," he reflexively replied, before tensing up, realizing what he said. An irritated expression crossed Cameron's face.

"Excuse me, I am no ma'am," they corrected.

"Fuck, I'm sorry I realized I shouldn't have—shit I mean, sorry I —" he was cut off by them holding up a hand.

"If you *must,* 'sir' will suffice. I will be honest with you, however, I'd like to avoid the whole affair of miss or mister. I'd prefer if you refrained from regarding me as either, as I view myself as firmly neither," they explained. Montague made a mental note to himself.

"Right… so neither then? Okay, sorry about that." He felt his face burning with embarrassment. Something about how filthy and covered in sweat he was made his cheeks burn ten times redder. "What do I call you then? Boss?"

"Just Cameron will do. Awkwardness aside, I wanted to ask you if you'd be interested in joining me for a drink? I know it's quite late already, but I would like to make your acquaintance," they added, nervously gripping one of their arms.

"Sure! But can I take a shower first?" He pulled at the neck of his filthy undershirt. "I'm feeling a lil' bit gross."

He did not want to reject their offer, even if the idea of alcohol after sweating so much made his stomach curdle. He'd done more physical labor that day than he'd done in years, and he could feel the lactic acid burning in his muscles. Cameron nodded and visibly untensed.

"Just meet me up at the house when you're done. I'll listen for you," they said before turning on their heels and disappearing across the now pitch-black lawn.

It just then dawned on him that they might have been expecting some form of violence. It had not even occurred to him that perhaps being mistaken for a woman in the past may have had unforeseen, and rather negative consequences for Cameron. They had no way of knowing from how Montague presented himself that he couldn't care less about how someone dressed or referred to themself. It was no more his business than who a person wanted to sleep with. He did wonder however, for just a moment, if Cameron was interested in men.

Monty grumbled to himself as he washed the day off in a cold shower. Cameron took up most of his thoughts as he did so. He knew they existed before this, but mostly as a vague concept, not a real person in Dr. Giovanni's life. She never spoke about them more than the occasional off-hand mention. The way she referred to them had always made it sound as if they were far younger. He expected

Cameron to be a child, twelve at most, not someone his age.

Cameron didn't feel like a fully flesh blood person when they stood right in front of him either. They had an air about them that made them feel like a ghost with how they carried their body. They could have had hollow bird bones and been made of nothing at all. He didn't understand how a living person could look like a memory when you were staring right at them.

He put his hands against the wall and let cold water clean the hot summer sweat off his soft body. He watched the water drip off his necklace and hair idly for a moment. His skin was already beginning to take a warmer glow after being outside for just a day. The cool water soothed the fresh burns blooming on his shoulders.

Perhaps the reason Cameron made him feel so strange had to do with the circumstances of their inheritance. Here they were with a massively decaying burden of an estate, effortlessly handed to them mere months after their mother's death. He wondered if they had been as blindsided by Dr. Giovanni's death as other people were. He was also intrigued by the level of opulent wealth that had been left to rot for far longer than the doctor had been dead. There were more and more, possibly too invasive, questions bubbling up in him. These thoughts simmered in his mind like a stew as he dried off, got dressed, and sauntered up to the mansion.

Monty felt the darkness swallow him whole as he entered the back entrance of the old Victorian. The halls felt as if they were breathing, cool air on the back of his neck, pushing him forwards into its maw. He shuffled down the dim corridor like a lost moth towards a single beckoning light he assumed was the kitchen. He was correct in his assumption.

The kitchen was just as grandiose as the rest of the manor, although it clearly had been redone sometime in the fifty's. Cameron was crumpled on one of the stools situated around the kitchen bar. One of their hands was resting on the stem of a very full wineglass, the other fiddling with a small golden object around their neck. Montague cleared his throat, causing them to jump and swiftly slip the pendant down their collar.

"O-oh! It's just you," they let out a sigh of relief.

"Sorry, I didn't mean to startle you," he apologized.

"It's okay. Come have a seat," they offered, pulling out the stool next to them. Montague obliged and sat down. They placed a wineglass in front of him and poured him a very generous glass before proceeding to top themselves off.

This was the closest he had been to Cameron. The poor fellow looked incredibly anemic in the kitchen light. Their lips were nearly blue. Their skin was too thin, gray, as if they'd never been in the sun. The circles around their eyes were tinged purple and yellow with mild jaundice. Up close, he realized their eyes appeared lavender because they lacked any pigment at all. Even under his scrutinizing gaze, they oddly looked more like a photograph than a living being.

"So, does it get lonely living all *alone* in a creepy old house like this?" Montague asked before taking a sip of his wine. Only after the fact did he realize just how bad the opening question sounded coming out of his mouth. Cameron let out a sigh.

"Naturally, though it was lonely here before I inherited the estate from my late mother."

"I'm sorry for your loss."

"Don't be," they said flatly.

There was an uncomfortable silence as Montague nervously took another swig of his wine, trying to shove down the thousands of questions he was burning to ask.

"So, what about the other house staff? I know you mentioned a previous groundskeeper?" he asked.

"He obviously was not able to keep up with the workload in his old age." Cameron paused, tensing as they spoke, "I know this estate is bad. Trust me, this is not how I want to have things. I'll hire more staff eventually. I don't know much about running an estate, but I promise you won't be the only one tasked with fixing this mess *forever.*"

"That is good to know," Montague nodded with a forced laugh. From the way they spoke, it appeared to him that Dr. Giovanni hadn't had house staff, which struck him as odd. Maybe he just didn't understand how rich people worked, and he was being presumptuous. Cameron was clearly embarrassed by the state of the property to some degree. He decided to change the subject.

"What do you do for work?"

"I don't."

"Oh, well then what do you... do?"

"I write poetry mostly, and compose music. I'm not really trained in much, but I find it's better than sitting quietly with my thoughts."

"What sort of music do you compose?" he asked. He tried his best not to speculate just how much money the Giovanni family had to have where Cameron did not even *consider* working.

"Solo piano pieces for now. I would love to write an opera someday, but I feel like I'm not at all ready for such a feat," they said as their face softened.

"I'd love to hear some of your work."

"It's not very good, I promise, but maybe sometime," they said with a nervous, melodic laugh.

Montague noticed their lavender eyes were lazily studying him. They lingered on the small hamsa hanging around his neck. He wished he could glean even a little sliver of what they were thinking. Their face was just as inscrutable as their mother's, stern and observing, as if they were trying to dissect his thoughts by merely looking into his eyes.

There was an oppressive heaviness in the air between them. It made him feel like there was a cloud slowly seeping into his brain. The fog creeping into his head was making him forget how to interact with another human being. Maybe it was the wine? He felt as if there were tendrils of shadows writhing around him. He was slowly being coiled in a tight embrace of confusion. The sensation was giving him tunnel vision. The kitchen melted away, and for just a moment the person sitting next to him was the only thing left in the world he could remember. He felt ever so faint in that moment.

"Is that actual silver?" Cameron asked, pointing to his necklace. Their soft voice poured directly into his ears as if they were inside his head.

"Yeah… why?" Monty reflexively put his hand to the pendant. The room around him suddenly came back into focus. As if by magic, the strange sensation of confusion crawling in his flesh receded.

"Just curious," they said. They looked strangely disappointed. "I've never seen a symbol like that before. Is it religious?"

"Sort of… It can be for some. For me, it's to ward off the evil eye," he explained. "It's called a hamsa. This was a gift from my mother. I'm not personally superstitious, but it can't hurt, you know," he added nervously. Cameron merely nodded pensively.

"Ah, so like a *cornicello*?"

"Yes?" he replied, not too sure what they meant. They merely let out a breathy laugh.

"It's an Italian talisman that wards off the evil eye. At least I think?" they explained. Monty nodded, pretending he understood. He was still waiting for the usual slew of bigoted questions that came with inquiring about his jewelry and appearance.

"Your name is—"

"French, yes, only like a quarter or something like that on my dad's side though. My mom's family immigrated here from Lebanon before she was born," he explained, "I've got some Greek in there too, I think, not sure what else. Guess I'm mostly an American mutt," he drunkenly joked, regretting his verbiage as he heard himself say it. Cameron merely nodded as if this meant little to them.

"Are you close to your mother?" they asked after a while.

"No, not really," he paused for a moment. "I'm not actually on speaking terms with any of my family. I haven't talked to them in years now. Hence why the family tree is a lot of guesswork," he explained. The wine was loosening his lips more than he would have liked. Cameron's expression was impossible for him to read. They looked simultaneously sympathetic and confused.

"Well, you know how it is," he let out a nervous laugh, "my coach caught me and my teammate under the bleachers after practice. The school didn't like that and kicked us *both* off the football team. Of course, then news made its way back to my old man that I liked *boys*, and well that was that." He cringed as the words left his mouth. He really was drunk now. His lips were buzzing, and he could also tell he was slurring his words. He felt stupid.

"So you were excommunicated over such a thing?"

"Well," Montague paused, stopping himself from continuing to overshare, "I imagine your family is a little more lax with gay stuff then? Sorry, I mean, I'm assuming you're gay, right? With the whole cross dressing neuter thing you've got going on?" If he could have dropped an anvil on his own head to make him shut up in that moment, he would have.

Cameron shook their head with a laugh. "I don't care about the gender of my partners anymore than I care about my own. As for acceptance, it's just different with my family." They appeared bemused, but not completely offended by Montague's jabbering.

"Was your mom supportive of you?" He asked. Now, *this* was the wrong thing to ask. Cameron's face instantly twisted into something awful.

"My mother and I were not on good terms before her *accident*," Cameron said very coolly. Something dangerous had suddenly taken up residence behind their eyes.

"Why say accident? She killed herself, I thought? Am I mistaken?" Montague wanted to shut up, he really did, but the words continued to slip out of him like vomit.

"Yes, my mother committed suicide. I don't like to put it so bluntly," Cameron narrowed their eyes.

"I'm sorry… It must have been hard. It felt so sudden, at least to us in her classes, I mean. Do you know why she did it?" Montague could feel his face burning from alcohol and embarrassment as he continued to pour more and *more* of the wrong words from his maw.

"That's not your concern," they snapped.

"Right… shit… I'm sorry," he apologized. His head was swimming. He had to get out of here before he made poor Cameron hate his guts. "I think I've had too much to drink. I'm sorry. I should probably go get some sleep," he remarked with a forced yawn as he stumbled to his feet.

Suddenly Cameron stood and grabbed him by the arm. His heart jumped from a mixture of fear and some misplaced excitement.

"Sorry." They dropped their grasp faster than they had reached for him. "I just have one thing I have to say before you go."

"I'm listening."

"I must warn you against snooping around. Do you understand?" Cameron warned sternly.

"No… I'm not too sure I know what you mean?" He frowned.

"You are not the first person I've met who knew my mother," they continued. "I know you want to know more. It may surprise you, but you are not the first person who's asked me why she did what she did…" they trailed off before lowering their voice, "very bad things have happened in this house, Montague."

"You gotta know how curious that makes me," he forced a laugh, but Cameron's expression did not change.

"If you want to work for me, you must respect that I'd prefer to not talk about that vile woman. Do we understand each other?" There was a look of fear in their eyes.

"I understand." He nodded as the reality of the situation came back to him. Cameron sat back down with a sigh. Montague anxiously slipped away into the night, feeling like he'd thoroughly made an ass of himself.

# CHAPTER FOUR

THE conversation Montague had the night prior still clung to every fold of his brain the next morning. Cameron's bewildering warnings haunted him throughout the course of the day. He had never really taken the time to question Dr. Giovanni's relationship to her only child. When she did rarely allude to their existence, there was never an indication of disdain or animosity towards them. However, it was clear from Cameron's behaved that the feeling was not mutual.

He decided it was in his best interest to finally give Mina a call. The cell service was just as bad as he had been warned. There was a strange dead zone that choked out the property. It was like there was an invisible forcefield around the house and woods that made everything just spark out and die. Even trying to tune in the radio in his minivan was difficult once he got all the way up the drive. If Mina had been trying to get in contact with him, there was no way of knowing. It had only been a few days, but he knew that enough missed calls would raise suspicion with her.

The trees were steaming as their dew evaporated into the morning air, vapor clouds lingering like cigarette smoke. He could feel the heat of the day beginning to broil as the sun rose in the early morning. He was already sweating as he walked down to the front gate.

He had learned rather quickly that the only spot on the property that had reception was just outside the rusting front gate. It was just past the same spot that the radio would begin to buzz in and out. Maybe the electricity in the gate had something to do with it? He doubted it though, feeling stupid that he didn't understand how these things worked better.

He was distracted from his plan for a moment. The post box at the bottom of the drive caught his eye as he noticed the little flag had been set up. He peeked to find there was just one letter inside. He pulled it out to inspect it. It was battered the way something that had spent too long in the postal system often looked. "Arianna Giovanni" was the name on the return address, which was from somewhere in Italy. He wondered if that could have been the other woman whose portrait hung in the drawing room.

A misplaced cool breeze blew past that caused him to tense. He could feel eyes on him, lingering somewhere in the foggy woods. There was something lurking in the treeline just out of sight. He stared into nothing. Despite seeing only trees, he felt like he was making eye contact with *something*.

He felt light crawling on his flesh. He broke nonexistent eye contact from the invisible threat to see a small spider climbing from the envelope to his hand. He swiftly shook it off and replaced the letter, taking it as a sign he was not supposed to be looking through Cameron's mail like some freak.

His attention lurched back to why he'd come down the drive in the first place. He dialed Mina's number on his tiny gray flip phone. Her phone rang just twice before she answered.

"Hey big guy! How's the new job treating you?" Mina chirped from the other end. She had a bright and plucky voice that could wake the dead, even over the phone.

"Dude, it's fucking creepy as hell up here," he paused. "I wanted to know if you'd wanna meet up at the diner this weekend?"

"Sure, let's do Saturday night–it's creepy up there?" Mina

repeated as a question, cutting her own train of thought short. Monty held still for a moment.

"Yeah. There's absolutely no reception here… and you know how it is in the off season," he lied, unsure how long he would keep up the ruse.

"Sure. I have a *lot* of questions about this new job of yours," Mina mumbled. He could tell she knew something was up.

"Well, save them for Saturday," he teased. "Does seven work for you?"

"Sure, sure. Seven is fine. Are you okay, by the way?"

"Yeah, why?"

"You just sound tired, is all," she explained.

"Oh yeah, it's just a lot of physical work. I think I'm a little out of shape," he laughed.

"Don't forget to hydrate, dude. It's been scorching lately. Ugh, I'm getting a call from the shop. I gotta go, but I'll see you Saturday!" Mina added before they both said goodbye. Monty clapped his phone shut. He gave one last look into the trees before he decided to go back to work. His uneasy sensation had vanished.

*Probably was just a deer or something,* he thought to himself.

He got started on tackling the front lawn that morning. He found himself swinging the scythe around without abandon. As he was cutting back the grass around the woodpile that sat neatly stacked on the side of the mansion, an aggravated garden snake came out from the logs. Without thinking, he sliced the head of the little snake clean off. A sputter of crimson leaked from its severed body as he glared at the blood on his blade. He kicked the side of the woodpile with a boot. A cacophony of angry hissing came from the pile of logs. He jumped back as a dozen perturbed snakes came slithering from the old wood.

*How does Cameron get wood for the fire without getting bitten?* He wondered. He would need to ask them about how to better deal with this at some point.

He moved on to battling the oppressive woodland that had once resembled hedges in the front of the mansion. They had begun to swallow up the porch thoroughly. Some of the vining plants had their roots growing into the very wood that made up the railings. In some spots, the wisteria was wholly indistinguishable from the wood of the porch. There was additional greenery growing cancerously, engulfing the entire western half of the house in ivy. He did not want to go into the sunroom to find the source of the ivy. Even up close, he could see nothing but green through the dingy glass.

He could hear the porch groaning miserably as he worked. He continuously found himself nervously staring up at the third-story balcony. He swore a strong wind could bring it crashing down on him if he stood under it for too long. His mind lingered on how easily one could land on the fountain below if they managed to stumble just right over the railing. It was a gruesome fall, noticing how the cherub in the center of the fountain's stone wing stood up. He tried to shake the grim thought out of his head.

There was a second balcony on the mansion, at the back on the second story. He wasn't very interested in walking out onto that one either. A tumble from that one would yield a similar sculptural falling hazard by the pool. He wondered what rooms they were connected to. He wondered if Dr. Giovanni had really jumped to her death. A chill ran through him at the thought of her cracking her neck on cement, or worse.

The days melded together with little interference from his employer. The work felt monotonous and unending. Every time he felt he'd finally tamed one portion of the property, another part seemed to grow wilder. The strangest thing was that the greenery engulfing the porch appeared to be growing back almost as soon as it'd been tamed. No matter how many times he tried to rip the wisteria from the rotting porch roof, it managed to vine and crawl back the next day. He wondered if it was even possible for plants to grow that fast. He would have to ask Cameron about ripping the greenery up at the roots, unsure how else to cull their rapid growth.

He spent the rest of his week cleaning up the pool-shaped swamp. He had found an instruction manual stashed with the nets and chlorine. Pool maintenance was incredibly complex to him. No matter how many times he reread the instructions, he felt unprepared. There was no way the chemicals in the tool shed weren't at least semi-expired.

He carted the questionable supplies up to the pool area. The green mucky water was swarming with mosquitoes, all too happy to feast on his exposed arms. He'd covered as much of his skin as possible, putting up with sweating profusely to protect himself from the little bloodsuckers he so loathed.

He felt bad just dumping chemicals into the water, knowing the pool had become the home of hundreds of frogs. He frantically tried to scoop as many out of the muck as he could with the pool net. That proved harder than expected. As he swung wildly at a few little green creatures in the middle of the pool, he slipped on sludge and careened down into the shallow end of the pool.

He swore as his bottom collided with algae and concrete, the net flying from his hand, landing half a yard away in muck. The smell of the stagnant water caused him to gag as it soaked through his boots, socks, jeans, everything. He let out a long groan of discontent. He glanced up at the balcony directly across from where he'd taken his disgusting spill. For a moment he swore he saw someone looking through the curtains of one of the doors that opened out onto the balcony.

*I hope Cameron didn't just see that.*

☽ ✧ ☾

Amidst the heat and dirt, the weekend came faster than he'd expected. He hopped into his trusted rust-bucket and headed out. He swore his head felt clearer the second he'd left the dead zone. After getting off the property, it was only a short drive to the small town twenty-four-hour diner that he and Mina liked to frequent.

Mina was practically bouncing with excitement as she came up to sit in the booth Monty had saved for them. She chucked her pastel pink motorcycle helmet onto the seat next to her and placed her backpack on her lap as she sat down.

"Man, I feel like I haven't seen you in ages!" She proclaimed before she began digging in her backpack. She was decked out in pastel pink motorcycle gear from head to toe. The handle of a fresh dagger tattoo on her neck was peeking out of her collar.

"It's been like a week and a half," Monty laughed as he leaned back in his seat.

"I know, I know, I guess I got used to you always being around," Mina joked as she pulled a small parcel wrapped crudely in pink paper, flecked here and there with mechanical grease. "Got you a lil' housewarming gift." He took the little parcel from her hands. Mina had small but extremely calloused hands with short nails that sported chipping pink pastel polish.

"You shouldn't have," Monty chuckled as he shook the package next to his ear.

"Oh, shut up and open the damn thing!" His friend said, watching him eagerly as he pulled away the paper. Bright cobalt blue glass shined back at him. "An evil eye, you know, since you moved into a new place? I remember you telling me how it was good luck to give those to people when they move," Mina explained. He smiled, shifting the large round glass eyes in his hands.

"I forgot I told you that. Thank you! I will hang this up by my door. I could use it. The place is creepy," he said, pocketing the glass disk in the front pocket of his denim jacket.

"Again with the creepy?" Mina pressed, narrowing her eyes. "Which resort are you working at anyway?"

"It's not actually a resort job," he admitted. It was either dig a deeper grave, or come clean. Mina just raised an eyebrow and drummed her fingers on the table for a moment. She was waiting for the rest. "It's a groundskeeper job at a private estate."

"Why didn't you just say that in the first place? No wonder it's creepy! All those old estates are *haunted* around here," she punctuated "haunted" by wiggling her fingers to imitate a ghost, before huffing and crossing her arms.

"I thought you might try to talk me out of taking this job. It's such a good deal, I didn't want to pass it up," he added, fidgeting with his necklace. He resisted the urge to put the silver pendant between his lips.

"Why would I try to talk you out of that? It's not like there are that many jobs like that around here as it is?" It was clear she was struggling to piece together Monty's vagueness. Then her expression changed to surprise. "Hang on, wait—"

"It's Dr. Giovanni's old estate," he completed her thought before he was sure she had figured it out.

"You mean you're working at your *dead professor's* house?" She spat. "Why? Are you crazy? You're not trying to figure out why she died, are you!?" Monty held his hands up in defense.

"I'm working for her kid, Cameron. I saw the ad in the papers," he explained.

"Ugh, I totally forgot. When you got all your stuff, I noticed you left the papers at my house with the address and everything on there still. I don't know why I didn't put two and two together," Mina smacked a palm to her face. "You're such a bad liar too," she laughed.

"I just didn't want you to try to talk me out of taking the job because it was at Dr. Giovanni's place. It pays really well, and Cameron's obviously in need of serious help cleaning up that mess. I don't know what the hell the doctor was up to before she died, but it looks like the property has been abandoned for decades," he explained.

"How do you even know that's where she was living then? Maybe it's just in the same family?"

"Cameron said they inherited the place from her when she died," he explained.

"Hmm, that's weird it's in such bad repair if she was living there," Mina said after a long pause.

"Extremely weird. Unless I'm super wrong, it was where she lived, and I'm pretty sure, also where she died. I think Cameron has also lived there this whole time? I can't quite make heads or tails of the place," he admitted.

"What about Cameron? What's he like?" she asked.

"*They're* strange as the rest. It's funny, the way Dr. Giovanni spoke about them made me think they were a child, but like, Cameron's gotta be close to our age," he added.

"And he–they're just there alone?"

"There's no other staff at the moment. I think the doctor had other people working there, but I genuinely don't know."

"So it's just the two of you alone on a huge old property? Aren't you a little unnerved by that?"

"I mean yes and no. Cameron is a little off, but I'm not too worried about them. As it is, I barely see them at all. I do my work and they stay out of my business mostly," Monty explained, thinking back to the first day he'd worked and how present Cameron had been, right up until he started drunkenly sticking his foot in his mouth.

"My curiosity about what happened to Dr. Giovanni has only been piqued," he added.

"Yeah, but... dude, you should probably not be prying into that shit. I don't think anyone would want you to bug them about their dead parents, especially not from their employee," Mina pointed out.

"No, I know. I'm not just going to walk up to them and be like, 'tell me in excruciating detail how your mom offed herself,'" he scoffed. Although if his hazy memory was correct, he may have already done just that.

"Knowing you, I wouldn't put it past you," Mina teased. "Hey," she suddenly became very serious, "be careful, Monty."

"I will, you know —"

"No! Listen to me. Promise me you'll keep yourself out of trouble. Looking into someone's death that's been kept intentionally vague is not something to take lightly. The fact you're alone there too... you are walking into something that could be very dangerous. You don't know this Cameron person or what their deal is."

"I can handle myself, Mina."

"You don't know what you're getting yourself into."

"I'm walking into a mystery with answers worth getting. If you ask m—"

"Monty! I know better than anyone that your curiosity makes you do stupid shit. If you're only doing this job to look for closure, you're better off quitting now. You know you're welcome at my house. No matter how many times you leave, you can always come back," Mina said sternly. That was the final word on the matter.

"I know, and I appreciate that." He took a moment. "I promise you I won't get myself into anything I can't get out of."

"Just don't fuck yourself, Monty," Mina sighed just as the waitress walked up to their table.

# CHAPTER FIVE

A woman's dying screams echoed in Montague's head. He sat up in bed, his heart pounding as the dream slipped away from him like the sand pouring through hourglass. It was early Sunday morning, light pouring through the large window in his sparsely decorated bedroom. Dust gently danced in the dappled beams of sun coming through the trees. Waking up here still felt like waking up in a strange motel, where the only thing he recognized was the smattering of dirty clothing on the floor.

He rubbed the hourglass sand from his eyes. The day was already scorching despite the sun clearly still evaporating the dew off the grass. Cicadas enthusiastically sang their morning songs as he lazily crawled out of bed. The only thing covering his body was a slowly growing layer of sweat.

He groggily began making his coffee, regretting not having made any ice to cool it off after brewing. No ice either to help cool down his blood with a glass of water. The tap itself was lukewarm at best. The most he could manage was sticking his shaggy head in the empty freezer for a moment to enjoy the respite from what was surely going to be a 100-degree day.

A soft knock on the front door of his cabin sent Monty's heart into his throat.

*Cameron!?*

He quickly slammed the freezer shut and frantically hopped into a pair of dirty pants and tossed on a gray undershirt. Another knock, firmer this time.

"Yep! Hang on!" He shouted as he frantically tucked his shirt in. His eyes lingered for a moment on the bright blue glass of the evil eye Mina had given him the night prior, now hanging by the front door. He yanked the humidity-saturated wooden door open, realizing he had left it unlocked overnight.

Standing like a dark cloud before him was Cameron. A huge black parasol over their shoulder blotted out the sun. They looked fresher than the last time he had seen them. Their face was flushed pink, likely from the heat of the day. Their many gold rings glittered in the sunlight, along with a small golden locket hanging across their chest, which glinted into Monty's eyes. They were more appropriately dressed for the weather in a flowing skirt with a long black ladies' bathing suit cover-up as a top. He could see Cameron's scarred skin underneath the sheer fabric. A myriad of pale lines and keloids were strewn across their chest and arms, which only raised more questions.

"Apologies for the early intrusion," Cameron smiled. The way their sunglasses obstructed their face made their strange expression appear far more pleasant.

"It's alright. What's up?" Monty asked. He realized it was hard to look at them, even though he felt himself staring. Just being face to face sent his heart up into his throat. He looked for somewhere to put his eyes other than Cameron's exposed skin.

"I noticed you were absent for quite some time. I wanted to see if you were alright, or if you'd decided to leave already," they said with a twinge of genuine concern. He realized they must have noticed him leaving the other night and gone to bed before he'd come home.

"I was out with a friend last night," he shrugged, leaning

casually on the door frame.

"Oh, I see. I am glad you're okay then," Cameron visibly relaxed.

"Do you want to come inside?" He offered after a moment of staring at his employer. The heat of the morning was already becoming too much for Monty. Despite not having a fan yet, inside his cabin was less harsh than the day itself.

"Yes, thank you," Cameron nodded as they walked in and closed their parasol. Monty turned his attention back to his morning coffee as Cameron closed the door behind themself. They sauntered over to the dusty couch. Monty leaned against the wall across from them, not wanting to sit that close to them.

"I've been looking over your work, and I'm quite impressed by how much you've achieved so far," they complimented. Monty nodded with a forced smile as he took a sip of his cheap pour-over coffee. "You aren't pushing yourself too hard though, are you?"

"Oh, no! I've been taking my time, don't worry," he assured them, not wanting to admit he was extremely sore. He was not sure if this was a test, or if they were genuinely worried about him.

"That is good to know," they remarked before turning their attention to the white envelope they pulled from a skirt pocket. "Here is your weekly pay. I will be here every Sunday with it for you, along with pointers on what I'd like you to do, if you are okay with that?"

"Oh sure, that's fine," he remarked, grabbing the surprisingly thick envelope. He peered inside, shocked at how much cash five hundred dollars was in hand. He realized this was the most money he had held in his hands at once. It sent a current of electricity through his fingertips.

"What would you like me to focus on this week?"

"If at all possible, I'd like you to wash the siding and fix the shutters and gutters. The fall rain will be here before you know it, and I would like to keep the place from springing a leak."

Montague nodded. "Consider it done."

"Just so you are on the same page as me, I would like you to fix the porch after that, to the best of your ability of course. Some of the boards are so rotten I fear they will give way any moment," they instructed.

"Yeah, about that. I tried fixing up the porch a little already. The wisteria seems to keep coming back no matter how much I try to cut it back," he explained.

"Odd," they mumbled to themself. "Well, at least try. Perhaps you require better cutters?" Monty merely shrugged.

"I would not worry about it too horribly, just cut back what you must to replace the boards." Cameron continued, "I also want the fountain back on and running. I really want these things to be done before the weather starts to turn. Once the outside is at least passable, your services will be needed inside the mansion."

"That's a lot to remember," Monty admitted, feeling slightly overwhelmed.

*Not like I wasn't warned about how much work this would be.*

"See what you can get finished this week, and I'll remind you next Sunday of what still needs to be done. I am trying to keep a log of everything. I may be absent, but I'm observant." And with that, they gave another weak smile before getting up and leaving Monty with his cash and coffee.

☽ ✧ ☾

Monday's heat was no less brutal. It was now truly the "dog days" of summer. The sun mocked all who dared enter its scorching rays. Everything Monty tried to do took him twice as long as he expected, like the heat was melting his bones. He was elated that he'd finally got the pressure washer working. The light misting of water on his face as it splashed off the old siding was a heavenly treat.

His mind wandered away from him as he worked, forgetting the external repairs he still had on his plate. He was instead far more focused on what tasks Cameron could expect him to do inside the manor. He secretly hoped it would offer him an opportunity to make more sense of the mess Dr. Giovanni had left in her absence.

Another week of mind-numbing manual labor flew by before Monty's eyes, mostly spent pressure washing siding and leaf-stuffed gutters. He felt like he was going slightly insane. Twice he tried fixing several of the hanging shutters only to wake the next day to find them exactly the way they'd been before. He must have been using the wrong tools? It baffled him as he climbed the ladder once again to see how the thing had managed to come loose. He was even further perplexed when he couldn't find the nail holes from his previous attempts.

It felt like the house was fighting back against him. It was a silly thought, but simple repairs like this should not have eluded him. He knew how to drive a nail through wood and remedy a hinge. His handiwork couldn't have been *that* incompetent. Maybe it was a strange phenomenon from the heat, making the wood expand and contract unpredictably?

Now that he was working closer up to the manor, he noticed Cameron left the property more often than he had originally thought. Their car was often missing from the coach house in the early evening, when the sun was just washing the sky pink. He did not see them return most nights.

That Friday night, however, time had gotten away from him. He had been preoccupied with furiously replacing every single last hinge on the front shutters, having given up on repairing the old ones. He ignored the limitations of the setting sun by hooking a shop light from the shed to his belt. He was so focused on completing his task, the fact that it was well past ten at night never even crossed his mind.

Finally satisfied that he was finally done fighting these old Victorian shutters, he wrapped up his equipment. His hands ached from the week of gripping onto screwdrivers and unattended ladder rungs for dear life. As he made his way into the treeline, he noticed Cameron's old black Cadillac come up the drive. Soon after they parked, a young man sprung out of their passenger seat. The man looked fit and chipper, sporting the uniform of one of the near by ski resorts, likely a seasonal worker. Monty couldn't help but spy from the trees in the dark, partly paralyzed with fear he would be seen snooping.

The young man was laughing and cracking jokes to Cameron, who, on the other hand, had a pitiful look of disinterest on their face. They merely gave the man a polite grimace here and there. The ski slope boy giggled a bit, possibly intoxicated based on his drooping eyes. He slid his hand around Cameron's waist, teasingly pulling the blond to him, before the both of them disappeared into the house, lights never turning on.

*I wonder who that is?* Monty thought to himself as he quickly slunk away into the darkness. *It's not my business...*

But he wanted it to be his business. He so desperately wanted it to be his business. There was a sickening feeling blooming in his chest and stomach as he contemplated exactly what Cameron was doing with that man. He did not want to admit to himself where that feeling was coming from. It was inappropriate. It was unprofessional.

Monty tried not to stew in his thoughts as much as he could the following day. He shoved down his odd pang of jealously as best he could. He had more important things that needed his attention. That morning he had seen a coyote snooping around the edge of the woods near the pool. He didn't want animals getting so comfortable coming that close to the mansion. The last thing he wanted was to yank open the shed and be met with a confused and angry scavenger. He figured he would have to check the edge of the woods and scare the pup off.

That afternoon he threw some D-cell batteries into an industrial flashlight he'd found in the shed and made his way across the lawn. As he drew closer to the woods, his pace slowed. He was unsure what his actual plan was if he *did* encounter something. He assumed he'd puff himself up and shout. He really hoped that what he had seen was a coyote, and not something more fearsome like a wolf or black bear.

The night was strangely quiet and still, as if the wind had suddenly forgotten to blow. As he walked into the trees, he couldn't even hear the whirring of the pool pump. He no longer heard the song of the nighttime frogs, nor the crickets. There wasn't much to remark on beyond the silence. It was just a patch of dark, quiet woods.

Despite that, his mouth felt incredibly dry, like his gut was dreading what he was looking for. This was reinforced by the fact that, the further he went, the more he noticed a putrid smell that was punctuated by the sound of restless flies. He wrote it off as a dead deer and decided not to go any further. He did not want to encounter its carcass in the dark. A decaying animal must have been what was drawing the coyote. He was smart enough not to want to uncover such a thing and run into a toothsome canine having its dinner. Not in the dark, at least. He would come back in the morning to take the carcass deeper into the woods, and away from the mansion.

*Problem solved.*

He decided that his curiosity was sated enough, and he turned back to leave the woods. The beam of his flashlight caught a dark figure for a split second before it darted into the trees. The figure's eerily fast movement made him freeze in his tracks. His heart jumped into his throat.

"H-hello?" his voice cracked. "Is someone there?" he called into the dark. He could have sworn he'd seen a humanoid figure. His sense told him he was not alone. There were eyes on the back of his neck. He was met with silence. He could feel his nerves frying as he involuntarily shivered. His heart attempted to escape his chest as he strained his ears to listen for any movement. There was just the sound of flies buzzing angrily around him on an all too quiet night.

He took a deep breath and bolted. He sprinted out of the woods as fast as his long legs would carry him. He ran all the way across the field, looking over his shoulder repeatedly into the darkness. Nothing was chasing him, but his instincts told him otherwise. He ran into his cabin and slammed the door shut. With his back pressed against the door as he panted and swiftly locked the deadbolt with a shaking hand.

He was not sure what he'd just seen. Maybe it was another deer, an angry buck on its hind legs. The sounds of nighttime filtered back into his ears, the screeching of frogs and chirps of crickets returning as normal. He listened to the rhythmic sound of the night, his heart still pounding in time.

A moment later his landline rang. His heart skipped a few beats, and he let out a yell, startled by the sound. He stared at it in bewilderment, letting it ring several times before shakily picking up the phone.

"I would not do that again if I were you," said a soft voice on the other end.

"Cameron?" he asked, his voice trembling with fear.

"It's dangerous in the woods at night. I heard you running and could see your light streaking across the yard from my bedroom," Cameron said. It sounded like they were panting on the other end. Monty let out a breath of relief realizing what he was most afraid of having seen in the woods; it was them.

*What an odd thing to think…*

"Right, yes. I just wanted to make sure everything was okay... I thought I saw something sniffing around there," he explained.

"It's in your best interest to stay out of the foliage at night," they instructed with a huff. "In fact, it's best to stay out of the woods altogether. Do not do that again, please."

"Do you want me to take care of what's been attracting the coyotes in the morning? It smelled like there was a dead deer or something in—"

"I would rather you wouldn't, I do not want to interrupt the ecosystem in the woods. Best not to meddle in nature's designs, you know?"

"Understood. Sorry to wake you up like that," he said. His heart was still pounding.

"Good night," they said before hanging up the phone. Monty stood with the dial tone in his ear for a moment before hanging the landline back up on the wall. Cameron had sounded out of breath, which was perplexing and a tad unnerving, for reasons he couldn't quite place. There was a twinge of something sour in Monty's aching chest as he triple-checked his locks.

# CHAPTER SIX

A heavy feeling of anxiety lingered in Montague's mind even as he woke the next morning. His heart never fully came back to its resting pace. He was unsure why he was so horrified by what he saw that night, or rather what he expected to see. He wanted desperately to go back and look in the daylight, to confirm it was a dead deer decaying in the woods. Though perhaps Cameron did have a point about not meddling with the environment. He was not thrilled at the idea of searching for an animal carcass, even in the daytime.

His employer did not come in the morning that Sunday. He spent most of the day down the drive, sitting in the dirt by the road, talking on the phone with Mina. He told her about the figure he'd seen in the woods. She insisted he must have seen a deer, reminding him of how tall bucks are when they stand on their hind legs. She eased his mind a little. Their conversation only ended when his cell phone ran out of battery juice.

The sky was splattered deep orange by the time Cameron finally knocked on his cabin door.

"Good afternoon," he said, opening the door. The sun was nearly all the way down, and he realized Cameron was donning a dark veil instead of their normal parasol. They held up the fat envelope of cash in their thin hand.

"Delivery for you," they said, waving the cash playfully before placing it in Montague's hand.

"Thank you," he chirped, already peeking to count the cash.

"Could I bother you for a bit?" Cameron asked.

"Sure, what do you need?"

"Would it be possible for you to come join me up at the manor?"

His heart skipped a beat at the proposal.

*Am I in trouble?*

"No problem, let me get my boots on," he nodded. He placed his cash neatly on his dresser and hastily threw his shoes on. Cameron just stood in the doorway waiting for him.

"What do you need me to do?"

"I just want to ask your opinion about a few things. There's arguably more work I'd like you to do inside than out here," they explained. Monty untensed a bit and realized it was simply business. He made sure he locked up his cabin behind him, still a bit on edge from the night prior.

"You sure? I've got a lot of work left outside. It feels like the plants are fighting me," he explained as they both walked up to the mansion. "I was also thinking of dealing with the rusted lock on the coach house before we got to that point."

"I know it's a lot of work for one man," they agreed, "but it will be winter soon and some things can wait. I want you inside once it starts to get cold. For now, I would like to know what you think is possible with your skill-set."

"I got ya," he nodded. They both walked into the dimly lit back hallway.

"Most pressing is the mouldering wallpaper. It's particularly bad on the third floor. I would love it if you could remove it and replace it with fresh paint," Cameron began as they walked through to the front of the house into the foyer with the magnificent chandelier.

"A paint job is no problem," Monty nodded.

"Do you think you'd be able to clean this?" they pointed up to the dusty light fixture. Monty hummed to himself, thinking about how heavy that thing had to be.

"I don't think I can get that down," he admitted. "Not without hurting myself or destroying it. You should probably hire a professional for that job."

"I'd really like to limit who comes in here," Cameron sighed, "but if you don't think you can manage, I'll see about finding someone who can properly service all the chandeliers. I have a few in my bedroom and in the ballroom that could use some work too."

"The ballroom?"

"Yes. What do you think all the space in this huge house is used for? A bunch of parlors?" Cameron laughed dismissively. Monty felt embarrassment come over him again.

"I've never actually been in a house this big before," he admitted.

"I'm sorry, I must have made myself sound like a privileged snob just now... there's a lot of interesting rooms here, and they all have very different needs in terms of repairs," they apologized, looking as if they had embarrassed themself, though it was hard to see if they were flustered beneath their veil.

"It's okay. For now, I think I should just focus on one project at a time," he suggested, trying to brush past the air of awkwardness. Cameron nodded in agreement. They were quiet for a moment.

"Say, Monty, if I can call you that, would you be interested in joining me for a drink?" They asked politely.

"Sure! I wouldn't mind a drink," he said without thinking. The moment he agreed, he felt regret.

*Why'd I say yes to that?*

Cameron motioned for him to follow to the kitchen. Instead of stopping there, they went straight to what Monty assumed was the cellar door.

"I feel inclined to treat you as a guest. After all, you and I are the only ones here, and I think it's in both of our best interest to get to know more about one another," Cameron said as they unlocked the cellar.

Montague's gut told him it was a bad idea to follow, but his feet betrayed him. He wandered down the groaning steps after the figure clad in black. Cameron flicked on a bright light, revealing the basement. He was pleasantly surprised by the extravagant wine cellar he entered, not entirely sure what else he was expecting.

"This is a *lot* of wine," he remarked, walking past racks upon racks of wine, some of which surely cost as much as one of his paychecks and then some.

"It's a family collection," Cameron said with a laugh to themself. Monty remembered being given a key to this cellar, now realizing it was a gesture of immense trust.

"How much wine is even down here?" He asked, realizing the cellar was more like a catacomb. He bet himself that the price of this collection alone was enough to buy a small property.

"More than I could probably drink myself before it's all corked," they joked.

Cameron pulled their veil away from their face to better look at the bottles in front of them, clearly looking for something specific. Monty was taken aback at how flushed and warm their face was. Their eyes sparked with a youthful radiance he had not yet seen. They were still a tad sickly looking, but there was a unique softness to their features that had been previously absent. There was an urge inside him that made him desire to move closer. He once again felt himself staring and made to avert his eyes.

He snooped around and looked at the racks. Most were organized by the variety, year, and where they came from. There was a rack of bottles that all had handmade labels. He wondered if at some point the Giovanni's had a friend with a vineyard. He examined the little homemade strikers. The few he saw simply had a seemingly random first name and year scrawled on them.

"Ah, here it is!" Cameron exclaimed, plucking a bottle from high. "1993 *Domaine de la Romanée-Conti La Tache Grand Cru Monopole, Côte de Nuits*, France. It's a very good Pinot Noir." They tapped a finger against the glass. Their French was well pronounced, though perhaps a bit pretentious. He walked over to see the bottle cradled in their hands. He had no clue about wines of any kind, so he had to take their word for it.

"Here, under the bar there should be a bottle opener if you would hand it to me," they gestured to the small bar set up in the cellar for tastings and parties, no doubt. It took him just a few moments to find the bottle opener. They gracefully took it and swiftly executed the most flawless and speedy opening of a wine bottle Monty had ever witnessed.

Cameron pulled two glasses down from the rack over the bar. They blew some dust off them and poured generous glasses of the expensive vintage. They picked up their own glass and gave it a good swirl before taking a deep sniff.

"Give it a try, it's very good," they encouraged with a half-smile. His stomach flooded with butterflies as he followed their lead, taking a cautious sip.

"Real good," he remarked, certain this was a better vintage than the first one they had offered him. He noted the feeling of wine mingling in his empty, never-stricken stomach.

"Mmm, I've been told you should decant this, let it breathe, or something, but I always forget," they said, wistfully looking at their glass. Monty felt uncomfortably aware of his tongue in his mouth and just how warm his face had become.

"I have to ask, why share this with me?" Monty put his guard back up. Cameron gave him a suddenly mournful expression that seemed to crash through their previously chipper emotions like a mack-truck.

"I'm terribly lonely, all things be told," they admitted in a low voice. "You are a captive audience to entertain," they explained.

"You're lonely?"

"You're the only other person on the property most of the time. It gets very quiet at night," they explained. They must not have meant that literally, since every night Monty could recall had been full of coyotes' howls and the screams of tree frogs.

"It's lonely for sure, but I can't lie, I kind of like the solitude," he admitted.

"Yes, but it's not even been a month since you got here. After a good long while, the solitude *wears* on you," Cameron explained. They gave him a somber salute and took a healthy swig of wine. It was almost criminal how they gulped down such an expensive vintage.

They leaned closer to him. They were both sitting opposite each other at the bar. Cameron's eyes drooped as they studied Monty's face, their gaze lingering on his silver hamsa necklace again. They gave a pseudo laugh before taking another swig of their wine. Monty desperately wanted to pull away, to look away, to stop staring deeply into lavender blue eyes.

He felt tendrils of something weaving into his flesh. A sensation of something intangible crawling through him and stitching him in place. A subtle caress in the flesh of his skull, between his gums. He wanted to look away. Darkness was tugging at the corners of his eyes in the way lights popped in your vision before blacking out.

"Do you think it makes you a little crazy after a while?" Monty asked in a whisper, not even realizing how quiet he had gotten. He could see them studying his lips before looking him up and down. He couldn't help but do the same, greedily taking them in like the wine in his glass. His heart raced, and his mind was pulled along on the thread of spectral webbing weaving through him. He wanted to run his hands through those strawberry-blond doll locks and—

*I cannot fuck my boss! What am I thinking!?*

"Hmm, I guess a little bit. The sound of your own mind gets very loud when there's nothing else to listen to," Cameron admitted, shifting on their stool slightly. Their voice was swimming in his gray matter. He tried desperately to push his inappropriate thoughts down.

"Don't you go into town often?" he asked, trying to stay on topic. He remembered how frequently their car was gone. His voice was still softer than he meant it to be. Though he was continuing the conversation, most of his mind was drifting to other places, wondering what the wine-stained lips in front of him tasted like. Cameron's half-lidded gaze elevated his heart until he could feel his own pulse screaming in his veins. He could feel the ethereal crawling sensation coiling up him, squeezing him tight like the grip of some beast.

"Not enough to fill my emptiness. I still spend far more time isolated here than anything else. It's hard to find meaningful connections. I need more than mindless small talk; do you know what I mean, Monty?" Cameron asked, leaning even closer over the bar. They were practically kneeling on their stool inches from his face. Monty was dizzy as his palms sweated. The shadows in the room around him were encroaching, wrapping around him like a fly being wound in a spider's web. He was swallowed into the depth of the shadows, imprisoned by threads of desire, as he spun into their pallid gaze.

*This is too much!*

He finally managed to pull away from Cameron's hypnotic beauty and took another swig of wine, hoping it would calm his nerves.

"I'm n-not entirely sure I know what you mean," he said with a surprising tremble in his voice.

"Oh, well… if you stay here long enough, you will eventually understand," they said, sitting back down on their stool looking slightly defeated.

As soon as they sat back, the dark tendrils crawling around Monty receded. Everything around him snapped back to reality, like he woke from a partial dream. He was mildly confused and aroused. For a split second, he wondered if he should have given in to his instincts instead of pulling back. The swarming emotions in his gut clouded his ability to parse out what was going on. He simply wanted to remove himself from whatever *this* was.

Cameron took out their golden cigarette case, reflexively offering one to Monty, who just put up his hand again to decline.

"I'm sorry. I appreciate this," he tapped his glass, "but I really should be going." He reflexively looked at his watch and squirmed off his seat. "It's getting late."

Though Cameron's expression was visibly put out, they simply sighed and said, "I understand. Have a good night."

"Good night." With that Monty slipped back up the cellar steps, trying to keep his feet from fleeing until he was out the back door.

# CHAPTER SEVEN

MONTAGUE was *still* trying to fix the porch. He got fresh lumber from the hardware store in town and now was undertaking the arduous process of replacing the rotten boards. Half the planks creaked and groaned under his weight, threatening to throw him down to the crawl space below. He had the strangest sensation while working here; it felt like there was an angry parent watching over his shoulder, just waiting to scold him for doing something wrong. Every board he tore up and replaced with fresh planks of pine left him feeling like a kid ripping up something he wasn't supposed to; like a child scribbling on the walls with a crayon. He was perplexed as to why he felt this anxiety of "getting in trouble." Cameron had explicitly told him to fix the porch, yet he was left feeling extremely unsure about what he was doing.

At least the shade of the porch was a welcome respite from the summer heat. The wisteria would not stop growing, to the point he wondered if trimming it had only emboldened it to sprawl more aggressively. He had given up trying to save the roof from the twining vines. He would have to wait for the plants to go dormant in the winter chill to actually remove them from the building.

He noticed now, while he was working out front, he often saw what he assumed—*hoped*—was Cameron, peeking at him from the old windows. He couldn't shake the feeling of being watched, even when he was certain he was alone on the property. Sometimes it felt like the house itself was watching him, the windows huge, soulless eyes monitoring his every move.

As soon as the sun set, he felt an overwhelming desire to run, to hide, as if night itself turned him to prey. This feeling was alien to him. He'd always felt more than capable, even in rather dangerous situations. He was not a slight man by any means, but the moment the sun set nowadays he felt so tiny. Everything in the dark set his teeth on edge. Now a mere breeze would send him stumbling home with his tail between his legs.

A few days later, Montague decided to tackle the fountain, knowing that putting it off would not do him any good. It needed to be scrubbed clean. Just touching the thing sent chills through him. The stone sculpture had taken on a rather impressive coating of moss and lichen. The basins were filled with dried leaves and an odd ruddy staining that he could have sworn was old blood, or maybe just rust.

He looked up at the stone cherub reclining at the very top of the fountain. Its cheeks puffed and poised to spit out a steady stream of water that no longer flowed. One of its stone wings stretched up to the sky, moss and a rusty color coating its intricately carved feather. Water stains across its youthful carved face looked like dried trails of ruddy tears.

Splayed out in a gory portrait was a woman's body impaled on the cherub's wing. Blood sprayed across her body, dyeing the water of the fountain crimson. She was face to face with him, short blond hair askew and her head lolled back, slack with death. There was no light behind her open amber eyes. Despite the terror frozen on her face, she was still recognizable. Dr. Giovanni's gored corpse was staring right into Monty's eyes. In a flash, the image was gone from his mind. The fountain was dry; no bloody corpse to be seen.

The feeling of a hand tapping on his shoulder caused him to

jump out of his skin.

"I'm sorry to startle you like that," Cameron said, backing away, parasol in hand, car keys in the other.

"Oh... I'm sorry, I was just having a bad daydream," Monty said, rubbing his face to assure he was awake. Why did he imagine such a thing just now? Was that how she died, or was that vision some paranoid fabrication of his heat-fried mind? He returned from his thought and felt embarrassment wash over him, realizing he was wearing just cargo shorts and boots. He'd been working with his shirt off in a vain attempt to even out his horrible farmer's tan.

"That's quite alright. I'm going out for a while. I wanted to ask you if you could do me a favor and start the wash? The machine is on the second floor, east wing. I'm in a bit of a hurry, or I'd do it myself, here's instructions." Cameron handed him a slip of paper with scrawling script written on it.

"Sure thing," Monty nodded, looking at the paper.

He heard a "thank you," and when he looked up, Cameron was already in their car.

Monty turned his attention back to scrubbing dirt and rust stains from the fountain. No matter how much force he used, he couldn't get it fully clean. He wondered if there was a special cleaner of some sort that would work better than the soapy water he was using. The red stains had seeped deep into the pores of the stone. He gave a resigned sigh.

He walked along the tree line back behind the mansion to return his things to the shed. His attention was suddenly caught by the sound of rustling in the forest. Right by the same patch of woods had gone into that previous weekend. He stopped in his tracks, listening. Mostly he heard the screams of cicadas and the occasional buzz of something flying past his ear.

Another rustle of something moving.

He would just peek. He knew Cameron had said to leave the dead animals be. However, if it was luring coyotes and bears this close to the property, he had to get rid of the thing, no matter what his employer wanted. He didn't want to be the next person who had to call animal control because a bear decided to take a dip in the pool.

He crossed into the trees, armed with nothing more than a bucket and scrub brush. If he hadn't been on the verge of heatstroke, he might have secondguessed this choice. The sun was still shining brightly overhead, so it was easy to see through the foliage now. Though the leaves were beginning to tinge yellow, the forest was still very lush green with minimal leaf litter underfoot. He was not entirely sure what he was looking for.

He tried to follow the smell he had discovered a few nights prior. To his dismay, and honest surprise, he could not find the putrid aroma at all. It had only been a few days, not nearly long enough for a corpse's scent to completely disappear, even if the animals had devoured it. He searched for longer than he'd hoped but —*no*—there was nothing, no deer's corpse, no human remains, no bones, no evidence there was anything here ever at all.

Dissatisfied and mildly concerned, he left the wilderness be. He returned to his cabin to take a break. He dunked his head in the sink to cool off and then tossed on a t-shirt. Then he remembered Cameron's favor.

He trepidatiously entered the dark and empty beast of a mansion. It was quiet enough to hear a pin drop as he climbed the stairs to the second floor. The whole manor felt suffocating, a musty kind of heat that would make anyone choke. He couldn't wrap his head around how Cameron could stand being inside this building with no airflow. The place felt like a claustrophobic crypt despite how much space there was to explore.

The hallways were dark as night. He fumbled around until he found a light switch of some kind. He flipped it on, and the electric wall sconces down the eastern hallway buzzed to life reluctantly. They protested and flickered as though they were not used to being turned on. He felt a creeping sensation come over him as he realized that every single frame on the walls of this hallway was covered in heavy black shrouds. He wondered if this was some sort of mourning ritual he was not privy to.

Curiously, he pulled back a shroud to find a dark-haired, sun-kissed, and very disgruntled man staring back at him. It was a mirror. He looked behind the cloth of another large gilded frame, another mirror. He walked past several, looking behind the veils. Every single ornate frame had a fading silver-backed mirror in it. Not a single painting, photograph, or the like, just a hallway of shrouded mirrors. This mansion continued to bewilder him.

The washer and dryer were newer than he'd anticipated, neatly tucked in a closet that had been conveniently left open. He mindlessly stuffed the white sheets into the washer as he read over the instructions again. He marveled at the amount of bleach written in the note, finding it excessive for one set of king sized sheets. Cameron's scrawling handwriting was hard for him to read, so perhaps he was mistaken. Just as that thought passed his mind, he noticed a rather large red stain, likely from wine, on the sheets.

*Please let that be wine.*

Somewhat disgusted, he quickly shoved the sheets in and set a timer on his digital watch to check back when it would be done.

Curiosity still buzzed around him like a headache. He was already inside. He wondered if he'd be able to see where the second-story balcony led. Often at night he had felt a presence there, watching him. At least his instincts told him so. There was nothing wrong with taking a peek at something he'd been curious about. He just wanted to know the line of sight from that back balcony.

He constructed a mental map to figure out which door down this unnerving hallway would most likely lead to it. He decided on one of the very tall, heavy wooden doors. As his hand curled around the crystal doorknob, he was astonished to find that it was unlocked.

He instantly regretted letting himself through said door, however, as he rather quickly realized he'd entered what could only be Cameron's bedroom. He noticed there were actually two doors from the hall that went into this room. Another floor-length gilded mirror sat between them. It too was covered with a large black shroud. It stood almost eight feet high from the floor. The heavy golden frame was made of intricately entwined serpents, with the family crest proudly displayed at the top. Through the thin black shroud he could faintly make out the unmistakable spider webbing of shattered glass, its nexus just a little below his face.

The room itself was huge, with a beautiful hardwood floor, a small portion of which was covered with a large bear-pelt rug. Hung from the high ceiling were two grandiose ruby chandeliers that stared down at him like a beast's angry red eyes, watching his every move.

There were two additional doors on either side of the room; he could only guess where they went. On one side there was a beautiful old turntable cabinet filled with records upon records. He crept into the room and curiously peeked at the music selection. Most of it was Italian classical music, operas. The other half of the collection was mostly post-punk. *Violator* by Depeche Mode was on the turntable as if it had been recently listened to.

On the other side of the room, there was a large writing desk. It was the only messy thing in the otherwise pristinely kept room. On the desk there was a clunky, ancient typewriter. There were many assorted notebooks, splotched sheet music, and scattered pens on the desk as well. It took all of his self-restraint to resist inspecting the contents of the notebooks.

In the center of the room, between two curtained doors to the balcony, was a king-size four-poster canopy bed. The posts were intricately carved wood with serpent motifs that matched the rest of the house's style. It was shrouded in thick black velvet curtains around it, as if it had been for mourning a passed relative, rather than for sleeping. It felt like an empty tomb to him.

He wondered if this room had always been theirs. It was lacking in decoration other than the intricate woodworking of the house itself. The ghosts of missing picture frames in the wallpaper led him to believe that this might have originally been their mother's room. The thought of sleeping in her bed so soon after her departure left a weird taste in Monty's mouth.

Leaning up against an end table with a rotary phone was a golden fencing sword. There were a plethora of empty wine bottles around the bed and one perched on the desk. He noticed they were all bottles that had the strange handmade labels. He looked at the bottle on the desk. 'Florence 1995' was written on the simple label in scrawling handwritten script. He examined the lone wineglass on the desk and gave it a sniff. The smell of stale wine made him gag.

He remembered why he had even come into this room in the first place, deciding he'd meddled enough with Cameron's things. To his ultimate surprise, the balcony door on the right was unlocked. He slipped out onto the back balcony and into the night air.

The moon was full, and a cool late summer breeze was blowing across the yard that ruffled his hair as he stepped out. His anxieties were right; not only could he see his cabin from here, he could see *into* it. You could see right into his bedroom through those large windows. It was also easy to see the pool from here, its lights underlit him in a dazzling array of blues as the wind disturbed the water's surface.

"Oh my, now this is a surprise," Cameron spoke calmly, coming through the left door to the balcony. All the blood drained out of Montague's body. "Didn't anyone ever tell you it's rude to snoop in another's bedroom?" They asked him.

"How? I-I saw you leave..." Monty stammered, backing away from Cameron as they advanced towards him. He had not heard them come back. He didn't hear anyone move in the house at all. He was certain he should have heard them come in at least. The absence of anger on their practically glowing face was terrifying.

They encroached on Monty until he felt his back press against the stone balcony railing. Cameron's figure somehow loomed over him despite their size difference. Slowly, a crawling sensation writhed under his skin as he felt himself become paralyzed in place.

Tendrils of shadow crawled from the night itself, stitching his fearful body in place. His head spun ever so slightly. Cameron trailed a long pale hand languidly up from his waist to rest just under his chin. Even the slightest touch of their fingers sent strange electrical currents through the tendrils of shadow coiled around him. They grabbed his jaw and tilted his head to meet their gaze. Their grip was firm but not meant to hurt. Their eyes glinted red in the moonlight. They looked hungry, pensive, intoxicated.

"I did not say when I would be back, now did I? I asked you to do something simple for me inside. As a trust experiment. Just to see if you'd stick to your word, to not go looking for trouble, like I asked. It didn't occur to me you'd be so rude as to rifle through *my* bedroom," they said in a dangerously cool tone. They paused for a moment and cocked their head to the side inquisitively.

"Looking for something of mine, hmm?" they teased. They looked from Montague's lips to his elongated neck. Cameron gently pulled his jaw to expose him even further, eyeing him over like a piece of meat.

The feeling of the darkness of the night continued to encroach on Monty, lights popping behind his eyes. He was an insect trapped in a web, prey. His knees quaked at Cameron's touch. Their icy hand held against his warm flesh burned in contrast. The pool just below him taunted his mind. He would be lucky to make the water if he were pushed any further back.

"Please don't kill me," he pleaded, closing his eyes, waiting for something. He was met with cool breath, like the breeze against his neck, causing sparks to fly through his body. He felt the faint trace of lips against his jugular.

"Kill you?" Cameron laughed quietly against his neck. "No, no, I'm just messing with you," they added before letting go of Monty's jaw just a tad too roughly. "Why would you think I'd do such a thing?" they asked with a lingering laugh in their voice. As they backed away, the darkness in his vision receded again, just as it had before in the wine cellar. Despite feeling as if he'd been freed from a sticky web, his feet stayed planted right where he was.

"Wh-wha—?" he stammered, frozen by a strange mix of fear and excitement. He could feel his shorts becoming painfully tight with his arousal. He was shocked at how excited by their touch he had become.

"I'd like you to keep out of my room unless *invited* in," they teased, still standing painfully close to him. He nodded, trying to swallow, though his throat was horrifically dry.

"I'm sorry. I shouldn't have done that," he apologized, his voice still trembling to his dismay.

"I will forgive it just this once. You are... *dangerously* curious, Monty," Cameron remarked, backing away now. His neck still tingled where they had teased him.

"Sorry, I don't know what I was thinking," he apologized again, heading for the balcony door. Cameron gripped his arm with incredible strength, stopping him in his tracks. He was taken aback, for how thin and frail they appeared, they were horrifically strong, nearly swiping him fully off his feet.

"If you keep snooping around looking for something, you're eventually going to find it, and I can only warn you so many times before it's too late," Cameron hissed, severity dripping from their lips like venom. He stared at them in bewilderment for a moment.

"What?" He was still dumbfounded that they had nearly pulled him off his feet with such a slight gesture.

"I know what you're looking for, even if you don't, and when you do eventually find it... there will be nothing I can do to help you," Cameron continued.

"I wish you'd be less cryptic."

"Stop looking for answers about my mother," they sighed as they released his wrist.

"How do you—?"

"Well, you are either a pervert interested in discovering the color of my underwear," they began, narrowing their eyes, causing

Monty to burn with embarrassment, "or you're snooping in places you ought not be because you've severely misunderstood the nature of your relationship to my mother. Which I feel I should mention, most people have had that experience with her."

"Now go," they dismissed him. Completely at a loss for words, Monty fled the balcony.

)  ✧  (

Despite drawing the curtains shut tight in his room, he was still paranoid about the fact that it was so easy to see into his cabin from the mansion.

*I'm the one who gets in trouble for snooping*, he thought, *but who's the one spying on me?*

He lay awake for some time in the dark, staring at the exposed beams in his bedroom ceiling. As he lay restless, he listened to something scratching and sniffing around the foundation of his cabin. He brushed it off as a curious raccoon, too preoccupied with his thoughts to really pay it more mind.

He felt shame searing through him. He wholly could not ignore his attraction to Cameron, and the fear they instilled in him only made things worse. The excitement caused by being touched in such a violently teasing way would not leave his mind. It danced around in his stomach and mingled with the terror he felt from that encounter. He didn't understand why Cameron had handled the situation that way. For a moment he really thought they were going to hurt him, which now felt silly. Besides, he was sure he could snap them like a toothpick. Still, they'd demonstrated nearly inhuman strength to stagger him like that.

Their warnings too rang in his head. What *was* he even looking for? What could have been in Cameron's room that he had missed? There was something they were obviously trying to hide... Or maybe he was completely out of his right mind to be assuming they were hiding anything personally. He'd gone into Cameron's private space completely unwarranted. He would have reacted far worse if he'd come home and found them in his bedroom, uninvited. He was assuming the worst of someone he barely knew, and he was the one who was being an utter creep in the end.

He let out a long, frustrated groan. They could have just yelled at him, or told him to get lost. Instead, he was left feeling aroused and baffled. Cameron surely knew what they were doing. He felt cornered, like a rat in a maze. He got the impression they wanted to eat him whole, rather than sleep with him. He still had a growing suspicion about Cameron that twisted his insides around into confused knots. He had to know *how* Dr. Giovanni died. He had to know if Cameron was the reason *why*.

# CHAPTER EIGHT

MONTAGUE sat bolt upright, drenched head to toe in sweat in his bed. Despite sleeping in the nude, he was panting like he'd been cooking on a grill. He ran a hand through his drenched shaggy hair and let out a ragged sigh. The details of his nightmare evaded him.

He could hear the tinny sound of Evanescence coming from his CD player, letting him know he'd not been asleep that long. He turned the CD player off. His ears rang from how silent the room became, not even a single cricket chirping in the distance. It was as if he'd been defended.

Moonlight was pouring into his room. The mansion and pool were completely dark. The moon itself was struggling to cut through the cloud cover. He got up to look out at the lawn through his open window. The lawn was painted in hues of indistinguishable grays. The trees were still as if the night itself was holding its breath.

His blood froze. Someone was standing out in the middle of the yard. The dark figure did not move. Monty blinked several times to clear his vision, to make sure of what he was seeing. They were still there. He could not see their face, but his animal instincts knew they were looking right at him.

He heard a soft hissing in his bedroom that distracted him from the window. He looked around aimlessly in the darkroom. His eyes were guessing where things could have been from memory. Another long, loud hiss. It sounds far too large and angry to belong to a common garden snake. He looked over the dark floorboards but saw nothing. He cautiously approached the bed to see if there was anything underneath. He found the big yellow flashlight. He carefully reached for it and switched it on. Nothing under the bed. It was quiet for a moment. He looked back up at the window.

His flashlight caught the face of the person standing just outside. Paper-white skin stretched over a long, stern face, with a slack-jawed silent scream. The fog of death clouding over once amber eyes now staring like two golden marbles. Through the center of her chest, there was a gaping void of gore, slipping organs glistening with fresh blood.

*Do not be fooled by the monster!*

Her voice rang in his head like tinnitus. Montague could not scream. He felt terror fix his body in place. A nauseating, dizzy sickness overtook him as he recognized those golden eyes glittering back at him. His flashlight faltered, buzzing and sputtering before going dark. The figure disappeared with the light.

Bright sunlight and the onslaught of hundreds of different birds singing their morning songs dragged him from his nightmare. He sat up slowly and watched dust motes dance in the sliver of golden morning light pouring through the crack in his curtains. He sat there for a while trying to remember his dream, but it slipped away from him with every passing moment. The gnawing need for coffee to soothe his exhausted body overtook his mind. He decided to get started earlier than usual. Despite feeling like he'd not slept a wink, he was far too awake to get himself to lie back down and sleep anymore.

He was almost done with all his exterior tasks. The last thing he needed to do was simply to get that wretched fountain to turn on. After a stomach-sickeningly bad cup of caffeine, he dressed and went to face the day. The morning air was surprisingly pleasant and soothed his tired body. The morning dew dampened his work boots as he walked across the freshly cut lawn up to the front.

He felt eyes on him as he looked over the lawn across to the woods by the mansion. Standing there just past the trees was the largest coyote he had ever seen. An unfamiliar person might have assumed it was a wolf from its size. There was some gore on its muzzle, as if it had just been feasting on some carrion. Montague froze in his tracks, realizing the hound had its sights fixed on him. Their eyes were locked; he didn't dare look away.

The coyote only gazed at him unblinking, blood dripping from its muzzle. The air stood still. It blinked slowly at him before shaking the viscera and dew off itself. It turned away and walked back into the woods. Where had he seen those eyes before?

*Forget it... stop acting like you've never seen a wild animal*, he scolded himself as he quickly strutted towards the mansion.

There was a faucet hidden just next to the porch he was sure was hooked up to the fountain. The rusty handle fought him for a moment before letting out a sharp squeak, relenting, and returning the water supply back to the roundabout's centerpiece. Rust-tainted water sputtered from the cherub's mouth like a cut artery as the fixture sprang back to life. It took a moment for the water to turn from a ruddy brown back to clear. The pipes must have corroded from sitting dormant. It took a surprising amount of time for it to fill both its basins and quit its sputtering. He couldn't help but think to himself how wasteful and vain having a fixture like this was. However, the running water did make the manor look simply dilapidated, rather than flat out abandoned.

He'd done all he could. It looked significantly better outside, and yet the old Victorian seemed no more inviting than when he had started. Everything was still crumbling, eating itself faster than he could ever possibly fix. It was an impossibly deep rot; there was no way to scrub it clean. Still, he didn't know what else could be done at this point. He felt he should find his employer to let them know he was ready to move on and possibly get some further instruction.

He let himself in through the front door and was blinded for a moment by the dark interior contrasting with the sunny day outside. He stood and listened for a moment to see if he could guess where Cameron was in the vast bowels of the home. He stood at the base of the massive central staircase. He stared up the steps at the gaudy family crest, casting red and gold light down at him. He didn't know much about family crests, having only ever seen them in films and old dusty books, but he still thought a snake was an odd choice.

"Hey, Cameron?" He called cautiously into the mansion. "Fountain is working. We should talk about what you need me to do next," his voice echoed through the halls. He waited for a painfully long minute.

It was so quiet and still. This house was such a vast space to go looking for one lone person. He wondered how this house had been run before it fell into Cameron's care. Dr. Giovanni had not, even once, maintained a single thing on the vast estate. He knew she spent most of her time at the college, either teaching or researching in the campus labs. Perhaps she never had the time to keep the place. It was possible she'd had it tossed in her lap already in a sorry state, similarly to Cameron. That was his most logical thought as to how an opulent historical building like this could fall into such disrepair.

"Why didn't you just call me?" Cameron asked from just behind him. Monty startled at their voice, having not heard them move at all. He gripped his chest and turned around to see them standing in the doorway to the main living room. They looked tired. It was evident in their mannerisms that they too had not slept well that night. Their expression quickly turned from irritation to something that resembled pity.

"I'm sorry," he sighed.

"It's fine. You are here now," they said. There was a cigarette hanging from their mouth, a maroon smoking robe hung loosely on them. Monty averted his eyes, realizing that was the *only* thing they were wearing, clearly not expecting company.

"I wish I'd had some warning you were going to come in," Cameron said, uncrossing their arms as they leaned in the doorway. They dug in their pockets for a moment before holding out their cigarette case again. "You look like you've seen a ghost. Are you sure you don't want one?"

Monty's eyes darted to the gold case full of expensive cigarettes. The ones in their case this time were thin with champagne pink filters. He eyed the case delicately perched in Cameron's long, thin hand.

"Oh, fuck it. Yeah, I'll give it a try," he felt himself finally crack. Cameron gave one of their forced half-smiles and plucked one from the case, before snapping it shut and slipping it back into their pocket.

"Here," Cameron handed it to him. He felt odd as his dirty, calloused hands lingered next to their pristinely manicured ones. After a moment too long, he put the filter in his mouth. Gently, they grasped his wrist and pulled him closer to light his cigarette on the butt of theirs. Their eyes locked as he drew his first drag, the head rush coming almost instantly to him. He did his best to hold in a cough.

He lingered on their eyes for a moment, mesmerized by their strange lavender color. They were studying him, but there was no malice in their expression. There was a smell of something metallic mingling with their floral smoky aroma. Cameron backed away.

"Rose flavor, you like it?"

"Yeah," was all he could muster. He continued to hold in his urge to cough. His anxiety waned as the nicotine relieved some of the aching from his sleep deprivation.

He couldn't help but think about how different Cameron's

demeanor was this morning compared to the night prior. It was almost as if they had wholly forgotten the encounter, or perhaps they wanted to brush past it. It was difficult for him to parse out what their feelings were, and perhaps that was by design.

"Come in here," they beckoned him into the drawing room. It was still just as filthy as when he first arrived for his interview. If anything, it was more of a mess, as he realized the floor was covered in notecards and papers, looking like a conspiracy board. Heavy velvet curtains were drawn over the large windows, blocking the sun and leaving a gloomy cast over the room.

"Don't mind my work," they said, watching Monty carefully step over the mess of papers on the floor.

"Do you do most of your work here?" He asked, looking over the notecards with a tinge of curiosity. Cameron's handwriting was beautiful but wholly illegible. Seeing it now sprawling across notecards, it reminded him of a doctor's handwriting. It was not much different from their mother's.

"I do now and then, mostly when I'm too lazy to go up to the ballroom to practice. You've caught me in the middle of trying to decipher the plot of an operetta. I like to toss bad ideas into the fire," they said, gesturing to the lit fireplace. They placed an ashtray in front of Monty and laid on their side along the couch. During the day, the fire made the room absolutely broiling hot.

"Destructive," he mumbled, trying to tear his eyes away from their exposed chest. Thin collarbones framed the golden locket that hung around their neck. He realized their locket looked identical to the one in Dr. Giovanni's portrait.

"I know, but still I'd like you to not ash on the parts I've chosen to keep," they pointed out. Monty realized his cigarette was ashing everywhere other than the tray in front of him. He hastily put out his half-smoked cigarette in embarrassment.

"So... I came here to ask you about what's next. Paint right?"

"Correct," Cameron nodded. They pulled out a blank notecard and began scribbling. "I know the hardware store in town? They should have this color. Get whatever tools you think you will need. Bring me back the receipt and I'll reimburse you," they continued, not paying much mind to Monty, who'd found himself entranced at their reclining form.

Their legs were long and smooth in a way that reminded him of a playboy model with how they stretched out on the couch. Their ankles were ringed with what looked to be scars in the dim light. He found it was hard to look away or even pay attention to what was being said to him. This choice of dress was a stark contrast to the elaborate, yet modestly full coverage outfits they normally wore.

"Monty?" He snapped out of his trance, realizing Cameron had had their arm outstretched with the note.

"S-sorry," he mumbled, sheepishly taking the paper from them.

"You can call here if you have questions," they added. They looked like there was something weighing on their mind.

"Yes?" Monty pressed their pensive expression.

"Why did you come in? You could have just called me?" they asked, blowing a cloud of smoke up to the ceiling.

"Oh, I..." he didn't know how to answer. He didn't actually know why he had not considered that. "I'm sorry about yesterday," he finally said, unsure if that was the crux of it. Cameron raised one thin eyebrow.

"I already said you are forgiven," they blew a plume of cigarette smoke from their sharp nose. They hummed to themself in thought.

"I know, but I still feel stupid for invading your privacy so carelessly," Monty admitted, feeling the full weight of his shame.

"I'm not used to having privacy, so what does it actually matter," they said nonchalantly, waving a hand dismissively.

"You're alone here?"

"Yes, I mean–forget it."

"No, please."

"Don't you feel it? The unrelenting feeling of being watched, observed?"

"I do, but..." Monty trailed off. It was Cameron who he had thought had been watching him. In that moment, he became acutely aware of the portraits staring down at him from the wall. He wasn't sure if the fire was the only thing making him sweat now.

"She's watching you too. I know she is. I can tell from the way you act, something is haunting you," they elaborated.

"You believe in ghosts, I'll take it then?"

"And you don't?"

"I don't know," he admitted. "I'm warming up to the idea. I'm not a huge believer in the supernatural, but I won't deny I've felt weird here."

Cameron let out a snort, clearly finding something about his statement to be amusing. "You look like you've not gotten much sleep," they remarked. "Take the rest of the day off when you're done with the hardware store."

"I'll take you up on that. I *am* exhausted," he nodded and then got up to leave.

"Oh, and Monty?"

"Yes?"

"Give me a warning before you come in next time," they said, pulling on the open collar of the smoking robe, revealing more of their bare chest, a few long scars catching in the firelight.

# CHAPTER NINE

SINCE Montague was already in town, he decided to stop by Mina's shop and pay her a visit while she was at work. She was a mechanic at a fairly small family-owned auto shop that specialized in motorcycles and mopeds. It seemed to be a slow day as he let himself in through the open garage door. The smell of motor oil and gasoline wafted over him as he walked inside.

There were two people working on bikes inside, one of them being Mina. She had her dark hair pulled back in a messy bun and sported her motor oil covered, baby pink overalls. Her sleeves were rolled up, showing off her impressive collection of blackwork American traditional tattoos on her muscular arms.

"Monty!" she practically threw the wrench in her hand with excitement. "What in the hell are you doing here?"

"I was already in town to pick up some stuff for work, and I decided to come say hi," he explained. Mina wrestled her tools free from the muffler on a huge trike she'd been tinkering with.

"Dude, I hadn't heard from you in a minute! I was starting to get worried," she remarked as she wiped grease off her hands.

"I'm sorry, I've been caught up with work, I guess," he said with a shrug.

"Don't take this the wrong way, but you look like hammered shit, dude," she noted. He followed her around the shop as she cleaned up.

"I didn't sleep super well last night in particular," he admitted.

"I can see," Mina said, pulling on her under eyes. "Give me a sec, I'm gonna go talk to Kev and see if he's cool with me clocking out forty early."

"Didn't realize you were almost done with your shift. I'm glad I didn't dawdle," he remarked, earning a snort from Mina.

"Give me one min'," she said, putting up a finger before slipping into the office. Monty crossed his arms and waited around, looking over the bikes in the shop in varying states of repair. In the shop's lot there were even more bikes parked, including Mina's, which was unmistakable in a crowd. She was the only person he'd ever met who'd have a pastel pink bike with Hello Kitty decals all over it.

*You could practically see it from space,* he laughed to himself.

"How much time do you have?" Mina asked as she returned with her bike jacket on and her helmet in hand.

"I'm off for the rest of the day," he said.

"You want to come over? You can have dinner with the fam," she offered.

"That would be great," he said with a smile.

"Sweet. I'll meet you at my place. I need to get my bike home," she said as she threw on her helmet. He gave her a thumbs-up and went back to his van.

Mina's house wasn't far from the center of town. He couldn't help but think about how the woods that were behind her house must have connected to Giovanni's property. Almost all the other properties in this county connected to the same forest, considering most of the space apart from the surrounding little towns and ski resort was undeveloped. There was a lot of wealth in this area, and the woods kept it private. The Kimura family was by no means even close to as wealthy as the Giovannis appeared to be, but they were "comfortable."

Sometimes he envied Mina and the fact that she never had to worry, purely working for her own benefit. Her parents supported her every ambition, cherished her, in a way he couldn't even picture his family extending to him. Even though they treated him like their own son, if he dwelled on it too long, he would feel a misguided bubble of jealousy surface.

He did his best to put these thoughts out of his mind as he pulled up to his friend's house. He slammed the door of his car shut just as he saw Mina walking out of the garage, her pink bike parked neatly inside.

"I hope they don't mind you coming by without warning," she joked, knowing that Monty still had a copy of the front door key.

"I'm sure I'll get the usual lecture," he played along. Mina let them into the house, where they both promptly took off their shoes and trotted into the living room. Monty sat in front of the glass coffee table on the sage green sectional, and Mina booted up her gaming console. She chucked a controller his way. He snatched it from the air reflexively in one fell swoop.

"Ready to get your ass kicked again?" she teased.

"You wish! I let you win last time," he snarked back as they waited for the game console to boot up.

"So, what have you been up to?" she asked.

"Still just hacking away at that old house. I'm in the process of undoing what feels like decades of neglect. I was actually in town to get paint since I'm going to start working on the inside of that crazy mansion soon," he explained.

"Oh, they're making you fix the inside too, not just doing groundskeeping stuff?" Mina asked. She tossed her motorcycle gear on the floor and jumped onto the couch next to her friend.

"Yeah, I mean they did warn me it was going to be a bit more like being a live-in handyman job at the start," he shrugged, fighter already selected in the player 2 slot.

"So why the hell are you so tired? Are they working you like a dog or something?" She asked, cracking her knuckles.

"No, no... I just didn't sleep well last night. Can you pick your character?" He shifted in his seat and ran a hand through his increasingly shaggy hair.

"Oops, yeah," Mina's cursor snapped to her character, filling the player 1 slot. "You look worse than just having one bad night to be honest," she added.

"I'm not sure how to explain it, but weird stuff has been going on around the property."

"Like?"

"Well... remember how I mentioned I was worried there might have been a dead deer or something in the woods drawing in coyotes?"

"Sure," she said. Neither one was looking at the other as their conversation was underlined by the furious clicking of plastic buttons.

"I went back yesterday to check it out, and it was gone," he explained, biting his lip in concentration.

"Like totally gone, gone, or like it got eaten?" Mina cocked her head to the side, eyes still glued to the CRT.

"No, like it had never even been there," he elaborated. She looked at him with a sense of confusion and concern, allowing him to knock her out of the arena.

"Hey!" she yelled before returning her attention to the fighting game. "Like you mean you imagined it?" She asked.

"No, I mean yes... but it felt so real, I could smell its rotting flesh. For something like that to just disappear overnight is insane," he paused, "and the coyotes are still lingering around the property. I saw a huge one this morning. It just looked at me and then walked off."

"That's freaky. But also there're animals around here, you might just be confused with the woods?" she asked.

Mina landed a final blow on Monty's character, ending the match.

*"GAME!"*

"I have no idea," he pondered, not sure of what he should and shouldn't share with his friend. "I could just be scrambled. I can't get the doc' out of my head, and... Cameron is... a really odd person."

"If I lived in that creepy place like that, I think I'd be a little 'off' too," Mina joked.

"No, that's not what I mean. It's like they don't make any sound when they move and weird shit like that. There's something they are keeping from me. It feels like they want me to figure it out but also simultaneously don't," he said, mulling over all the stranger interactions he'd had with his boss. He debated telling her more about how their flirtatious and foreboding gestures made him feel.

"You sound a little nuts, you know that?"

"I know... I keep having these intrusive thoughts, or dreams, I don't know what you'd call them. I just keep seeing the doctor splayed out all freaky and dead in the fountain they have out front." Mina was now looking at him like he had six heads.

"I don't think being all alone on that huge estate all day, every day, has been good for you, man," she said with a tone of severity. "I think you need to get out and get some more human interaction, and not just with me, dude."

"Yeah, but it's hard, you know? I'll be wiped out by the end of my day, and since the property is so far away, it's really hard to go anywhere. Not to mention I don't really have a lot of friends out here other than you."

"Alright big guy, why don't you come with me and my girl Leah to the bar this Saturday?" Mina asked, clapping a small, admittedly still dirty, hand on his shoulder. He paused and let out a sigh.

"Yeah... I think that would be a good idea. I need to spend more time away from that eerie place," he admitted. Mina nodded and gave him a concerned smile.

# CHAPTER TEN

MONTAGUE returned to the estate late that night after spending most of the evening with Mina's family. The painfully loud drone of frogs was the only thing keeping him awake in the warm summer night air. The property was disturbingly dark as he pulled up to the shed of a coach house, parking his minivan in its usual spot. Despite having fixed the porch lights, the house was completely dark, save for one window that was lit.

He realized it was the room connected to the third-story balcony. The doors were open; the night breeze blowing the curtains gently. He could almost make out the room. He could see a chandelier through the gaps in the fluttering lace curtains. In the warm night air, he vaguely thought he could make out the sounds of someone playing the piano. He wondered if he was imagining the soft melody. He checked his watch. It was nearly one in the morning. Maybe Cameron was having another fit of insomnia. Maybe Monty needed to go to sleep himself. He walked swiftly with his head down along the trees to his cabin, the melody of soft piano blending in with the chirps of crickets.

He was pleasantly surprised to wake the next morning after a dreamless night. For once, he was shocked awake by his little watch's alarm clock. He prepared himself for the day as always. It was now beginning to feel like autopilot. Wash face, make coffee, get dressed, brush teeth, boots on. The only true difference this morning being that it was the first overcast day that was not already scorching with heat by the time he'd gotten up. He wondered how long until he would have to cover the pool. The thought of managing autumn leaves filled him with a twinge of dread.

He pulled the plastic landline off the receiver, remembering his employer's request to warn them before barging in. The phone rang for a very long time. The anxiety of waking Cameron stewed in his stomach as he listened to each ring. After what had to be the second to last chime, he finally heard the phone pick up. It was silent for a moment, causing his stomach to knot with anxiety further.

"Monty? Please tell me this is you," an extremely groggy voice said on the other end of the line. There was a tone of dread in Cameron's voice, as if they might have been expecting a call from someone they did not want to speak with.

"Yes, it's me. I'm so sorry to wake you, but you told me to warn you before I came in. I'm gonna be getting started upstairs," he nervously shifted his weight in front of the phone as he spoke.

"Mmm… yes, right. I plan to be sequestered in my room all day," they paused for a moment. "I have a rather unpleasant… hangover." They sounded unsure of themself, but he fully believed that they would be in such a predicament.

"I'll do my best not to bug you," he assured.

"Okay. I think the roof might be leaking up there. Let me know if you notice anything while working. I might see about getting the roof replaced if it's urgent… Oh, and Monty?" they paused.

"Yeah?"

"Just stick to where you plan on working, okay?"

"Right, understood. I'll keep an eye out and won't fuck around."

"Good," they mumbled and hung up the phone.

Cameron sounded wrecked, the way someone who had only spent a few hours sleeping typically did. They might have spent the entire night playing piano. He could imagine them losing track of time, especially if they'd been drinking. Then again, their musings the night prior sounded quite good for an intoxicated player.

The overcast day left a muggy sensation looming in the air. The sky was turning shades of gray and would likely stay that way for the coming months. The humid heat was ten times more unpleasant inside the mansion. The moldering rot of decades of unmitigated mildew felt ripe to bloom in this weather. His throat practically burnt from the scent of mold on the third floor. The peeling yellow floral wallpaper was the primary source of the scent. Its ornate surface was marred by dark blooms of black.

Cameron had taken it upon themself to remove all the frames from the walls for him. The empty spaces against the peeling paper left a saturated ghost of darkness, unfaded, safe from sun and nicotine. He wondered if the missing frames were also all mirrors, like on the second floor.

He got busy taping down tarps to protect the floors against the violence he was about to enact on that god-awful wallpaper. The patterns had the same effect as the wings of a large butterfly, giving the illusion of hundreds of hungry eyes watching. The paper was warped and bubbling in spots, places where moisture from the plaster had already eroded the glue.

Oddly, the only thing that truly made him feel exposed was the wide-open doors to the ballroom. The majority of the third floor was taken up by the ballroom. The large ornate doors to the very room were wide open as if they were begging him to peek inside.

A blur of movement caused him to stop in his tracks. He paused and peered into the room. He saw nothing inside, but he could have sworn he heard the faintest tune of music. He slowly found himself wandering in through the open doors, just to see, just to look.

The ceiling was high, with a grand chandelier that rivaled the one in the entryway, hanging heavily from the gilded rafters. The dance floor was a black and white checkerboard marble tile, like a huge chessboard. There were decorative columns pretending to hold the ceiling up around the dance floor. Rows of chairs sat stacked and covered in dust cloths along the burgundy-draped walls. The balcony was centered with the dance floor, its doors closed, the white lace curtains still. A gorgeous white grand piano sat next to the doors in the far-left corner of the checkered tiles.

On the wall there were golden fencing swords, delicately mounted in a way that made him unsure if they were for display or use. He didn't dare touch them, but he looked for just a moment. There was space for four, one in the center missing, likely the one that he'd seen in Cameron's bedroom.

This room felt like it could belong in a castle. It was almost a shame it was stuck in a place like this, disused and vacant, tucked away for just one person's enjoyment. Montague didn't notice himself wandering onto the dance floor. There was the faintest tune playing from the piano. His body was drifting along the melody, wandering across the checkered floor. He was drawn towards the beautiful doors that opened out onto the balcony.

*Mon~ta~gue*

He heard his name softly, sweetly, called from somewhere he could not see. It pulled him further forward. He was entranced by the somber melody in his ears, and before he knew it, he had walked all the way across the floor. His feet did not feel like they were on the ground. He was floating along in a dream.

The moment he stepped off the dance floor, the doors to the balcony slammed open and standing there, just feet away, was Dr. Giovanni. Her eyes dead, the blood still pouring from her stomach and mouth as she stood close enough for him to smell the decay.

*Leave this place, Montague!*

She shrieked in his ears as she lunged for him. Cold hands forced him back. He yelped in terror as he fell hard onto the tile floor. It felt as if he'd been tossed back off a ladder as he was shoved down. Her putrefied and bloodied face was inches from his, mouth stretched wide, shrieking her warning.

Then she was gone, and silence rang in his ears. The piano had stopped. Now only a humid late summer breeze blew over him from the open balcony doors as he lay dumbfounded on the ground. The smell of rot was replaced with overwhelming ozone. He could still feel his heart trying to escape his ribcage, a stinging pain coming into his wrist that broke his fall. He let himself lay back flat on the cold tile. He gazed up at the dusty chandelier, some of its crystals swaying in the breeze.

*Why am I here?*

He wondered if all his commotion had woken Cameron. Despite the horrific and bizarre experience he'd just had, he was far more scared of them finding him here like this. He mustered his willpower to get up and close the balcony doors.

*I'm really losing it now*, he thought to himself as he rubbed his throbbing wrist.

He'd seen her. He *felt* her touch. His insides squirmed at the gory image that was burned into his mind. His memory of her was slowly beginning to warp into a decaying nightmare.

Curious, he inspected the piano, which he had only just now realized had been playing with no one to possibly tickle its ivories. It was a beautiful but unremarkable grand piano. He gently smacked his face, trying to ground himself in reality. He was surely cracking from being alone in silence with his thoughts for far too long. Too much alone time, too much black mold.

He walked out of the ballroom and attempted to lock it behind him. When he actually got to the part of locking it, he realized that none of his keys fit the doors. This was possibly one of the aforementioned rooms that he'd been meant to keep out of. The dread of what had just happened began to sink in even further with this realization. Perhaps his dread was exacerbated by the fact that his left wrist now had a heartbeat of its own.

"Is everything okay up here?" he heard Cameron coming up the steps. He was unsure what to say, still in shock. He stood dumbfounded in the hallway, clutching his wrist, which was really beginning to hurt now as sparks of pain were pulsating up to his elbow. They stopped short upon seeing him.

"What happened?" They asked. They looked sick. Their face was horribly gaunt with dark circles around their eyes.

"I... I fell off the ladder," Monty lied. "I hurt my wrist in the fall," he said, showing his obviously sprained wrist to them. It was already swelling and turning shades of purple. There was a strange expression on their face looking at his bruised wrist. Their eyes darted from him to the closed ballroom doors.

"Do you need help? That looks awful!" they asked, walking towards Monty, who reflexively backed away. Cameron looked so much like their mother that their face reactivated his fight or flight for a split second. His name being screamed in his ears was still ringing through his head.

"I'll be okay. It would be nice if you had a brace?" he asked, still keeping his distance.

"Here, come downstairs and I will get you some ice." Cameron spoke tenderly. It was clear they were exhausted. There was another emotion in their eyes Monty couldn't place. He hesitated for a moment before following them down the steps.

"You fell so hard I could have sworn that someone was physically shaking me from my sleep," Cameron continued as they walked down to the first floor. He followed them into the kitchen and sat on one of the stools at the kitchen bar. They produced an ice pack from their mostly empty freezer.

"I know I got spooked," he admitted, debating how much truth to tell.

"By what?" Cameron asked. "Here, give me your wrist." They slipped onto the stool next to him. They gently took his tender wrist and applied the ice. Their touch was shockingly delicate and cold from the ice. Their soft hands sent sparks into Monty's skin. His desire to feel their touch was the only thing keeping him from recoiling with the amount of pain the ice elicited.

"The ballroom door was open, and I don't know how, but the doors to the balcony slammed open while I was working. It scared the hell out of me," he said. What little color Cameron had left in their sickly face drained as they looked up at him with wide eyes. Their grip unconsciously tightened on Monty's throbbing flesh.

"The ballroom was open?" they asked.

"Yes? I assumed you left it open last night. I saw the light was on in there when I got home late," he explained. He knew that this was not the right thing to say, seeing the look of what he could only guess was terror on Cameron's face.

"I... must have been sleepwalking again. I could have sworn they were still shut," they said slowly. This only unsettled him further.

"Are you sure? The doors were wide open when I got up there," he asked, his voice cracking a bit, catching somewhere around his Adam's apple.

"Maybe... maybe I forgot... But I don't remember being in there last night," they said. Monty knew his bewilderment must have been evident on his face.

"When I came home late last night, I saw the lights on, and I could hear you playing the piano?" he remarked. Both of them were perplexed now.

"That's strange. Even if I had managed to practice in my sleep, I'd never turn the lights on in that case," they rubbed their face furiously, clearly also wondering if they were dreaming. "Excuse me. Let me go get you something to wrap your wrist with. I think I have something upstairs. Stay there, I will be right back," they instructed, handing the ice to him.

Before he could look up to thank them, they were gone. Dread filled him as he was alone again. It felt as though he were in a nightmare. His own name still rang in his ears. It felt like Dr. Giovanni's horrible face was burned into his eyelids every time he tried to close his eyes. For the first time, he admitted to himself that he truly felt terrified of being alone. Every moment of waiting for Cameron to return was agony.

His visions of Dr. Giovanni shook him, but not knowing the full story behind her death made her specter even more foreboding. He couldn't tell if she was trying to warn him, or terrify him, or if he was simply going insane. Cameron had given him some reason to be wary of them. They had nearly pushed him off a second-story balcony purely to fuck with him, and yet now they were tending his injuries. Thinking about them made his head hurt. Cameron silently walked back into the kitchen.

"Here we go," they said as they resumed their spot next to him. They took his wrist again and began to wrap the brace bandage around it. Monty hissed with pain as they did so.

"Thank you," he managed. It felt like his heart was going to leap through his throat at Cameron's touch. Their soft hands released him, and he rubbed the bandage reflexively. He noticed how his mouth had become incredibly dry.

"I think you should spend the rest of the day resting," they said to him, their eyes drooping as if they were fighting to stay awake. He went to protest but was cut off before he even began. "Actually, why don't you take the rest of the week and just start fresh Monday. I'm sure you can't feel good after taking such a fall," they instructed. He wanted to object but chose to shut his mouth.

"You didn't hit your head, right?" they asked. His head *was* still buzzing, but he was sure he'd only landed on his wrist.

"No, no, I'm fine," he replied quietly.

# CHAPTER ELEVEN

THE next day was brutal. It was the sort of warmth that made everything unpleasant to do or touch. The flamethrower of summer's death-cry that finally forced leaves to crisp up and change for the impending storms. Montague was afraid that the very glass in his windows could melt, the last day of extreme heat. This weather was always followed by thunder and lightning, the sort of rain that suddenly froze your bones and made the summer fauna run off.

He sat in front of the little box fan in his window that he had purchased from the hardware store in a vain attempt to stay cool. His shaggy hair drenched, tank top and shorts glued to his body in sweat. The thick overcast humidity was giving him a headache. He stared into space as he rolled an ice cube around in his mouth. He was positively bored out of his mind as he cooked in his cabin. With not even the mind-numbing whine of a cathode ray to soothe him, for the first time in his life, he missed television.

Somehow, taking time off only stressed him out more. Despite only spraining his wrist on the marble floor, it hurt far more than he'd expected. It had been a long time since he had injured himself and felt something other than the dull ache in his body from working. The pain was not his main issue. It was more so that every time he felt his pulse in his wrist he could remember Dr. Giovanni's rotten face. Nightmares were nothing new to him, but the waking visions were something else. They felt so real, and yet there was no explanation for what he'd seen, other than he was simply going mad.

Cameron buzzed in his mind like a swarm of angry horseflies too. They had warned him about how the seclusion messed with one's mind. Monty assumed he was finally cracking from being alone, spending every night feeling hunted by scavengers. He wondered if Cameron had been seeing the same visions as him. They'd mentioned feeling watched by her; it could have been more than guilty paranoia. Perhaps they too were terrified of the night. That could account for why they acted so strangely, and why they seemed to disappear for days on end.

He couldn't *stop* thinking about them. They were beautiful in a way that hypnotized him. The feeling of their soft hands wrapping his wrist still lingered on his heat-flushed skin. Just the mere memory of their lips next to his neck excited him. He wished it didn't. He found it increasingly difficult to imagine anyone else when he pleasured himself. It was alarming the way their face and body invaded his thoughts. If anything was haunting Monty, it was the desire to taste their lips.

He was startled out of his thoughts by the sound of a knock on his door. He got out of his chair sluggishly. He trudged through the hot air and yanked his front door open. It gave a loud CRACK as the heat-swollen paint stuck to itself. He pulled with such force that he shook the evil eye off the wall, shattering it in the process. The muggy summer air from outside hit him in the face like a ton of bricks before he even saw Cameron.

"Oh, shit." He looked down at the perfectly split cobalt glass on the ground. He turned his attention back to Cameron. "Hello?"

"I'm sorry," they said, looking at the broken eye.

"I was being clumsy," Monty said as he shook his head.

"It's unbearably hot. May I come in?" they asked, their face obscured by sunglasses and a wide-brimmed sun hat. They cast a dark shadow over the entrance with their parasol.

"Sure," Monty said with a twinge of curiosity. He hastily picked up the split evil eye and placed it on his kitchen counter.

"I came to see if you needed anything? You hurt yourself quite badly from what I could tell," they said plainly, their back against the front door, clearly not meaning to stay long. Monty crossed his arms.

"I'm fine. You could have called me," he teased, pointing his goatee towards the phone on the wall next to them.

"I just—" Cameron was visibly flustered. "I just thought you must be bored, considering we have no reception up here. That and the fact I haven't been able to get cable or dial-up yet either," they said more so to themself as if they were making a mental note.

"I *am* itching for something to do, not gonna lie," he said as he pulled more ice from his freezer to cool a glass of water. "You want?" he offered. Cameron shook their head.

"Well, I do have books. A lot of books, actually. I was left a very well stocked library."

"I'd love to have something to read."

"I have quite a wide selection, however," they hesitated, "as you know, my mother worked in researching... hematology, so there's a lot of texts regarding her work." They looked sick to their stomach as they explained that fact.

"I know. I was in her intro to hematology and diseases of the blood classes. I don't really want to think about school, or *that*, so something else would be nice. Nonfiction if you can. Surprise me? I'll take any entertainment I can get," he tried to laugh off the oppressively tense air the mere mention of Dr. Giovanni invited in.

"If you hate what I chose, you merely have to tell me and I'll bring you something else," they smiled softly.

"Thank you again."

"Oh, it is no trouble. Is there anything else I could do for you?"

Monty paused for a moment. It was so hot all he could think about was the pool. Asking to take a dip felt unprofessional, but then again, it was becoming clear Cameron did not see him merely as an employee. "Would it be weird if I asked to go for a swim?"

"Oh? You absolutely can use the pool," Cameron said with a bit of surprise in their tone. "I would just avoid getting that wet," they pointed to the brace on his wrist.

"Don't worry, I'll take it off." He merely let out a laugh.

"I will be back. Help yourself, Monty, you're my guest," Cameron said before slipping back out into the hellish summer heat.

*But I'm not?*

He was perplexed but decided he didn't care how strange he felt. He just needed to cool off. He quickly slipped into his swim trunks and loosely tied his boots on, wishing he'd had flip-flops, or sandals, or honestly anything else to wear. He half ran across the yard with a bath towel over his head, shielding his eyes slightly. Despite the overcast, it was still scorchingly bright outside. The humidity smelled of ozone and metallic sweat.

The water of the pool was so cool and soothing, although maybe a bit incorrectly chlorinated, he realized, now swimming in it. There was a strange chemical smell to the water that worried him ever so slightly. He decided not to think about too much. It was likely fine, since Cameron had not said anything.

Taking a dip would have been a pleasant experience if it weren't for the graveyard of cherubs that seemed to follow his every move. Their round little faces, obstructed by elemental damage, made them feel out of place. Taking a dip on an overcast day in his boss's pool did not help with the surreal feeling of it all. It felt like Cameron did not know there was a social contract that was supposed to be between the two of them. It was as if they'd never really been out in the world with the way they acted.

"I grabbed three I think you would like, but I am only guessing," Cameron's voice came from behind him. He turned around to see them standing near the deep end of the pool.

"Can you drop them by my boots?" he asked. They nodded and walked over to plop down the three rather thick hardcovers.

"Victorian medicine and surgery, a book about New England's history of vampires, and one I have not read about, *I think*, the history of Coney Island," they said, pointing to the stack. "This is the best I could muster. Most of the books I have read in the library are fiction or are about hematology."

"Nice! No, these are great. Thank you," he smiled up at them, appreciating the broad shadow their parasol cast over him. Even though he could not see Cameron's eyes, he could feel them fixated on him, no less burning than the creepy sculptures that surrounded the pool.

"Do you mind if I join you?" they asked. Monty shook his head.

"Of course not," he said.

Cameron kicked off their sandals and hiked up their skirt, slipping just their feet in the water, taking care to keep themself covered from the sun. They pulled out a little pocket reader, flipping it open with their free hand. As they kicked their feet around, Monty couldn't help but notice they had mangled scars around their ankles. Their skin looked as if it had been rubbed raw over and over at some point years ago. The rest of their legs were impressively smooth.

"It's not polite to stare," Cameron teased with a slight smile, not looking up from their book. The light reflecting off the pool created a glimmering effect against their dark shades. Monty felt all the blood in his face rush to his cheeks despite the fact he was sure they were just staring at him moments ago.

"I'm sorry—I wasn't—" he stammered, realizing how long his gaze must have been fixed on their exposed skin. "I was just thinking you might wanna join me?"

"I can't swim," they said flatly.

"You can't!?"

"No, I was never permitted to swim in the pool," they explained.

Monty thought for a moment before swimming up to the ledge to look up at them.

"I can teach you? If you want?" he offered. Cameron looked up from their book.

"Teach me? What about your wrist?"

"I'll be careful. Come on, get in the shallow end, and I'll at least show you how to float," he smiled, making his way over to the shallow side of the pool. Cameron nervously looked up at the sky.

"I'm going to burn," they sighed to themself.

"It's overcast?" Monty remarked. Cameron just shook their head as they stripped down to their bathing suit, a plain black one-piece, and their long-sleeve mesh cover-up.

"You don't burn?" they asked.

"I do sometimes, but I've never gotten any color with cloud cover like this."

"I envy that. The sun and I don't get along," Cameron joked. They did not remove their sunglasses either as they cautiously entered the shallow end.

"You're not gonna take those off?" Monty pointed at his face.

"The sun also hurts my eyes. I would be rendered temporarily blind if I took them off. Not all of us are blessed with big, beautiful brown eyes," they said as they cautiously waded into the water to join Monty, who was standing about waist deep.

"You're the first person I've met who had eyes your color," he admitted, trying not to blush at their comment. He didn't realize he was walking back into deeper water as Cameron approached him until they looked distressed.

"It's a genetic condition," they said matter-of-factually. "Now, if you got any further, there's a drop. I'm pretty sure I'll just sink like a stone." They were now standing up to their shoulders.

"Right," Monty approached them, "we should start you here. I'm going to help you by lifting you up so you can lay on your back. All you need to do is relax, and you'll float," he explained, standing next to them.

"Are you sure? That sounds wrong," they inquired nervously.

"Hear look," he proceeded to demonstrate, spreading his arms out and letting his body relax.

"Start to lay down and I'll help lift your legs. I won't let your face go under the water," he promised as he returned to stand on the bottom of the pool. Cameron let out a nervous sigh and laid back, their hair splaying around them in the water like a gold halo. Monty gently raised their legs up and kept his good arm under the small of their back.

"I f-feel like I'm going to sink."

"You're tensing too much. You have to *relax*, try not to hold your breath. I've got you," he reassured them. Cameron took another deep breath and finally relaxed. Monty slowly let go of them. They stayed that way for just a moment, before anxiety overtook them and they began to sink.

"*Cazzo!*" they panicked. Monty quickly grabbed them and held them up in the water. They wrapped their arms around his neck. Even out of the water, he was fairly sure he could hold them with one arm.

Monty noticed through their mesh cover-up how scared their thin arms were. Long keloided gashes in multiple directions littered their skin, along with what looked like track-mark ghosts of IVs that had been carelessly inserted. The scars were similarly violent to the ones on their torso and legs. Had they done that to themself, or did Dr. Giovanni do that to them?

"Not bad for a first try," he beamed, ignoring the questions swimming in his head. Cameron had just barely a tint of flush in their cheeks as their gaze met him through their sunglasses.

"It's hard to relax when I'm terrified of getting my face wet."

"There's an easy way to fix that–"

"DON'T!" they shrieked like a schoolgirl.

"I'm not gonna to dunk you, oh my god," Monty laughed,

putting them down. They reluctantly let go of him. "I was going to suggest you let yourself sink and hold your breath. I wasn't going to force you under!"

"I think this is enough for me. I feel my face might be burning," they said, touching one of their flushed cheeks.

"You *sure* that's sunburn?" he teased.

"You're burning too," they pointed to his shoulders.

"Touché."

They both laughed. Cameron's genuine laughter was like music to him, breathy and sweet. It made his chest bloom with warmth. Like a vining plant, that warmth sprawled through his body, and made every inch of his flesh hum with delight.

# CHAPTER TWELVE

THE following day was just as drearily humid, though now there were periodical summer showers scattered here and there. Thanks to the rain, that evening had finally grown just the tiniest bit cooler. Montague found himself anxiously pacing the length of his cabin, thinking himself in circles. His mind had become fixated on Cameron, who had been lingering in his mind for most of that day. His thoughts were consumed by his growing fondness towards them and the tortuous scars that littered their body.

The violent markings on their pale flesh led him to imagine the innumerable, gruesome ways such scars could have been made. The rough rings around their ankles looked as though they'd been tied up for a very long time at some point. Their arms were marred far worse than any simple cases of self-harm he'd ever seen. They looked more like someone had been bloodletting them. The scars across their torso were rough and faded. He wondered if they'd been hit with a switch as a child. He found it incredibly difficult for him to swallow the genuine possibility that they'd suffered such abuse at the hands of their mother. The image of Dr. Giovanni torturing her only child curdled his insides.

His mind wandered to what other places they might be scarred, not realizing until it was far too late he was undressing them in his mind. His purely inquisitive thoughts quickly turned to the insatiable desire to run his hands along their body. He wanted to feel each bit of raised flesh under his fingertips, to entangle his hands in their gilded hair. Their delicate arms around his neck in the pool came back to his mind. He had held them so close. The ghost of their laughter still rang in his head. He wanted to hear that again. He wanted to hear other sweet sounds from them too. He wanted to —

*Stop being a pervert!*

Montague, on the whole, was finding it increasingly hard to focus on other things besides this fantasy. He tried several times that day, and failed, to read any of the books he was given. He kept picking up *The Complete History of Connecticut Vampires*, reading a chapter, and putting it down slightly bored. He found it somewhat ridiculous that this outdated folk tale was deemed "nonfiction." He didn't doubt the panic of backward towns-folks in an era before the popularity of science. Rather, he found it funny that the text took their superstitions so seriously. From what he had read, most of the "signs" someone was undead were merely normal symptoms of decomposition. The signs that someone was being plagued by such a creature sounded more like tuberculosis, or perhaps a severe case of anemia.

Thinking of anemia brought him back around to Dr. Giovanni. She had been making incredible strides in researching treatment for the affliction and its many causes. Maybe that was part of what rattled him so much about Cameron's appearance. They were clearly suffering from some kind of hemoglobin deficiency, and yet they appeared as if they'd never been properly treated. He could tell their health had been neglected for a very long time just judging by the thinness of their pallid skin and jaundiced eye bags. This only bolstered his suspicion that Dr. Giovanni could have been the reason for Cameron's mangled flesh.

Something in the back of his mind was trying to connect the

dots, but his thought was half-formed. His mind buzzed and hummed like the pool pump as he tried to get his head on straight to no avail. Being alone all day was making him think fantastically. He decided he needed to get some fresh air.

It was getting dark now. The clouds had finally parted, leaving the air cool and moist. The moon dimly illuminated most of the estate, leaving the woods in dark, writhing shadows. He didn't know where he wanted to go, so he just began walking across the empty backyard. Maybe he'd go looking for Cameron. Maybe he'd get in his van and go for a night drive. Maybe he would just up and leave.

A chilling gust ripped through him as he walked along. After such scorching heat, even a sixty-five degree night felt frigid. Fall was crisping the edges of leaves and just beginning to whisper through the night. The scalding days would surely pass soon. Even the frogs had begun to quiet down in the evenings. He clicked on his flashlight to see across the yard.

*"Mon~ta~gue?"*

He could have sworn someone had said his name on the wind, but when he turned around, there was no one there. He was hearing things again. He looked up at the old Victorian for signs of life. There was a deep crimson light pouring from Cameron's room as he saw someone walking about on the balcony. He quickly remembered how much of the yard was visible from there.

"Monty?" he heard the voice again, louder. This time he realized a real person was speaking to him. Cameron was leaning over the railing of their balcony, calling to him. His heart skipped a beat as he quickened his pace to stand by the pool so he could hear them better.

"Yes?" he called up. Cameron was backlit in blood red light, making their face very difficult to see.

"What are you doing?" they asked with a concerned tone in their voice.

"I was feeling weird, so I came out for a walk," he called back up, giving them a shrug.

"It's almost eleven. It's not safe to be out here in the dark. You of all people know how the wildlife gets at night," they scolded. He stood there for a moment in silence.

"I know."

"Did you get lonely?" Their question rattled him. There was something teasing in the way they spoke. He realized they were smoking.

"It's hard not to," he said, resisting the urge to shine his flashlight at their obscured face.

After a painfully long moment, Cameron put out their cigarette and piped up again. "Do you want to join me for a drink?"

"Are you sure?"

"Yes, I'm perfectly lonely myself," they said. "Come in. Meet me in the drawing room and I'll bring a few bottles. Unless you'd like something other than wine?"

"Wine is fine."

Even when he thought better of it, he couldn't seem to resist entertaining their invitation. In the blink of an eye, Cameron had already left the balcony. Monty let himself in through the back door into the painfully dark house. He was glad he had the flashlight, as it made finding his way much less dangerous. He wondered how anyone could see at all in such a dreary mansion. The place did not have enough electric lights installed to illuminate most of its musty corners. Electricity felt like an afterthought when they were building this home's sprawling hallways.

He was impressed with how fast Cameron had moved. They were already waiting for him in the living room, tending the fireplace. Sat on the table between the two couches were three bottles of wine and two glasses. Stacks of papers had been hastily shoved out of the way to make space for a guest. He raised an eyebrow at the amount of wine set out for the two of them.

Cameron looked like they had not slept a wink. The dim firelight made it look as though their bones were attempting to escape their marble-white skin. They hadn't taken any color from the other day at all. Dark, jaundice-tinged circles were deep around their sad eyes. Their bun looked like a rose-gold bird's nest perched atop their head.

They were dressed in a frilly shirt with a deep V that was untied and hung open, just slightly slipping off their sharp shoulders. Said shirt was coming untucked from their high-waisted pants. He noticed the golden locket hanging from their neck glinting in the light from the fireplace.

"I told you the boredom and seclusion would eventually get to you," they said with a smirk, finally noticing Monty in the doorway. They blew a stray strand of hair from their face before disengaging with the fire. They looked oddly dashing despite being so disheveled.

He clicked off his flashlight and sat down in his usual spot. Cameron threw themself down across from him on the opposing couch and snatched up the bottle from the table, ripping into it like a hungry wolf.

"I've just had a lot on my mind, and not a whole lot to do," he explained, trying to justify his late night wandering.

"What's been plaguing you?" Cameron asked as they handed a glass of wine to him before taking their own, leaning back and crossing their legs. He hesitated for a moment. There was no way for him to explain every single thing that was racing through his head in adequate detail.

A regrettable portion of his thoughts not detected to the person across from him were occupied by Dr. Giovanni. The doctor's portrait stared down at him with disapproval from just above. He could feel her eyes blazing on him, trailing across his every movement. He could hear her screaming at him in the ballroom again as he sat there. He tried to shake her horrible voice from his head.

"Maybe you were right. The quiet is getting to me a bit. My mind is wandering to dark places," he said, taking a gulp of his own wine, desperately hoping it would calm his nerves.

"What do you mean by that?" Cameron asked. The bags under

their eyes mixed with their hollowed cheeks in the firelight made it look like their skull was coming out of their skin. Their eyes looked positively starving as they lazily trailed along Monty, their gaze burning. He took another generous swig of sweet wine before deciding to actually speak.

"Please don't think I'm crazy."

"I won't."

"I lied to you the other day. I didn't fall off the ladder. I'm not sure how to explain it. I sort of just fell? I don't know. I've been having horrible nightmares," he explained, still not sure if he wanted to be honest about everything.

"It's hard to not have nightmares with the creatures howling at night," they said into their glass with a flat tone.

"Sure, but I've been having them when I'm seemingly awake," he elaborated. Cameron merely gave him a lazy look as they swirled their wine around. They let their frizzy hair down. It cascaded over their exposed shoulders in a golden cloud.

"I don't think you're crazy."

"You don't?"

"She's watching you too." Their eyes flicked up to their mother's portrait. "You saw her in the ballroom, didn't you?"

"Yes, how did you know that's where I was going with this?"

"Lucky guess," they shrugged. The air was filled only by a crackling fire and gusts of early fall wind against the old, uninsulted front window that loomed behind them.

"You know… you can leave if you want to," they said, breaking the silence. At that moment, Monty considered it. It would be easier to go back to Mina's and just forget about whatever the hell was going on here. But that would be too easy, and the fact he'd gotten so close to this mystery would surely haunt him to his grave. His curiosity was binding him here like some sort of spell. Maybe it was more than pure curiosity binding him. He was mesmerized by the gentle rise and fall of Cameron's chest in the firelight as wine started to make his lips and fingers buzz. His desire may have been even stronger than his curiosity. He filled up his glass and downed half its contents before answering.

"I'm considering it. This place feels... wrong." Even he didn't fully know what he meant by that. Cameron merely nodded as if they understood.

"'*Wrong*' is a good way to put it." They followed his lead and poured another glass for themself. "I don't want you to leave, but I don't want you to feel like you're trapped here like me."

"You're trapped here?"

"I don't know if you could understand," Cameron replied rather shortly. Monty felt defeated, and a bit pissed. He finished his glass and poured himself another, finishing the bottle, realizing he was feeling so flustered.

"Sometimes talking to you feels like I'm talking to fucking drywall," he sputtered out. Cameron raised their eyebrow with a smirk. They opened the second bottle.

"Is that so?" they sarcastically chided as they yanked out the cork. "*Drywall?*" Montague realized what he'd said all a bit too late as regret flooded his body. Despite everything, Cameron was still his boss. Even though every single interaction they had made it seem like they did not remember this fact themself.

"I'm sorry," he apologized swiftly, nervously taking another swig of wine. His head was starting to spin faster now.

"No need to apologize, I can see how you must feel," Cameron said as they sat their glass down on the coffee table. Monty looked into his dark reflection in his glass of wine. Maybe the fire was a bit too hot for him. He could feel a ripping heat beginning to bloom across his cheeks and the tips of his ears.

"I'm surprised you're not offended," he said sheepishly to his warped face in the wine. The ripples in the liquid made his slightly bent aquiline nose look even more crooked. As he looked up, he saw Cameron step over the low table to stand directly in front of him. A lump formed in his throat at their sudden closeness.

"Oh, I didn't say I wasn't offended. I said, 'I can see how you must feel.' I know I've been obtuse," they admitted. They gently pulled Monty's wine glass from his hand and sat it down on the table. His heart began to pound, and his mind was confused as to what on earth they were doing.

"Perhaps it's the wine, but I feel like I need to clarify something to you."

"What do you mean?" Monty trembled out, surprising himself with how much he was shaking. He could feel his tongue in his mouth pressing eagerly against his teeth. Cameron proceeded to sit themself down, straddling his lap. Blazing electricity shot through his nervous system like a car battery being jumped at the highest voltage. His heart slammed up into his throat as he stiffened with shock. Cameron braced themself against his shoulder, holding him at arm's length while simultaneously pinning him back into the couch.

Their wiry frame hung over him like a starving coyote about to devour carrion. Their skin was cold to the touch in a way that perplexed him. He, on the other hand, felt his blood pooling hot in his flesh. Sticky tendrils of darkness slowly crept up around him, enveloping his senses, stitching his body to the dust-caked couch cushions.

"I really don't want you to leave," Cameron leaned forward and whispered into his ear. A slender finger hesitantly looped under his necklace as they pulled his silver hamsa charm behind him, cool digits lingering for a moment against his pulse.

"I've taken a liking to you," they added. Monty sensed he might be devoured by the darkness weaving through his flesh at any moment. He could feel shadows pouring into his mind and body, cool nothingness slipping between tooth and gum, through the muscles in his skull. Tunnel vision engulfed him as lavender eyes stared him down, firelight causing them to sparkle like pale crystals ringed in long pink eyelashes. Cameron placed a long hand on his chest against his ravenous heartbeat.

"I don't want to be alone again. I want you to stay here, with me," they whispered, their face now mere centimeters from Monty's.

Dumbfounded, he opened and closed his mouth several times in an attempt to say something, *anything*, but all he could muster was a half sound. He was mesmerized. If he could just lean forward, he could close that painful gap between them, but he was paralyzed. The world around him was dark and empty, pulsating with lights like a migraine. The only thing he could see was Cameron's glowing visage heaving in front of him.

Before he could ask a single question, Cameron leaned in and kissed him. Their lips were soft and frigid against his. They smelled sweet like jasmine and lavender, tasted like wine and metallic smoke. He couldn't help but kiss back with equal hunger. Their intoxicating aroma poured down his throat and flooded his lungs.

He wrapped his arms around their narrow waist, pulling them closer to him. Cameron's breath hitched as the force of the motion caused them to grind together through thick denim. Monty could feel his heartbeat in his ears. He could feel himself falling through darkness as his worries and cares seemed to be devoured with every soft sound from the strawberry blond in his arms. Light popped behind his closed eyes as he savored every single millisecond. His blood was pumping so hard it felt like his veins were going to burst. His head was spinning—*no*—the entire room was spinning.

Time only started moving again when Cameron finally broke the kiss. The moment they moved away, air flooded back into Monty's lungs, life coming back to his intoxicated brain. His grip around their waist was fighting tight. He was terrified that if he let go of them, they would just disintegrate into a cloud of fog. They both stared at each other unblinking.

"I hope my explanation makes sense?" they finally said in a low voice.

"Crystal clear," he croaked sarcastically. His voice was hoarse, weak and out of breath. "I-I'll stay, but under one condition."

"What is that?"

"Please, I need you to tell me what the hell you're hiding from me," he finally said. A sour expression washed over them as if he had asked for something impossible. They wriggled their way out of his grip, to his dismay, and put distance back between them. They shook their head "no," long legs stepping backward over the coffee table.

"What do you mean by that?" They laughed unsteadily as they sat back down across from him, pouring themself a fresh glass.

"I think you know. We both know we're seeing the same visions, but why? You don't have to tell me everything right now, but..." he paused, knowing he was going to regret his next words. "I need to know the truth. What the fuck did she do? To herself? To you? I don't know what you think you're protecting me from, but I can just live in the dark." He choked on his own words as they fought to escape his drunken lips.

"Did she really kill herself, Cameron?"

They dropped their glass, spilling wine across the floor. Abject terror sprinted across their face.

"You can't be serious?" They spoke so softly their voice was nearly inaudible.

"I'm—"

"No," Cameron held up a bony hand, golden rings flashing in the firelight. "Monty, *please*, I'll try to be more open with you, but... for my sanity, please don't ask me about *that*."

"I understand, but—"

"You don't!" They snapped. "Even if I could explain everything to you, you still wouldn't understand. I *know* what's going on inside your head. I saw you staring at my scars. I know that look in your eyes. You're not the first person to look at me like that. My mother was not a good person. I'm sure the version you knew of her was much different than the woman who raised me. I know you want to know what happened to her, and what she did to me, but..." they paused for a moment, searching for an answer in their mind, "horrible things have happened in this house, Monty. Can we just agree to leave it at that?"

"You can't push me out and simultaneously ask me to stay," he finally said after thinking carefully about how to phrase what he meant. Cameron looked tired.

"I think you would sleep more soundly if I left some things up to the imagination."

"That's what you think," he mumbled, thinking of his nightmares. For a moment, he swore he heard a familiar voice whisper in his ear. He whipped his head to see where the voice had come from, but there was just the painting of Dr. Giovanni staring down at him. Cameron let out a long, shaky sigh.

"I'm sorry, Monty. I just... I genuinely don't think you would even believe me."

"What are we doing here, Cameron? What's so horrible that merely knowing would put me in danger, like you claim? So complex I could never understand? We've both established we believe in ghosts! What's more insane than that?" He could feel the drunken word vomit coming now. He was only slightly aware that he was beyond drunk.

"Do you even know what my mother was actually researching?"

Monty sat for a moment, a million different thoughts swimming in his head. "No... I think I need to go to bed. I'd prefer to continue this conversation sober."

"Perhaps that would be best," Cameron nodded, their face gaunt with exhaustion.

Dr. Giovanni's mangled corpse filled Monty's mind again as he realized he was still staring up at her stern painted visage. He could see her twisted body in the ballroom in his mind's eye. The gaping bloody hole in the center of her rotten body, empty, and hollow, almost as hollow as Cameron's fearful gaze.

# CHAPTER THIRTEEN

MONTAGUE was quite hungover the following morning. Intense nausea and a soul-splitting headache met him unforgivably early. He was not sure how or when he'd even come back to his cabin. The events of the night prior were foggy in his mind as he desperately tried to parse out reality from dream. He knew he had acted foolishly, blaming the same thing that caused his head to throb. He could still feel Cameron's lips against his, still taste their floral perfume, still see the look of terror on their face at his questions about their mother. He wished he could remember his conversation more clearly. He had the sense they'd ended the night on an unpleasant note.

He wondered if they had witnessed her death. Though the images of her desiccated corpse rattled him to the core, he could not even begin to imagine what seeing that would be like for Cameron. His mind lingered on to the way they had shut down his lines of questioning, wondering what exactly "awful things" entailed. Whatever that was, it went far beyond the doctor's untimely death.

The idea of Dr. Giovanni hurting her child sat like a block of ice in Monty's stomach. It was hard for him to even believe she'd hurt anyone. The woman he'd known was the reason he made it to his fourth year of undergrad. She had been nothing but patient and nurturing with her students. And yet, at the same time, there was a look of palpable fear in Cameron's eyes every time she was brought up.

That expression was one Monty knew too well. It was the same emotion he knew he felt when someone asked him about his father. Fear, hatred, grief, all tied up in a neat package of words impossible to say. His father had only raised a hand to him a few times, and only really unforgivably beat him once. To him, Cameron looked as though they'd been tortured.

He mulled over all the things that had happened over the course of the past week. He was distracted and confused by the memory of Cameron in his arms, their lips on his. The hallucinations and nightmares. He dwelt on the lingering sound of Dr. Giovanni's voice in his head, urging him to run, warning him. There was still a nagging fear at the back of his head that Cameron had also done something horrible. It clashed awfully with his memories of their melodic laughter. It was dizzying, attempting to untangle the weeds of his emotions.

He did his best to clear his head as he drove his minivan into town to meet Mina. He was supposed to be meeting with her to unwind and maybe make some new friends, but all he could think about was reliving the utterly bizarre week he'd had. The idea of drinking again made him slightly nauseated, still hungover even this late in the day.

The sun was just disappearing behind the horizon when he finally got to the small dive bar. He knew Mina was already here, as there was a bright pink bike parked outside, next to a few other more modest motorcycles.

The bar itself was a dingy, stand-alone building by the train tracks that was normally fairly empty, even on Saturday nights. Inside the bar was surprisingly well lit. Most of the bar's floor space was dedicated to a large pool table, which currently had two leather clad women playing a game of billiards. Around them were several mismatched wooden tables and chairs filled with women in varying amounts of leather and spikes. In the corner a decrepit jukebox played a 90's hit he was only moderately familiar with.

Sat at the bar was Mina, talking to a rugged woman with cropped gray hair and several face piercings. Over the bar was a large CRT playing what looked to be the end of a women's rugby game that no one was paying much attention to. The bartender stopped what she was doing as she saw Montague approaching.

"I think you might be lost son," she said to him.

"It's okay he's with me," Mina said to her. She proceeded to make a motion with her hand, the universal symbol of "he's gay."

"Oh!" The bartender's expression instantly softened, "right, what d'ya' want?"

"Cheapest beer you've got on tap, please," Monty smiled, sliding onto the stool next to Mina and placing a ten-dollar bill on the counter. The woman raised an eyebrow, "don't worry about change." The bartender nodded with a smirk as she filled up a dinghy glass.

"You okay?" Mina asked him. He shrugged. She gave him a moderately concerned look, before turning her attention to the woman next to her. "This is my friend Leah," she introduced him to the spike clad woman.

"Nice to meet you," he said with a polite smile, feeling his awkwardness creeping in. Leah saluted him with her stout and a smile. The bartender placed his beer in front of him and happily snatched the bill in exchange.

"Monty, yeah? Mina talks about you a lot," Leah said with a bit of a laugh in her voice.

"Does she?" he asked, locking eyes with Mina.

"Yeah, she says you're working on that creepy Giovanni estate?" Leah asked. The way she phrased it caused him to tense up.

"Yes, I work for Cameron," he said flatly, sounding wrong to him as he said it.

"What's it like? You know his mom ate it on the property, apparently?" Leah prodded nonchalantly. Her question made his beer catch in his throat.

"Dr. Giovanni was actually one of my professors."

"Oh, I'm sorry."

"It's fine."

"How do you know she died there?" Mina asked Leah.

"Oh? You didn't see it on the news a few months back? It was a pretty big story even through the family kept most of the details pretty hush-hush. They said, 'the pressure from working at the college got to her,' or something like that. Poor girl jumped off her balcony and landed in the worst possible way," Leah added. Monty could feel his insides squirming as he could vividly see her gored body in his mind's eye as the older woman spoke.

"Could not have had a more freakish fall if you tried. Funny, she had *all* that wealth, and it still didn't cut it for her," Leah took a sip from her beer before continuing, "that Cameron kid had nothing to do with the whole thing apparently… But… you knew the woman, do you really think she 'couldn't handle the pressure from the department?' It would make more sense that her adult son wanted the estate, don't ya think? I mean, the kid inherited the place in the blink of an eye," she snapped her fingers.

"I don't like what you're implying," Monty spat with a level of venom he was surprised by. Despite this, Leah had been implying exactly what had been nagging at the back of his mind. He took a breath.

"You don't think it's a bit strange?" Leah pressed. He was unsure of what to say.

"I don't think I knew Dr. Giovanni as well as I originally thought," he began. As he tried to make sense of his thoughts, his eyes flicked up to the TV. A news report was now playing. A seasonal worker had gone missing from one of the ski resorts two weeks ago. His face was familiar, so familiar that for a moment Monty thought he recognized him somehow.

*The twink in the ski slope uniform?*

"Maybe we change the subject?" Mina suggested with a nervous laugh. Monty was preoccupied with the face of the missing man on the television.

*He really does look like that man Cameron took home a few weeks ago.*

"Aren't you at least a little unnerved working there?" Leah asked. Her meaning was earnest, but Monty had already grown terribly upset from the way she broached the entire subject. He could feel the beginnings of a panic attack boiling under his skin.

*Did they kill that worker? Bad coincidence?*

"I'm not afraid of Cameron, if that's what you mean," he lied to her and himself. "They're not..." he trailed off, unsure how to respond.

*They're not a murderer! They didn't—*

Leah had plucked a nerve he hadn't been aware of, like someone had poked a cavity with an ice pick. His hallucinations seemed to buzz around in his skull, taking over everything he could imagine. That stupid news report was still distracting him.

*They couldn't have!*

"Monty, are you okay?" Mina asked. He now realized he was holding still, his dark knuckles practically white from his grip on his glass.

"Yeah, I'm sorry, I think I need to step outside for a second. My — I mean, I think my phone was just ringing," he lied before giving Mina a "please follow me" look.

He heard Mina excuse herself and apologize to Leah. The older woman simply shook her head and said, "I'm worried about him... and you."

"I know, I'll talk to him," Mina whispered, before following Monty outside into the cool night air. The contrast with the hot, dingy bar eased his impending mental breakdown.

"What was that big guy?" she asked him.

"Mina... sorry. Just freaking out a little is all," he huffed as he felt like his lungs were going to collapse.

"What just happened? God, here, sit down on the curb, you look like you're about to faint," she said, sitting him down.

He took several deep breaths trying to get the jumble of thoughts and emotions to settle in his head. He felt like there was a scream of terror just knocking at the back of his throat. He tried to shove down all the swimming accusations and nightmarish thoughts knocking in his psyche.

*I'm imagining shit again.*

"Sorry, I was suffocating in that bar," he said after the cool air had been given a moment to clear his mind. "The way Leah was talking so nonchalantly... It was getting me way too in my head," he said.

He debated mentioning the man he'd seen on TV, but he now realized he was being ridiculous. His anxieties, Leah's accusations, it all felt ridiculous now that he was outside in the night air.

*I never even saw the face of that man clearly.*

He felt like his sanity was slipping away from him, and like ten thousand volts of awful were being shocked through his nervous system.

"Don't worry about it," Mina consoled him. "Now what's really going on, man?"

"I don't think Cameron would have killed their mother for the money. That estate was on the verge of being condemned when I showed up."

"Leah just likes gossip. I'm surprised she got that under your skin."

"It's dawning on me that, I think, I didn't really know Dr. Giovanni at all. I feel like I've been placed into a puzzle box. That house is rotten. There's something awful about the whole thing. Remember how last week I started the inside painting job?"

"Sure?"

"Well, when I was setting up on the third floor, something

freaky as hell happened. I'm still not sure if what I experienced was even real," he paused, "the doors to the ballroom were open—"

"The ballroom?" Mina interrupted as if he personally offended her.

"Dude, it's an old money mansion. It's got a lot of crazy things in it, you should see the place," he elaborated.

"Right, sorry, continue"

"I decided to go into the ballroom, or more like I felt like something was calling me in there. I could have sworn that the piano was playing itself. Then suddenly the balcony doors crashed open." Mina rolled her eyes. "And standing in front of me was Dr. Giovanni. She was mangled like in my nightmares. But she was also rotting? She screamed my name and then pushed me to the ground, *hard*, before disappearing," he recounted his encounter to his friend, holding up his wrapped wrist.

"I hurt my wrist falling back on the ballroom tile." Mina just looked at him dumbfounded.

"What? I'm sorry. I'm having a hard time understanding. You *saw* Dr. Giovanni? Like *physically* in their ballroom?" Mina asked for clarification.

"Yes, well, I don't know. I keep seeing her in my dreams. Even when I'm awake, I can hear her voice telling me to leave the estate. And then when I was with Cam—"

"Dude, I really think you need to quit this job. It's not good for you. Every time we talk, you sound more n' more unhinged," Mina interrupted him with a concerned look on her face. She'd heard enough already.

"I know I sound deranged, but this stuff feels so real. Cameron and I both think the place is haunted. I mean, the level of isolation might be doing something to me," he continued, only causing Mina to become more concerned.

"I think it's definitely doing something, probably all that black mold you've both been breathing in too. That or the old place has a carbon monoxide leak? I know it's a sweet job on paper, but you've got to get out of there, man. For real, I've never seen you like this before. You can always come back to my place and just rest for a bit," she said, putting a small hand on his back, attempting to relax him. He sat in silence, trying to make sense of it all.

"I don't want to quit… not yet," he said, failing to find an excuse as to *why*.

"Are you planning on quitting at all?" she asked.

"Yes," he stopped for a moment, "I told them I'm thinking about leaving."

"What's making you hesitate?" she asked him sternly.

"It's Cameron… I don't know what happened to them. Or what actually happened to Dr. Giovanni either. Every time I think I've found a clue, I'm left with more questions than answers," he said firmly.

"Dude! For real!? You know more than enough about what happened. You're gonna get yourself in deep shit going digging around that estate. I don't want to put stock in Leah's stuff, but, like, what if she's right? And then what happens if Cameron catches you going through their stuff? What then? You wanna get yourself disappeared? 'Cuz this is sounding like how you get disappeared!" Mina scolded. Monty was stiff-silent, not knowing where to place his thoughts. Mina's face softened slightly.

"This isn't your problem. I think you should leave ASAP," she pressed after taking a deep breath. "I don't know when you last looked in the mirror, but you're going gray, Monty." She gently pulled at a bit of the hair on his temple. He reflexively ran a hand through his now incredibly overgrown hair. Sure enough, there were strands of half-silver in his hand when he pulled it away.

"I'm not afraid of Cameron!" he lied again, "and I feel like I'm very close to at least hearing their version of the story." Something lit up in Mina's eyes as she studied him.

"You're developing feelings for them, aren't you?"

"What!?" He felt his face grow flush as he tried to renounce her accusation.

"You shouldn't shit where you sleep, Mr. Varon."

"I haven't slept with—"

"Yet! I know you! Don't you start making decisions with your dick again. Dude, if you keep talking crazy, I'm going to drag you home myself if I have to. You're fucking swinging a bat at a hornet's nest for Christ's sake!"

"I'm not! You don't know shit about them. I'm not going to get 'disappeared' by them or *whatever*. I wanna know what the hell happened in that awful house. I'm not going to screw myself over just because I want to fuck Cameron!" He froze, realizing he finally said it aloud. Mina raised an eyebrow.

"Guilty."

"Stop it! Stop treating me like I'm still some dumb kid," he shook his head, feeling hideously embarrassed.

"Then stop acting like a dumbass!"

"I'm allowed to care about people and want to know about their lives!"

"It's not your job to fix someone else's family just because you can't fix your own!"

"Are you serious? Fuck off! It's not like that, but why not just kick me in the balls while you're at it? I'm getting out of here." Monty abruptly stood up from the curb and fished in his pockets for his car keys.

"Where are you going?"

"Home!" he replied, turning and walking back to his car. Mina sat defeated and watched him walk away. She got up and went back into the bar.

Montague drove back to the mansion in total silence. He wanted to vomit as he choked his emotions down. His brooding silence was suddenly interrupted by the worst mechanical sound he'd ever heard. He felt the vehicle jolt and sputter as even the gradual incline became too much for his old rust bucket. Something had gone awry in the engine. He barely managed to get the van up into the coach house.

He turned the machine off and popped the hood to see what was happening. White smoke was pouring from the interior. He never regretted leaving Mina on a bad note more than in this moment, as he stared at his fuming engine in bewilderment.

# CHAPTER FOURTEEN

MONTY sat in his living room the next morning watching the gray clouds rolling above from his kitchen window. A storm was moving in, the kind that often peeled off the outer tendrils of the hurricanes coming up the eastern coast. He watched the trees sway as he tried to enjoy his morning coffee.

There was a rotten feeling in his chest from the night before. He knew he would have to call Mina soon, either for an apology or to address his smoking engine. He couldn't help dwelling on what Mina had said to him. What did she know of a broken home? She had two parents with enough love in their hearts for more than just her. Mina didn't understand abandonment. How could she?

A knock at his door pulled him from his stewing. He slowly made his way to the door, certain he knew who it was. It was Sunday after all.

"Hello Cameron," he said as he pulled the door open. Their appearance in the overcast daylight shocked him. They looked hollow, bloodless, transparent and washed out like a faded Polaroid. Their too-thin skin was stretched impossibly taught over their muscles and bones. How long had it been since they had last eaten or slept?

They gave a weary smile. "I'm sure you already know why I'm here then?"

"Yes, do you wanna come inside?"

They nodded and crossed the threshold into his sparsely decorated apartment. He closed the door behind them and raised his mug to them. "You want some coffee?" They put up a tendon-bare hand and shook their head.

"No thank you," they said flatly before presenting Monty with his paycheck. "Here you go. I took the liberty of adding reimbursement for the paint as well."

Monty peeked inside to count the cash. They had given him a bit more than he was owed, seeming to avoid breaking a large banknote. Something about that made him feel odd, like a misplaced apology.

"Thank you," he mumbled and tossed the envelope on his kitchen counter. It slid into the broken glass of the evil eye he'd forgotten to throw away.

"Do you mind if I sit for a moment?" Cameron asked. They looked like they were about to fall over.

"Take a seat. Are you all right?" He asked. They sat down slowly on the couch and crossed their legs. He sat next to them, studying the dark rings around their eyes.

"Oh, yes, I am quite fine, just a bit tired is all," they explained, rubbing the heel of their palm across their face. Their lips were stained with dark wine. They smelled of their sickeningly sweet lavender musk. Tobacco smoke lingered on every part of them and soured their overpowering perfume.

"No offense, but you look awful," Monty remarked, putting his cooling coffee on the low table in front of the couch.

"I haven't been sleeping well is all," they sighed, "but I'm not here to complain about my insomnia."

"So then...?"

"I wanted to apologize."

"About?"

"I think I made a fool of myself. I realized my actions might have been seen as inappropriate," they explained. Monty felt fidgety and nervous.

"You're not typically supposed to make out with your employees, if that's what you're talking about?"

"I realize this," they sighed. He found himself leaning closer to Cameron. "I know that we were both a bit drunk."

"I was plastered, to be honest with you," he admitted with a half laugh. He was barely paying any attention to the conversation at hand. His mind had been drawn back to them sitting on his lap, their cool lips against his. He wanted more.

"I don't mind though... even if it's bad form, or whatever," he lamented. His throat had become incredibly dry. They were studying him with pale eyes. Even looking half dead, there was something about them that uncontrollably drew Monty in.

"There is an imbalance here, worse than you may even realize." Cameron murmured, their eyes lingering on his mouth.

"Sure..." Monty knew indulging in this would not lead to anything good, "but who cares?"

Time was moving as slowly as honey. Even though at this moment he was fully sober, he felt out of control of his own body. It was like an invisible force was puppeting him as he slowly leaned forward. He gently slid a hand behind Cameron's skull and pulled them into a deep kiss. They did not protest, instead melting against him. Their arms slunk up and around his neck, pulling him even closer. Their exhausted body was ice cold like a corpse against Monty's super-heated arousal.

He felt them push their tongue against his lips, and he parted them, allowing them to explore each other's mouths. Thick perfume poured down the back of his throat, making him dizzy. It settled down in his lungs like dry ice as he inhaled more of them. The slipping sensation of eclectic fog parting his skin and fascia ran through his whole body. He was being internally flayed by this ravenous sensation. His heart slammed against his ribs like it wanted to escape. Cameron's teeth felt sharp against his coffee-tinged lips.

They let out a soft sound of pleasure as Monty slowly crawled on top of them, caging them with his massive body. They were trembling under him like the wind tussled trees outside. He could feel his arousal protesting against his cargo shorts. He wanted to have them here, right this second. He uncontrollably bucked his hips, and they twitched against him as they let out another quiet moan. Their sounds were sweeter than anything his imagination could muster.

Trying his best not to break away, he pulled his shirt and flannel off his sweat-soaked body. He moved to pull up the hem of Cameron's shirt. Before he could even graze their torso, they slid their hands down his strong chest and pushed him back, breaking their kiss.

The two of them were panting and dazed as they stared at one another. Even exhausted, the image of Cameron below him made Monty's brain short-fire. They were disheveled, hair tangled around them on the couch, lavender eyes half-lidded with lust. They were heaving as if it was hard for them to breathe.

"Stop," they whispered softly, "we shouldn't do this. Not here, not now." Monty nodded, allowing them to free themself from under his body.

"I'm sorry, you're right," he huffed out, crying inside slightly from his need for release.

"I want to… very badly… I'm just not sure this is a good idea," they added, sitting back up and putting a little distance between the two of them.

"Oh, I'm well past making good choices at this point," Monty chuckled to himself.

"Besides my kissing you, how much of the other night do you remember?" they asked.

A pang of guilt bloomed in his chest, "more than I would like to admit. I'm sorry for the way I acted," he apologized. "The conversation got away from me. I genuinely don't remember it all, but I know I was kind of a dick."

"Same here. I'm also sorry..." they trailed off. Their eyes were searching his face for an answer of some kind. He could practically see their thoughts rolling around in their wine-stained mouth. Something was eating them, and for a moment they looked like they would tell him what it was.

"I still stand by what I said. If you want to leave, I won't keep you here. I really want to tell you the truth. I truly do. I want to explain everything, but I-I-I just can't. I don't think you would want to stay here either if you knew *everything*."

"Then I can't stay here, not if you won't tell me *anything*," Monty countered. Mina was right, as she often was; he couldn't keep this up. It was subtle, but he could see a bit of fear slide into Cameron's expression.

"You want to quit then?"

"No!" he answered far too hastily. "I mean, no, I don't *want* to quit, but if you won't even give me an inch, I think I have to. Look, there's obviously something going on here," he gestured between the two of them, "but I genuinely don't know if I can trust you if you're going to keep playing with me like this. The less you say, the more I have to speculate, and I don't like the conclusions I've been coming to," Monty admitted, trying to gain some composure. Cameron nodded.

"I'm not trying to toy with you, Monty, but I know that doesn't change how you feel. I'm sorry, some things are best left unsaid."

"Then I'll be leaving at the end of the fall," he practically choked on his resignation.

After a somber moment, Cameron stood up and headed towards the door. "Monty, I pray you never understand why I must be so opaque," they sighed. "I hope you know my feelings are unchanged. I cannot and will not keep you here any longer than you wish to stay. Whatever you decide, I will honor," they finished before heading out the door, not giving him time to say another word. He felt a bitter, tight sensation in his chest and a nuisance between his legs.

☽ ✧ ☾

Monty lay in his bed watching the trees in the dark beat upon each other, the wind of the impending storm threatening to tear the roofing off. No rain yet, just the oppressive building pressure of hellish humidity. His mind wandered again to Cameron. Any distance he'd been trying to build had been broken. No amount of scolding himself or denial could keep him from his desire. He finally let himself give in to his urge to imagine them how he wanted to. With a low roll of thunder, the rain finally broke.

Panting from the heat, Monty turned his head to look out the window again. The glint of two huge, hungry eyes caught his attention. Standing there just a few feet away was a tall, ravenously thin coyote. Its fur clung to the exposed bones of its ribcage as water drenched the beast. The creature did not growl or move, merely keeping its shining red eyes locked on him. He could feel his lungs begin to burn with the sharp pain of anxiety. He was transfixed by the canine. He could feel his pulse throbbing in his neck.

Rather than jumping with terror, or attempting to scare the creature off, he merely slid out of bed, moving against his will. He opened one of the huge floor-length windows in his room and crawled outside to stand in front of the coyote. The beast huffed, and despite the hot air, steam rose from its nostrils in the rain. It then turned and walked off into the night. Cool rain drenched his exposed body.

*Monty, Monty, oh Monty please.*

He could hear Cameron calling for him in the night.

*Please, Monty.*

Their soft whines entangled with the distant sound of the piano. His feet slipped on the wet grass as he scrambled through the increasingly heavy rain.

126

*MON~TA~GUE*

And then their voice changed, causing him to whip his attention to the pool.

*Lei sta arrivando.*

Dr. Giovanni's voice crooned from somewhere he could not see. He tried to call out to her, to ask what she meant, but his voice was hoarse nothingness.

He walked up to the edge of the pool, looking down at the water. Again, he saw his reflection in dark liquid, distorted by the pouring rain. The pool looked impossibly deep, a sheet of onyx underfoot.

*Leave before it's too late.*

Her voice said, seeming to come from every drop of water at once, cacophonous, though not loud.

*Every second you stay brings you closer to a painful death.*

Her voice pleaded with him. It was so familiar, a voice he'd heard her use hundreds of times when she was trying to help him. She was trying to save him.

*Leave!*

The rippling dark water below parted. Cameron, or so he thought, began to crawl from the pool. Their face was obscured by matted soggy hair, their skin seeming to glow in the dark. They looked demented, with every tendon in their body exposed under too-thin skin.

Their twisted bony hands gripped his ankles and pulled him swiftly under water. He tried to cry out, but all that came from his lungs were the gurgling sounds of drowning. As he felt himself pulled below the water's surface, a whip of lightning struck, scorching his world in white.

Monty let out a scream, shooting bolt upright in his bed to the sound of lightning striking the pool outside. At least that was what it had to be, the sound still ringing in his ears like a bomb.

# CHAPTER FIFTEEN

THE streak of good weather had truly finally come to an end that Monday morning. Before Monty could even get the lights on, his dark room was being lit by strobes of electricity. The weather made his healing wrist hurt with a dull thrum. He sluggishly peeled himself from the comfort and safety of his bed. Sleep tugged at the corners of his eyes so viciously he could cry. He tried to forget his dreams as he got ready for the day.

He marched to the manor under his umbrella, assaulted by the buckets of rain pouring down on him. He had tried to warn Cameron he was coming up to work, but they didn't pick up when he called. He let himself in through the back into the dreary mansion. The only thing he could hear were his own footsteps through the dusty halls and the storm outside. The rain battered the old casement windows, threatening to break them in, as waterfalls cascaded over them.

It was a rather lonely and quiet day. He was genuinely relieved to have an uneventful morning for once, filled only with the sounds of hand tools and thunder. The rhythmic melody of rain and meditative motions of his hand sander allowed his overactive mind to wander. He simultaneously hoped and feared that Cameron would come and check on him. His feelings for them continued to intensify against his better judgment. They grew inside him like the ivy that climbed up the walls of the western side of the mansion, crumbling all that it took root in. It was as if the vines were growing through his veins, rooting so deep he would never be able to truly pull it all out, even now, when the feeling was still so green. The mixture of fear and longing sent his emotions swinging back and forth like a pendulum.

Though it was not the first time he had felt this way for someone, there was something different about this. Perhaps it was some kind of bias, considering they were the only other person he saw regularly, lending his mind to fixate on them. Perhaps it had to do with the fact that every time they were in the room, he felt small, like a young buck running from a coyote. It was a feeling of fear that, to his own surprise, he loved. Or maybe he just loved being looked at by someone with hunger in their eyes. No matter what it was, the more time passed, the harder his chest pounded when he thought about those sad eyes peering oh so deep into him.

He had managed to prime all the upper hallways by the end of the day without a single peep from Cameron. He wondered if the darkness of the gloomy day had led them to sleep the entirety of it away. He would not have been surprised. The last time he saw them, they'd looked painfully exhausted, almost edging towards death. He wondered again when the last time they'd eaten.

The next few days melded together into one long task. Monty painted the third story's hallways with little to no interruption. He had in fact not heard anything at all from Cameron since the previous Sunday. Their silence was tortuous to him, leaving him to sit and stew in his thoughts, all the while covering himself in paint and primer. He wondered if he'd said something horribly wrong.

*Of course I did*, he thought to himself. *They're probably angry with me for deciding to quit.*

His mind hummed with thousands of different way that scenario could have gone. He was certain he'd once again made a fool of himself. His frustration transformed into genuine concern as the end of the week approached.

That Friday, after he'd finished painting the upstairs hallways, he decided to go looking for Cameron.

Another worry had begun to edge into his mind, one that made him ache. They'd looked so unwell the last time he'd seen them. He did not know if lack of sleep would kill someone, but he knew starvation could. He was not blind. Cameron was clearly starving and falling apart. Whether it was self inflicted, or stress-induced, he couldn't say. Either way, he worried they might not last much longer without intervention. He wished he'd gone looking for them earlier in the week. He'd been preoccupied by selfish feelings of rejection, and now he felt shameful anxiety clawing at him.

He made sure he wasn't tracking paint as he clambered down to the second story. Down here, the hallways were longer, darker, snaking through the bowels of the manor. The wallpaper peeled and curled like bark off a tree. Alone in the dim, the shrouded mirrors that lined the hallways felt menacing. Rows of black cloth appeared to breathe with the howling winds. The smell of mildew from the rain was overwhelming as the toxic scent of latex paint waned.

He could feel himself trembling. He stood still, listening for any kind of movement. For the most part, he heard the drone of rain hammering the roof of the old mansion. Then, at the very far end of the hallway, he heard soft footsteps.

He crept down through the dark, checking for open doors along the hallway. Every door he found was closed, including Cameron's room. He stopped just outside in hopes of hearing them moving about, or the muffled sound of a record playing. However, it was dead quiet; if they were in there, they must have been sleeping.

Again, he heard footsteps and what sounded to be the rustling of papers down the hall.

All the way at the very far end of this wing was a door that, he assumed, led into the rounded tower on the easternmost side of the estate. The door was slightly ajar, as if someone had gone in and not bothered to fully close it behind themself. He braced himself to find Cameron inside, but no such luck. He had opened the door to a visibly abandoned room.

It was gloomy. Thick layers of dust coated everything, as if no one had entered the room in months. The window across from him flashed the room bright white with the cracks of frequent lightning. The small bit of daylight that came through the rain had an eerie green cast to it that illuminated just enough to see. Sat in the middle of the rounded room was a desk, covered in papers and such, with a large leather armchair behind it.

There was also an open spiral staircase in the back of the room going both up and down to the other stories of the rounded Victorian tower. It was one of those rickety old iron ones that was held up with tension wires. The kind that was a risk to anyone who'd set foot on it. He briefly imagined it collapsing under his weight five steps up.

He lingered in the doorway, his palms sweating with excitement. A paper peeking out from a stack on the desk confirmed his suspicions; this was Dr. Giovanni's office.

He stepped over the threshold into the office and approached it like a museum. He carefully closed the door behind him. A crack of lightning made his heart leap again as it illuminated a grinning visage of white teeth. It was merely an anatomical human skeleton staring at him from the back of the room with its empty sockets. Its loosely strung bones rattled with the rolls of thunder. He took a deep breath.

There were many locked metal filing cabinets. He debated wrenching them open, but thought better of himself. The utilitarian bookcases along the walls were filled with numerous plastic binders, fat and mangled folders, and a plethora of mismatched notebooks. Nothing stood out to him. Nothing told him where to start with all of this. A lifetime's worth of hematological research. Backlogs and charts that would tell him very little.

He cautiously peeked at what was left on the desk. There were a smattering of dusty pens and a very full crystal ashtray amongst the refuse. Most of the desk was taken up by an ugly electric IBM rollerball typewriter, keys yellowed by nicotine. He had expected at least a desktop computer here, but just like everything else in this mansion, her office was outdated.

There was a forlorn D-ring binder labeled *"Weekly Charts 1998-2000"* along the spine. He carefully flipped it open to see tables that told him nothing of meaning. The binder only had tables and graphs, numbers scrawled out that lacked clarifying context. He shut it with a small puff of dust, dissatisfied.

He rummaged through the drawers of the dust-caked desk to see if he could find any of Dr. Giovanni's journals. He knew she kept them. He'd seen her writing in them during her office hours when she thought she was alone. He wondered if they held any clues as to what had happened to her, or what had happened to Cameron.

Sure enough, there was one of her leather-bound books jammed in the top middle drawer of the desk. He thought he could feel her standing just behind him, egging him on, but he dared not turn around to confirm it. He instead ignored his racing heart and opened the journal. He nervously skimmed through its scribed pages. Her handwriting would have been utterly illegible if he'd not read it so many times before.

He was rattled by her long anecdotes of pain and punishment. Though she seemingly never once used their name, she wrote extensively about disciplining Cameron with "necessary" corporal punishment. Most of Dr. Giovanni's handwriting was frantically sloppy. From what he could read, she frequently lamented a failed experiment and a deep fear of a woman she referred to only as her "sister."

She'd been trying to augment a strange blood disorder. He was unsure what she was trying to accomplish, but it was clear that Cameron was her primary test subject. There was a lot of talk of blood, transfusions, alterations. She spoke of purposefully prolonging an infection "gifted from sister," a grueling long-term disease of the blood. He'd expect boring hematological research, or personal life stories, not a book brimming with partly unintelligible scrawlings of madness and cruelty. He let out a sigh of disappointment and looked up from the pages.

A jolt of adrenaline coursed through him. Standing in front of the desk, dead-eyed and bloodied, was the corpse of Dr. Giovanni.

"What did you do to them?" he whispered with a quiver in his voice, as another crack of lightning illuminated the room.

She said nothing, her death-glazed eyes fixated on him, the bloodied hole through her chest festering with putrefaction. She slowly walked over to the spiral staircase. The bottom of his gut dropped out as he realized she was trying to get him to follow. Despite his nerves protesting, he felt his body move automatically to ascend the stairs after her.

The staircase groaned and swayed under his weight as he carefully spiraled up. His palms slipped along the banister. His core had gone cold to the point he could have sworn wind was drafting through the house and directly into his soul. At the top of the steps, there was a battered door. It was outfitted with an obscene number of locks, mostly chains and deadbolts that could only be opened from the outside. This room was meant to keep something in, not to keep people out. His hands shook violently as he gripped the handle of the door.

"What the..." wood creaked underfoot as he entered the room, "...*fuck!*"

He nearly leaped out of his skin as thirty or more Montagues looked back at him. The walls were covered in large eight-foot mirrors, like a gutted carousel. The door behind him was battered on the inside. Long gouges made by a beast's claws splintered the wood. The only light came from the skylights in the high conical ceiling. The putrid smell of stale blood and mold caused his nose to crinkle.

The room was predominantly empty. Sparingly furnished to resemble possibly a child's bedroom. There was a heavy bed with a rusted frame. It was fitted with disgusting sheets and had an empty IV stand sitting next to it. A well-put-together looking Dr. Giovanni sat on the edge of the bed. She looked full of life, untouched by decay, adorning her crisply ironed slacks and a squiggly plastic headband that kept her short bleach-blond hair off her face. The way she had always looked.

A teenager, no older than fifteen, sat in front of her on the ground as she ripped a brush through their matted strawberry blond hair. They were dressed in a loose white gown, heavily bloodstained down the front of it. There was a metallic muzzle-like cage around the lower portion of their face. Their ankles were rubbed raw and bleeding from the loose chains that held them to the bed. It was hard to explain, but they cast a half-reflection in the mirror surrounding them. They looked more like a forgotten memory, a faded photograph left too long in the sun.

Monty was petrified in his tracks.

"What is this?" he whispered to no one in particular.

"S-stop, it hurts," the teen whimpered. It was undoubtedly Cameron's voice; however, it was softer, younger. Their mother pulled the brush from their hair and smacked the side of their head with an audible WHACK, causing them to yelp in pain.

"Silence. Be grateful that I am not punishing you more severely for what you did," she hissed. She gripped them by a fistful of their hair and forced them to stand with her.

"Maybe I should just cut this mess," she shook their head before forcing them to lay on the bed, chains rattling as they let out a grunt.

"*Mi dispiace*," they moaned.

"Your behavior today is the precise reason why we cannot have company," Dr. Giovanni said evenly, coldly, glaring disapprovingly at her child.

"I'm just so hungry. Please resisting the urge to feed *hurts*. I didn't mean to hurt them, I promise I didn't mean to, *mama*," their small voice cracked as they lifted themself to look at their mother. The metal muzzle around their face rattled with their body's trembling.

"A little discomfort is not a good excuse to warrant ripping the throat out of another human being," she scoffed at the sobbing teenager in front of her. "If you cannot control your hunger, you will find there is much worse in this world than my discipline. Be lucky your aunt was not here to witness such lack of control. Perhaps I should take a leaf out of her book, *hmm*?"

"No, *mama*, please, don't! I'll be good, I promise," Cameron cried softly.

"Listen to me! If you do not learn discipline, these urges will drive you to madness. Unfettered feeding will lead you to lust for only blood. It will create a state so craven you'd devour even those you love without realizing what you are doing," Dr. Giovanni scolded them, before turning to something that was set up on the dresser. She picked up a fresh scalpel and a tray of empty blood vials.

"I'm sorry, *mama, mi dispiace*, I'll be better. *Capisci, capisci, capisci*," they curled into a tiny ball on the filthy bed, crying like a small child.

"This is my fault for being too lenient with you. I've listened to that awful woman and let you grown too strong. You need to learn how to handle this bloodlust," their mother said coldly.

She loomed over them and roughly gripped one of their arms. They did not fight here. They merely held in sobs as they looked away. Dr. Giovanni slit their forearm swiftly and carelessly. Blood quickly bloomed to the surface. She squeezed their flesh like a writing juice from a fruit, as the red fluid poured into a glass vial in her hand. Cameron's face contorted in agony as tears streaked down their face. They groaned, their free hand gripping at their muzzle's straps. The skin on their hand sizzled as it made contact with the metal of the silver buckle.

"Hold still," she hissed, shaking their bloody arm. Once the flow from their wound had slowed, she slit another part of their flesh, repeating as needed. Cameron's groans began to morph into snarls, their eyes shone red, their teeth gnashing as they tried to forcefully pull the muzzle from their face. They shrieked in pain as their hand seared against the metal of the cage. Dr. Giovanni clicked her tongue before she wrestled their arm away, stopping their blistering flesh from burning further on the muzzle. She forcefully maneuvered them so she had both of their arms pinned behind their back. The gashes she'd made stained the white fabric of their gown.

"I said, hold still," she hissed in their ear. They let out a whimper like a kicked dog as she continued bloodletting them. She only stopped after she'd collected just a bit more than what might be considered safe to donate, more being carelessly spilled in the process.

She finally let their raw flesh go as they looked on the verge of fainting. Dr. Giovanni hastily wrapped their yawning wounds without care for infection or scarring. Cameron lay there utterly despondent, eyes glazed over as they watched her gather up the vials of blood.

"You may come out again once you've calmed down," she scoffed before walking towards Monty, who'd been frozen, forced to watch this scene play out. She walked directly through him, the vision of young Cameron fading as the feeling of ice being pumped through his veins lingered.

"Why show me this? What the hell is wrong with you?" he spat as he turned around to speak to the specter. His moment of bravery melted the second he came face to face with rotten flesh. Dr. Giovanni had been standing just behind him, a worm-eaten grin across her hollow face. Her sweetly rotten scent caused saliva to pool in his mouth, threatening to spill the little lunch he'd had.

*Let me show you the truth.*

Her voice echoed through the air, sounding disappointed. Without thinking, he found himself stepping through her ghostly apparition. The feeling of sickness only twisted in his gut for a moment. As his foot made contact with the step below, he was suddenly standing in the third-story hallway.

Confusedly he looked around, unsure how he managed to even get here. He noticed the smell of fresh paint eluded him, as he realized the walls were still covered in the mold-riddled yellow wallpaper. The doors to the ballroom were open. He instinctively entered the room. His chest felt like it was going to split open, dizzy from how fast his blood was circulating.

Cameron was standing in the middle of the room. They had an exhausted and miserable look on their gaunt face, not too dissimilar from the last time he'd seen them. They paced back and forth like a stalking dog, golden fencing sword in one hand, their knuckles white from the grip on the handle.

"What are you doing here?" Monty asked as he approached them. They did not respond or even appear to notice him. Standing across from him was Dr. Giovanni. Her hair was sloppily coming loose from her headband, her golden locket swaying around her neck. Her face was contorted with anger and shock, pale cheeks flushed.

"I said I am sorry! Is that not enough for you, ungrateful child?" Dr. Giovanni shouted, her own golden fencing sword at her side trembling.

"Sorry!? *Te fugo!* You think sorry means anything to me?" They spat at her.

"Do not take that tone with me! I am your mother! Stop acting like a self-centered brat!" she hissed, taking a stance showing she was ready to strike.

"Some mother you are! I'll talk to you how I please, *vai scopare Maria!*" They spat again on the floor. "After everything you've done to me—"

"Everything I have done *for* you!" Dr. Giovanni shouted at them.

"You've never done anything for me a day in my life. You've just used me like your little rat. You have never seen me as your flesh and blood!" they growled, advancing on her. The rattling of their sabers colliding echoed through the empty ballroom. Dr. Giovanni's eyes narrowed with venom.

"I have done no such thing. All I have done is discipline. What *am* I supposed to do with such a wicked child?" she spat.

"I'm wicked because you made me so," they retorted, jabbing their saber with clear intent to maim.

"You were given a gift!"

"Ha! A gift, she says!? I'm only here because you don't have the strength to lock me back up now."

"I cannot believe that horrible woman let you drink fresh blood!"

"I was *starving* to *death*, Maria! If Zizi had not come to help me when she did, I would have *died*!" Hatred seeped from their lips.

"Stop being dramatic! Ugh, I knew she'd meddle with things, I just never expected you both to gang up on me!"

"Gang up? You lied to her! She told me she gave you her blood to look for a cure, not make *more* of us!"

"I never lied! There was never supposed to be a cure. She is the one who's deceived you. I was to find a way to make her kind stronger, to make you stronger!"

"*Bugiardo!*"

"You were merely a necessary byproduct of my research!"

"Necessary, hah!? No, you did not have to do this to me. I hope you know now that I will unleash what you've done on the world. People will die at my hands because of *you*! I will leave a trail of death in my wake because of you," Cameron encroached on her, aiming for her face with their saber.

"*Figlio demoniaco!* I should have killed you while I still could. You are evil!" Dr. Giovanni screamed, her face beet red.

Cameron laughed uncontrollably as their fencing became more and more erratic.

"Evil!? EVIL!? ME!? HOW *DARE* YOU!?" they shrieked through chilling laughter, Dr. Giovanni's expression turned to mild terror. Their eyes grew wide and wild with a wash of crimson.

They were backing her towards the open balcony doors as she

stumbled to block their swings. Freezing air was wafting in from the winter night outside.

"After every single thing I've endured!? After every single thing you've done to destroy my body!? *My soul!?* This is all your own evil! I will *never* be free of this curse you condemned me to! *YOU* DID THIS TO ME!" they screamed through angry tears.

With one final thrust they buried their saber deep in Dr. Giovanni's stomach. She let out a shriek of agony and surprise as the golden blade burrowed straight through her, splattering her blood across the balcony. Cameron plowed her right to the edge, her bleeding body collided against the concrete railing. They buried their sword deeper until the guard was pressing into her stomach, crimson covering the hilt and their shaking hands. Her boiling hot blood steamed up into the cold winter air.

"How… how could you? *Il mio bambino*…I-I'm your *mother!*" she coughed weakly as she grabbed Cameron by the shoulder, pulling them face to face.

"You are *nothing* to me," Cameron said quietly before thrusting her up and over the edge, moving her skewered body as if it were weightless.

The sound of Dr. Giovanni's scream as she fell onto the stone fountain was not nearly as haunting as the sound of spilling guts into water.

Cameron stood heaving at the edge, looking at her body bleeding out in the fountain. Her blood made the water run red as her entrails oozed into the fountain. Tears streamed down Cameron's rage-twisted face, their hands painted red and trembling. Clutched in one blood-slick hand was their mother's dainty golden locket, the script G outlined in crimson.

) ✧ (

Dr. Giovanni's death rattle echoed in Montague's ears like tinnitus. He jolted back into his body like snapping awake from a falling nightmare. He felt like his circulatory system had been replaced with ice, shaking like the rain-battered leaves. The memory was gone, fading away before he grasped the full wight of its details. He noticed he was merely staring through the closed journal in his hands. He had never moved from the desk, still seated in the dusty leather armchair.

Cameron had killed the doctor after all. He was shaken after witnessing her version of that fight. Despite Dr. Giovanni's best efforts to characterize her child as an uncontrollable beast, a murdered none the less, she had also shown herself to be a monster all the same.

*I will leave a trail of death in my wake, because of you!*

He was undoubtedly a little scared of Cameron, even before now. Their behavior was unnerving at times, but hearing their voice trebling with murderous rage sent his teeth on edge.

Despite everything, he found that he sympathized with them. He could see himself in their shoes. Maybe he too was more violent than he gave himself credit for. The fantasy of running his own father through with something sharp was often on his mind. He understood that rage after seeing how Dr. Giovanni had treater her child. What was being thrashed by a man your own size a few times compared to the torture that had been inflicted on Cameron? Torture that which must have been the majority of their young life from what he'd seen.

But Cameron *did* kill Dr. Giovanni. It was not just a violent fantasy. If what he'd been shown was to be believed, they had done something truly unforgivable.

As he looked up from the journal, he realized the door was still open somehow. He shakily stood up from the desk to close it. Before he could grab the handle, the door slammed all the way open. Its knob collided with the bookcase behind it, causing folders to fall to the floor. Standing there in the frame was Cameron with a look of pure terror and rage stretched across their sunken face.

"How did you get in here?" Cameron asked softly with a

dangerous smile, their entire body shaking.

"I—"

"HOW!?" they shrieked as they backed him into the room, tears welling up in the corners of their eyes. Every single part of their body was vibrating. Their teeth were bared, exposing a set of razor-sharp fangs. Monty felt himself knock into the desk, causing it to push back slightly. He gripped the wood for support. He was unsure if he was about to be torn limb from limb. He tried hard to swallow, his mouth dry. His heart had been pounding so much his chest hurt.

"The door was open. I heard someone in here, and I thought it was you," his own voice stammered out. "I was looking for y—"

"The door was open!?" They laughed with a tremble in their voice. "This room has been *locked* since the day my mother died. The key to this room was *buried* with her. I made sure of it. How the hell was the door open?" They whispered their final question. If Monty had not been thoroughly horrified already, his stomach would have dropped further. Cameron's face twisted with horror as they pieced something together in their head. They began to hyperventilate.

"Oh my God," they whispered, covering their mouth to stifle a soft shriek, tears beginning to overflow. "Oh *dio*, oh *dio*! What did you see? What did she show you? Wat did you find? You know now, don't you!?" Monty was unsure what to say as he watched Cameron melt into screaming sobs of terror.

"I'm... I know what?" he tried to calm himself. "H-hey, Cameron, take a deep breath, please I—what do you mean?" Monty was still terrified of them, of what he'd seen, but watching them sob hurt more than his fear. Their face was warped by a sickening paler. He'd never seen someone look so close to death.

"You know, you know, oh *dio mio*! You're going to kill me! You're going to kill me, aren't you!? That's what she wanted with you this whole time!?" they sobbed in horror.

"I'm not going to hurt you, Cameron," Monty croaked out of his desert-dry mouth. It was bizarre to think he was far more worried they'd kill *him* after what he had witnessed.

"By all rights, you should! Oh, *dio!* This room was locked for a reason, Montague! She was right! Oh, after all this, I thought maybe you would be different. No, why could I ever think you wouldn't eventually discover the truth," they continued, their arms now tightly wrapped around themself. The image of their rage-twisted face staring down at Dr. Giovanni was unrecognizable in contrast to their sobbing, sickly visage.

"I haven't learned anything th—"

"Don't lie to me!" they hiccuped through a sob. "Go! Get out of here while you still can!" they sobbed again, pointing to the door. Monty tried to reach out to hold their shoulder, but they backed away from him like his hands were made of fire.

"Cameron," it hurt to see them weeping like a terrified child.

They began to back out of the room. "I don't understand why I feel this way. I've never tried so hard to keep this secret. I begged you to stop looking for answers! I told you, you didn't want to know the truth. How can you stand here still? I selfishly thought maybe if I could stop you... you wouldn't..." They broke down again into uncontrollable sobs.

Monty tried to find something to comfort them, to calm them down, but he could barely make sense of what they were saying. They tried to squeak something out, though nothing coherent came from their mouth as they turned and stumbled away to their bedroom, leaving the doors open behind them. Montague stood there, staring into the dark hallway at a loss.

# CHAPTER SIXTEEN

MONTAGUE knew it was stupid to stay. He had gotten what he wanted. He'd gotten the answer to both of his burning questions. He knew what had actually happened to Dr. Giovanni *and* what she did to Cameron all at once. He could leave now. There was no real reason for him to stay here and put himself in supposed danger. Yet the question of *why* still was not satisfied. He was even more confused now than before.

No amount of thunder could drown out Cameron's sobs that rang in his head. He trembled as his own emotions washed over him. He couldn't leave them, not like this. Not a terrified sobbing mess. His feelings for them had grown too strong. Seeing how they'd been abused only made his heart ache. He did not have to think too hard to fill in the blanks of where the hundreds of scars they bore came from. Once again, his feet began to move of their own accord.

Crimson light poured from Cameron's bedroom. He stood in the doorway surveying the scene inside. The blood-red chandeliers above, with their many ruby crystals, dimly lit the space like a photo-darkroom. There were a number of wine bottles with hand-scrawled labels scattered around the room, some lying forlorn, half-shattered with frustration. Forlorn books were scattered everywhere, their papers strewn about, and many records scattered haphazardly. Clothing and shards of broken glass covered the floor. They'd utterly trashed their room since he'd last been in it.

Cameron was lying on their bed with the black velvet curtains drawn open. Though they were face down with their hands over their head, it was easy to tell that they were still crying.

"Cameron?" he croaked out softly. His voice was barely audible, as if it did not want to come out of his throat. Their body froze as though they had just then realized they were not alone. The two of them held perfectly still for what felt like an eternity as the sound of rain and low rolls of thunder mingled with Monty's heartbeat. He stepped further into the bedroom.

In the blink of an eye, Cameron materialized in front of him silently, like they'd been made from wisps of smoke. Their hollow face was streaked with tears. Their wet eyes glistened red in the dim light.

"What are you still doing here?"

"I'm not just going to leave you like this!"

Cameron began to pace around him like an animal stalking its prey. "Do you not understand?" they cried, running their hands through their messy hair. "Do you still not realize what I am!?" They threw both of their arms to the side in frustration, their eyes wild and blazing. "How can you stay if you know the truth!?"

"I know th—"

"No, you obviously don't, or you would have been out that door the second I told you to run," they cut him off, pointing to the open bedroom door, "if you knew what you were up against, you would have bolted the second I gave you the opportunity!"

Monty stood there watching them heave, tears still rolling down their face. He was at a loss for words, all of them seeming to tangle in his throat like a lump of twisted roots. He could feel his own tears tugging at the corners of his eyes.

In a flash of dark smoke, Cameron appeared behind him and pushed him further into the room, and simultaneously locked the doors shut. The lights went out with a dull POP.

He was blinded for a moment, only getting a flash of the room with a crack of lightning. He stumbled over his own feet in the dark. He was pushed down with thunderous force onto the bear skin rug. His head collided with the footboard of the bed with a loud THUNK. He let out a groan of pain as he saw stars in the dark. The way they managed to move his massive body made it clear that he weighed nothing to them.

"What the hell are you doing?" he panted out as he rubbed the sore spot already forming on the back of his head. He was too bewildered, and now spinning, to fully grasp what was happening.

"I'm showing you what I've been hiding," Cameron spoke coolly in Monty's ear, causing him to shudder. In the same breath, they were again across the room, somewhere off in the dark he could *almost* see.

It felt as if all the shadows in the world were coming to swallow him whole, a dark beast closing in on him. He once again felt like prey, like a small creature being stalked by a starving coyote, and to his dismay, it excited him. He could hear his eager heart pumping in his ears.

He desperately scanned the room for the creature that seemed poised to devour him. He caught movement as his eyes finally adjusted. Standing in front of him, to where he could feel its frigid breath, was the same huge, underfed coyote that had been stalking him for the past month. Lighting illuminated its mangy coat that clung to its shuddering ribs. It paced back and forth in front of him, making sure he couldn't leave, its glowing red eyes now familiar to him.

"What the—*YOU!?*" he sputtered in shock. They continued to pace, growling slightly, practically circling him. He felt himself sweating. He was no longer certain they would not kill him. He could see them thinking as they stalked him. Their contemplating eyes in this beastly form looked no different from when they could not find the right thing to say.

They snapped there jaws at him with a snarl and lunged towards him. Monty's blood rushed as he reflexively put both of his hands up to shield his face. He could feel cold breath against his skin as two frigid hands pulled his shielding arms away with ease.

"Look at me!" Cameron's gaunt face loomed over him. Their eyes were wild crimson as they bared two incredibly sharp fangs. Their icy skin burned against Monty's flame-hot racing pulse in his skin. He tried to wrestle free from their grip, but they were able to effortlessly keep him in place. They were ten times stronger than him, his struggling barely registering to them.

"I'm a *vampire*, Montague!" They angrily sobbed. He froze solid like a deer in headlights. It hit him as reality as the words left their trembling lips. The denial and disbelief he'd been shielding himself was shattered.

They let his hands go and backed away for a moment. If he hadn't felt like he was drowning, he would have tried to leave. Either some trick of Cameron's or the sheer speed of his heartbeat made his legs feel like jelly.

"Don't look so surprised! You said you read my mother's notes." Their tone was accusatory, as if they assumed him to have already sided with Dr. Giovanni, as if he had already decided that they were a monster.

"I-I did but... I thought she was... she—" Monty stammered stupidly, only being able to crawl further back towards the foot of the bed. It was so dark now as rain poured down he could barely see their eyes in the void. His mind was short-circuiting as fear tore through his every nerve like a wildfire.

"I'm the monster she created! I'm dead, Monty! My heart has long since stopped from the poison that was forced into my body. My mortal soul was ripped from me slowly, over years and *years* of torment. Do you have any idea what was actually, truly, done to me? Do you know the things *I've* done with these hands? I killed my mother!" their voice continued from the darkness. He instantly thought of the room full of mirrors and just how more tortuous it was than he even originally understood.

"I killed her without mercy."

"I'm sorry—"

"And, oh Monty, so many times I tried to make myself kill *you*! Over and over I tried to lure you in, but at the last minute I just couldn't make myself do it." They reappeared in his line of sight, a bottle with a hand-written label in one hand.

"What do you think it is that I eat?" they practically whispered as they crouched down in front of him. They wafted the bottle under his nose. The smell of stale blood mixed with wine permeated his nose, causing him to gag.

"I've been trying to live on this. This 'blood-wine' never really cuts it. It's just supposed to keep me from starving to death between kills." They suddenly flung the bottle towards the wall, causing it to shatter in a shower of glass. The violent force of their carelessness caused Monty to jump out of his skin.

"I have to feed on fresh warm blood to sustain myself," they whispered inches away from him. His blood was pumping hard and fast. He could feel his pulse in his neck taunting Cameron, their face so close he could feel their breath fogging on his hot skin.

"You have no idea how much I want to sink my fangs into you and drain the life from your warm body. Do you understand how hard it is for me to control myself?"

Monty's lungs were on fire as sweat dripped into his eyes. In a final last-ditch effort, his nervous system sent a desperate signal to run. Before he even made it to his feet, Cameron grabbed his ankles and dragged him forcefully to the ground. He let out a yelp of pain as his heavy body made swift contact with the hardwood floor, only cushioned by the bear skin rug beneath him. They jumped on top of him and pinned him down with such force that he could barely move despite his squirming to get free. Pain bloomed from his sprained wrist, causing his elbow and shoulder to spasm under the pressure.

His heart skipped a beat as chills and shakes took over him. The darkness enclosing around his mind made him feel weak. Shadows were stitching his body to the floor.

"It's too late! I already gave you the chance to run!" Lightning cracked, revealing the wild visage of Cameron looming over him.

"Please, Cameron!" he pleaded, "I know you, and I know there's better in you. Please stop! I'm not on her side," his voice trembled. He shook violently under their grasp with a level of excitement that shocked him. It filled him with a strange shame. He knew what it felt like when someone was trying to kill him, and this was not the same.

His vision turned dark, tunneling so all he could see was the monster looming over him. Spots of light bloomed from the back of his brain, and his ears rang as he became dizzier and dizzier.

"Listen to me, Monty!" Cameron shook him violently as his wrists went numb from the pressure they were applying. Their voice was flooding directly into his head as if they were inside his brain.

"It doesn't matter whether or not I want to kill you! Do you not understand? I'm a beast. I can't fight my instincts forever!" What little color they had left faded from their face. "You have to run... do you... do you not understand how..." They panted heavily as their eyes rolled around, "...how hard I've been... trying t' keep m-m-myself fro—?"

Their eyes rolled into the back of their head and they collapsed onto him, their grip going slack. Suddenly Monty's head stopped swimming, and the room slammed back into focus, dark, but clear to him.

He was still shaking as he rolled Cameron over onto the rug next to him. They were terribly cold and still as the confusion in Monty's mind began to wane and his strength returned to him.

He hissed with pain as he forced his aching body to sit up. He could feel tears at the backs of his eyes as he rubbed his swollen wrist. He gently pulled Cameron's messy hair away from their face. Their thin eyelids fluttered for a moment more before they shot open, and they let out a gasp, coming back to life.

"That was your cue to escape," they moaned disappointedly.

"What?"

"Stab me through the heart? Be the hero and get out?" Their eyes darted over to their saber lying on the floor. It had been in plain sight just a few feet from where Monty's pinned hand had been. He could have easily grabbed it and defended himself.

"I've been starving myself so I would be weaker. I wanted to make it so even if the temptation took over me, I wouldn't be able to kill you," they wheezed out before closing their eyes. "I'm... so hungry," they mumbled. "I knew if I was weak, I wouldn't be able to actually kill you... I thought you would have tried harder to survive. I kind of assumed you'd try to kill me in the struggle and make your escape," they spoke feebly as they looked up at him, "but, you're still here?"

"I lack self-preservation instincts," Monty joked with a wince.

"I'm sorry I hurt you." They looked away. "You're a lot lighter than I expected. I wasn't going to kill you, but I thought you'd at least try to defend yourself if you believed I was."

"You had me for a moment, not gonna lie, but..." he took a deep breath, "wait, you were trying to goad me into assisted suicide!?"

"When you put it that way, I suppose yes? I thought you'd see my saber and instinctively fight me, put the monster out of its misery," they mumbled. "I don't know if it would have actually killed me, but I was ready to let you win."

"It didn't even cross my mind, Cameron. You're not a monster. I'm obviously not dead despite your desires, so... I'm not just going to leave you here, and I'm not going to hurt you. You're one of the few people I've met who's treated me kindly, made me feel something. I *want* to be here with you."

"Monty..." Cameron pulled on his paint-stained flannel to bring him closer, so that his face now loomed over theirs.

"Meeting you has made me feel like I've had my head pulled out of the water for the first time in my life. I don't know what's happening to me. I've never felt this way about someone before and... I'm horrified." They were trembling. He brushed their incredibly soft cheek with the back of his hand, and they closed their eyes. He sighed, thinking about just how shaken he still was. They gently grabbed his sore, calloused hand and softly kissed the heel of his palm, causing chills to run up his body.

"I'm sorry. I want you here with me, but I have never wanted to sink my fangs deep into your skin more than I do right now. I almost lost myself just now; I crave your blood so badly... I'm so hungry. If you stay... I need to feed. I can't hold myself back anymore unless you kill me," they said with their lips against Monty's pulse. He paused for a moment before pulling his hand away, rolling up his stained flannel sleeve. He was nervous about what he was going to let them do.

"Instead of trying to scare me away, why don't you prove to us both you have some self-control," he said as he took the brace off his pained left joint.

"Here," he said as he presented his tanned wrist to Cameron, who just stared at him wide-eyed.

"I shouldn't... What if I can't stop?" they asked. Their eyes darted from his face to his wrist, his pulse visible in the bulging veins under his warm skin.

"I trust you," he said after a moment of contemplation. They weakly moved so their head laid in his lap. Their head was heavy and cushioned by their cloud of curly hair. They slowly and cautiously pressed his wrist into their mouth. In this moment, he couldn't help but think that they were somehow even more beautiful than they had been in his intimate dreams. They closed their eyes and lingered for a moment.

Monty's breath hitched, and he let out a gasp of pain, throwing his head back against the footboard behind him as their fangs cut deep into his flesh like little white-hot knives. His vision momentarily flashed bright white. Their saliva burned his sore wrist like a festering infection within seconds of it entering his bloodstream. They drank with such fervor that some of his blood dripped down their chin. They held his wrist tight in their lips as if they would die if he took it from them. He began to feel faint, and his heart screamed in protest.

He started to pant and sweat as his life seemed to be draining into Cameron, their face becoming less sallow with every swallow. Circles under their eyes receded, cheeks filled, and what could only be described as a youthful glow returned to their skin. Monty, on the other hand, could feel darkness tugging at his eyes and mind. Different now, darker, further away than the previous void. Just as he thought he would lose consciousness, he felt the sharp pinch of fangs pulling from his skin. Cameron's mouth was glistening with sweet dark fluid.

*My blood...*

They lapped up the soft stream trickling down his wrist with a cool tongue that sent chills through his body. Cameron panted heavily as they propped themself up, looking from the blood smeared across his arm to his pained face.

"Thank you," they whispered with genuine gratitude. He looked down at the mess they had made of his wrist, the smell of his own blood churning his weakened stomach. He looked back to Cameron, their eyes half-lidded and chest heaving.

They leaned closer to him, slipping their slim hands around the base of his skull. Their cool fingers in his thick, sweat-soaked hair felt heavenly. They pulled his head forward into a deep kiss. Though they tasted faintly of flowers and cigarettes, most of what he could actually smell and taste was his own blood on their lips. The flavor of salty copper and something oddly sweet mingled in his mouth. Though the taste was strangely pleasant, he still gagged on the metallic flavor.

They abruptly pulled away. "Oh, *dio*, I'm sorry," they apologized as they wiped blood from his mouth. "I didn't think that through," they huffed out. They released his skull and trailed their hands gently down his body.

There was a charge in the air that reminded Monty of the feeling of one's hair standing on end right before being struck by lightning. The feeling buzzed through him as they both stared at each other for a good long moment. Their faces seemed to pull together again without realizing. He closed his eyes and took a breath in. Monty kissed them this time, softly, gently and slowly, only pulling back as his lightheadedness became too much to bear.

"Does this mean… I'll… You know?" he asked softly after pulling away. His head was still spinning from blood loss.

"No, no, my venom would have to mix with the disease in my blood for my infection to spread to you. I would have to make you drink my blood right this moment for it to spread," they explained, gently kissing his still-bleeding wrist before looking back at his face. "I'm so sorry." Their expression became painfully somber.

"For?" he asked.

"The way I've treated you, for trying to scare you away… for a lot more," they added. They gently tried to wipe some of the sweat off his brow with their sleeve, before wiping their own blood-covered face.

"Can't say I'm a fan of everything, but I at least understand now." Monty huffed out. He gently rested his sore skull on the footboard of the bed and felt his blood pressure slowly begin to go back to normal. The both of them sat in silence, listening to the pouring rain outside. The thunder was quieter and farther off now. Cameron leaned their head against his chest softly.

"I'm still scared of myself," they finally said after a long while.

"How could you not be? It seems like you've been conditioned to believe you're an uncontrollable monster."

"She's right."

"Obviously not." Monty felt insulted at their instant resignation. "You've shown me you can control yourself. And, *and,* also, if you've really tried to kill me as much as you've said it only proves my point more. You're not about to lose your mind and tear me apart."

"I can't stop these feelings… I've seen it happen," they whispered the last part.

"In your dreams?"

"In a way, sometimes asleep… sometimes awake. You've been having them too, the visions. I remember you told me," they replied.

"I honestly wasn't sure if you thought I was fucking crazy at that point," Monty laughed slightly.

"Her spirit has been here since before you arrived. I thought I was just going mad from guilt. But then the daydreams and horrible visions started. All after that first night I failed to kill you. She wanted me to, I think. There was something about the air around you," they paused and pointed to his necklace, "that silver holy symbol of yours kept you from falling under my hypnosis. I've never had someone be able to break free like that. And then after that, I started feeling this strange warmth in my chest when you were near me. I wanted to see you, be near you, so I could feel that strange feeling more. It's like she could tell, like she wanted to punish me for those feelings…" they trailed off.

They both sat for a moment listening to the rain, which was slowing now.

"You've never fallen for someone before, have you?" Monty asked them. Cameron shook their head.

"I've read about these feelings and desires in books, but I've never actually felt what it's like for myself," they admitted.

"It eats you if you ignore it, you know," Monty said, thinking of how consumed he himself had been. Enough to let them physically consume him. He turned his attention back to his wrist, blood clotting now. Cameron noticed his gaze on the bloody mess.

"Here, let me go get something to clean this up," they fussed, jumping up with sudden ease. They walked off into the room Monty had previously assumed was a bathroom. They moved through the darkness as if they didn't even notice the lack of light.

"You made my blood look so good," he joked, thinking about how he couldn't stop himself from gagging at its taste. Cameron stifled a laugh. He tried to sit up straighter with a grunt. His head was still swimming.

"Blood does taste good to me." They returned with gauze and antiseptic and crouched down to dress the wound on his wrist. "Everything other than blood and alcohol tastes vile," they explained softly as they wiped Monty's wrist clean. He practically howled with pain as the antiseptic burned out the poison from their fangs. "Sorry," they whispered over and over as he squirmed with pain.

"What does it taste like to you?" He panted out through the throb of his injuries being tended to.

"Blood?" They stopped for a moment to think, "I suppose it tastes like salted meat, wine, copper, but also sweet? All of those things in a good way though. I don't know if it's possible to explain." After wrapping his wrist tightly in gauze, Cameron paused again, looking like they were searching their mind for something. He could practically see the loop of their thoughts repeating behind their dilating pupils.

"Will you stay here tonight?" they asked, their eyes were soft and pleading.

"Wasn't all of this because I wouldn't leave?"

"No, I mean, will you stay here, in the house, with me in my room tonight?" they clarified. He thought for a moment, feeling his slowed pulse throbbing in his wounds. "Let me take care of you. I owe you that."

"Sure," he replied.

# CHAPTER SEVENTEEN

CAMERON brought Montague water and an apple from his cabin. He was grateful to get his blood sugar back up, quite certain that if he didn't, he'd simply faint when he tried to stand. He had no way of knowing how much blood he'd lost, but it was enough for him to nearly lose consciousness. And it was enough that Cameron looked significantly more alive. They had a spring in their step that he'd not seen in a long while. His blood had done more than just sustain them. It brought them back to a form of life.

He wondered if it would be possible for him to keep them healthy if he donated his own blood. The splitting pain in his head told him—*no*—doing so would likely kill him. It was still hard for him to swallow that Cameron had killed before, and most definitely would kill again. They had to, to survive. That much was clear to him. Still, a part of him wished that wasn't true, that there wasn't even a shred of truth to Dr. Giovanni's claims they were a monster.

Cameron was painfully quiet as they sat at their desk, watching him closely in the dark red light, a glass of blood-wine clutched in their slim hand.

"I can't read your mind… but I do have an idea of what's on it," they finally said to him as they lazily swirled their wine around.

"What do you mean?" he asked.

"I don't like having no choice but to kill to stay alive," they admitted.

"You know... You don't have to. Look at how much better you feel now, and I'm still alive," he pointed out.

"You're the first person who's ever voluntarily let me drink their blood. If I let my prey go, how long would I have to live before they came to put an end to *me*? As it is, I'd have to feed much more often, potentially hurting even more people in the process," they explained.

"How much would you need realistically?" he asked.

"I'm sorry, I don't understand?" Cameron cocked their head slightly to the side.

"My blood, how much of it would you need? To survive without killing?" he asked.

"Oh Monty, I couldn't do that... I don't think it would be good for you if I fed on you regularly. I don't think you could make enough blood," they sighed with a sad expression as if they had realized what he was hoping for.

"I could try to be enough for you," he said with a sense of desperation that took them both off guard. He took a deep breath. "I mean, I'm a big man, I'm sure I have enough blood to keep us both alive."

"No, absolutely not," they shook their head. Monty sat quietly for a moment.

"How much blood exactly do you *actually* need?" he asked inquisitively. Cameron sat for a moment, pondering.

"I don't have a precise measurement," they said to their glass of wine.

"Your mother was studying you, right? She must have made a note of that at some point?" He regretted his question immediately, realizing their expression changed swiftly.

"I don't think she ever even considered letting me be fully fed, never mind how much it would take. Neither before nor after the infection took hold of me," they said softly, the darkness around them hanging far more heavy.

"All I know is that I need more than this to stay alive. One person can't give me enough blood and sustain their own body at the same time," they elaborated. "I need the blood-wine to stretch out my time between victims. I can't keep up with consistent kills to keep myself full. I don't enjoy the affair, but I have to, or I let myself die... And, oh Monty, it hurts, it hurts so very bad when I'm starving," Cameron explained as the conversation died down again.

Montague's mind was still stewing, trying to pick apart the mess he'd landed himself in. He did not have the capacity to fully parse out how he felt about it all. He was far more preoccupied with the dreadfully ill feeling in his bones. His body felt as if it had been dehydrated in the sun for hours and then dunked into a pool of ice water.

He peeled his disgusting flannel off to let some of his adrenaline sweat evaporate. With a sigh, he closed his eyes and leaned his head against the footboard again. His head throbbed in waves, like the sheets of rain pouring on the windows. He felt disgusting and exhausted as he thought about Cameron's soft bed fitted with crimson satin sheets just behind him. He wanted to lay down so badly, but he couldn't feel comfortable covered in all this stale sweat.

"Do you want a bath?" they asked.

"A bath?"

"Yes, I have a bathtub that's quite deep," they explained as they put their wine down on their paper-covered desk.

"I guess so. I feel disgusting," he nodded.

They walked over and held a hand out to help him up. "Here."

He grunted as they effortlessly pulled him up from the floor. He took a moment as he felt his head rush at the change in his altitude. They steadied him and led him through the small black door into the master bath.

It was hard to see in the dim light. The floor and walls were black marble tile. The double sinks were the same black marble with a large old mirror hanging heavy over them. The counters were messy with strewn accessories and bottles of things he had no clue how to use. Hairbrushes, combs, a lone toothbrush, all sat in no particular order. The tub was a big, black clawfoot cauldron twice the size of any he'd seen before. All the faucets and findings were of a beautiful gold that matched the gilded tin tile ceiling.

He looked at them both in the mirror. Well, he was looking at himself and the silhouette of black clothing that appeared to float in the air in the aging silver-backed mirror. Montague's normally tanned olive-brown skin looked washed out in the dim light. There were circles under his eyes, albeit nowhere as severe as Cameron's had been. His far too shaggy hair was practically standing on end, and he was covered in paint, a shock of white becoming ever more prominent at his temple. He realized at this moment how purely insane and wild he had looked that whole evening.

He watched in the mirror as the black clothing floating next to him fell to the floor. He turned to look at Cameron, who was now starting the tub, fully nude save for their mother's locket. He felt the little blood left in him flood to his face. Cameron's skin was like milk against the tiles. They perched a thin leg on the ledge of the tub as they leaned over to check the temperature of the water.

He could now clearly see all the scars across their body. Long slices across every inch of their arms, gashes across their chest, long, ugly slashes around their torso as if they'd been cut open countless times, and their mangled ankles. He wanted to run his hands over every raised section of soft skin. They looked up almost as if they were surprised to see Monty still fully clothed.

"I'm sorry. Was I being presumptuous?" They asked, looking a little embarrassed. "I should have asked. Would you be okay with me joining you?"

"Oh! Y-yes, of course," he said, his dry voice cracking as he felt himself blush, "I'd like that."

"Why don't you get out of those disgusting things?" They pointed to Monty's sullied clothing. Without saying a word, he disrobed, catching a chill as he did so. He realized this was the first time in years anyone other than himself had seen his body fully naked. He didn't even really look at himself when he was alone. His body was more of a tool than anything else to him. That being said, he glanced in the mirror. He had horrible tan lines barely masked by his thick layer of dark chest hair. He was far more toned than he'd remembered, the shape of muscles just visible under fat, undoubtedly caused by all the physical labor he had been doing. He realized now that they were nude, that he was considerably bigger than Cameron. The way their gaze lingered on him made him feel self-conscious, and yet excited.

"I'm sorry," he nervously mumbled.

"Why?" they looked perplexed.

"I don't know. It's just... it's been a long time since I've felt this exposed," he admitted with embarrassment. The room was fogging up from the heat of the bathwater, and he wondered if they could even tell how hot it was. Cameron walked up to him, their slender spindly limbs swaying slightly.

"I like looking at you, you know?" they said softly, "all of you." They gently ran a hand along his chest. There was a soft, inquisitive look in their light eyes. Suddenly they wrapped their lanky arms around him and pulled him into a cooling embrace. Their body stuck to his as the steam reactivated his sweat. He could feel his blood rush as they held close to him. They let out a soft, smirking laugh.

Cool hands ran down his back, causing chills to run down his body with them. He was more nervous at this moment than when he was actively being hunted. He wrapped his arms around them, the coldness of their body rather soothing against his hot, flustered self. They both stood like that for a moment before Cameron abruptly broke away from his embrace with a soft curse under their breath, rushing over to stop the tap before the water overflowed.

"Oops, I guess we'll just flood the bathroom a little bit. I've done it before. It will be fine," they laughed to themself before getting in, causing some water to spill over the sides. They sighed and reclined against the large tub. Monty reassured himself before slipping into the impressively large tub as well. The water was nearly too hot for him, but it felt spectacular on his tight muscles. A large amount of water splashed on the floor as he got in, causing Cameron to let out an amused laugh.

"Definitely a mess," he sighed.

"Don't worry about it," they smiled. Monty let the rest of himself be soaked in the warm, practically pool-sized tub. He let out a long hiss of pain as his wrist made contact with the water. His vision flashed white for a moment from the searing-hot agony that shot up his arm, lingering in his elbow and shoulder for a moment. Cameron's bite mark stung like a hornet.

"Oh, I really hurt you badly," they said softly, realizing why he was reeling in pain.

"I'll be okay," he said as the shooting pain began to numb.

"Here, relax against me," they insisted, pulling him back into them. The larger man nervously obliged, still feeling like he could crush them. Their body was pleasant in contrast to the scalding bath water. They were so soft and smooth, their skin might as well have been made from vellum. They let out a soft hum of contentment, and their arms wrapped around him.

Every inch of their forearms was heavily scarred with the ghost of gaping slashes and many gruesome marks from past IVs in the pit of their elbows and along their forearms. Mangled, mutilated, disfigured surface scars were the least of the damage they had endured. He couldn't help but tenderly run his fingers over their scars. They tensed slightly as he did so.

"Oh, I'm sorry. Does that hurt?" he asked, noticing their movement.

"No... it's okay. I just haven't had someone touch them... like that," Cameron said with a slight shake in their breath. "I try to keep them covered as much as possible. Normally, by the time most people get to see them, it's... well anyway, you're the first person who hasn't met me with audible disgust at my scars," they explained. Monty gently lifted their arm to his lips and softly kissed their forearm. He could feel them shaking behind him as they placed a cheek against his tight back.

"Your body is not disgusting because it's scarred." He tried to turn around, but they held him too tightly, as if they did not want him to see them crying, even though he could feel their cool tears on his back. Cameron was quiet for a moment before taking a deep breath and planting a wet kiss on the nape of Monty's neck. They both were silent, just enjoying the warm water.

After a while, the both of them clambered out of the cooling water and dried off. They exhaustedly crawled into the dark fourposter bed. Cameron's bed was softer than he had ever imagined. He sank deep into the mattress. Their sheets were silk satin and so smooth he felt like he was swimming in water. Every inch smelled of Cameron, laced with musk and floral perfume.

There was a unique intimacy in lying in their bed. They had drawn the black curtains around them, making it incredibly dark now. He could not remember a time when he had been this calm. Perhaps the blood loss and exhaustion had added to his eagerness to simply sink in and relax. Maybe it was the fact that he was not alone as he drifted off to sleep for once.

"Close your eyes. You don't have to stay awake," Cameron whispered to him.

"You can see me?"

"Yes, and I can see you're staring at nothing. I'll be here in the morning, and we can talk more then. I promise. Now rest," they murmured, running a hand through his still damp hair.

"Alright," he snuggled up against their cold body and wrapped one of his arms around them before letting his mind relax into sleep.

# CHAPTER EIGHTEEN

MONTAGUE found himself standing in the musty second-story hallway. He could still hear the gentle sounds of rain faintly in the distance. He was unsure of how he had arrived here. Perhaps he had sleepwalked?

Down at the end of the hall, there was a figure. He thought it might have been Cameron for a moment. His eyes struggled in the dark of night to make out their features, their edges liquid with the black expanse before him. He was unsure if he was even looking at a figure at all until they started moving. As they turned to face him, he realized he could see straight through *her*, the mass of darkness interrupted but a clear gaping wound straight through her stomach.

*Mon~ta~gue*

She approached him slowly. It felt like his feet were rooted to the ancient carpet below. He wanted to run far away from the figure advancing towards him. Weather through fear, or some otherworldly power, he couldn't move his body even one inch.

Her approach was not a threat, though it was macabrely familiar to him. He could smell her rotting meat as she drew near. She gently placed her hands on his shoulders in a gesture of comfort and consolation. Though he'd felt this sensation before, it was now tainted by the hum of flies and the creeping decay that gripped her body. Despite her stomach churning putrefaction, her hands brought him the same comfort they had in years past. Despite being a head shorter than him, she had always made him feel like a small boy when she comforted him.

*What are you doing?*

She asked him softly. Her voice poured out from the mirrors along the walls, up through the carpets, and down through the dark ceiling. Her voice was in every particle of humidity that saturated the wood of the old mansion as she spoke.

Montague tried to reply to her, to ask what she meant, but his petrification had extended to his vocal cords. Her withering hands were mottled blue and marbled with the decay of veins beneath. The skin was so loose it threatened to slough off with the slightest of movement. Her hands traced from his shoulders up to his neck slowly, achingly, until they were wrapped around his thick windpipe, choking him.

*Is this what you want?*

He could not understand what she meant, and he sputtered under her grasp. He desperately tried to claw at her hands as panic flooded his oxygen-starved mind. He could not move his arms, nor could he fight the crushing weight that had spread from his throat down to his chest. He tried to scream, but the weight that had replaced air in his lungs asphyxiated him tenfold, as he felt himself fall backwards through the floor.

He gasped as air returned to his body. It was still impossibly dark as he found himself slumped on the ground. He looked around in a daze and was met with eighty reflections of himself in a round mirrored room. The reflections made it feel like his surroundings went on infinity. The ceiling was an unending black hole. The smell of stale blood and ozone-laced sweat permeated up from the floorboards.

He was startled by a pained groan from the rusted bed across the room. His body moved automatically as he approached the bed. A white sheet was stretched over the figure underneath, who was shivering and whimpering like a kicked dog. He pulled the sheet back. Curled in a heap of lanky limbs and frizzed hair was Cameron. Fixed to their face was a metal cage, a muzzle, its leather straps cutting into the tender flesh of their cheeks. Their arms were wrapped tightly in dirty bandages. The side of their torso was split and oozing from long angry wounds that looked to be the result of being whipped with the blade of a fencing saber.

They froze as Monty uncovered them. Their eyes snapped to his. Their expression was feral and laced with fear as they stared at him. They looked like a scared dog backed into a corner. His fingers gently brushed the muzzle, and they recoiled from his touch, as if his hands were made of fire.

"Leave," Cameron croaked out, "please."

Monty wanted to response but his voice would not come. His vocal cords were paralyzed in his still-aching throat. Cameron's gaze moved over his shoulder, and their crazed red eyes widened further in horror.

"Get out!" They sat up swiftly and pushed Monty back from the bed with intense force. He let out a groan of pain as his body made contact with hardwood.

Dr. Giovanni approached them both. It was strange to see her bluing flesh in this light. Her skin had come loose from the muscles now. Much of the fat she'd had had since liquefied and left her quite hollow in appearance, as though her sinew was being marionette by the flies living in her body.

"Don't do this to him," Cameron's voice was barely audible, "don't do this to me."

The rotting, bloody void through the doctor's body festered with flies, happily eating away at her decaying meat. No matter how much Monty wanted to, he physically could not turn his gaze away from her.

She turned to Cameron, who was cowering. They looked crazed, blood-starved, as drool leaked from underneath their muzzle. She looped a finger under one of the leather straps holding the silver cage to their face, loosening a buckle and slipping it off. Cameron's crimson eyes rolled in their head as they gnashed their fangs. They gripped face and trembled. They let out a slew of animalistic groans as their body writhed.

In a shock of dark smoke, a huge mangy beast collided with Monty. Cameron's canine maw made sudden and painful contact with his throat. Terror and agony ripped through his mind as he felt his flesh shred under razor-sharp teeth.

☽ ✧ ☾

Montague fell out of his nightmare with a sudden jolt, the real world coming to him in an instant. He heard his heart whooshing in his eardrums as he forced his eyes to open. The feeling of satin sheets underneath his weary body was the first sensation he noticed, a little confused as to where he was. In the dim morning light he looked up at a grotesquely carved ceiling, tracing the serpents coiling along the woodwork with his eyes. There was a spill of red spread across the ceiling, as light crept in through a crack in the nearby balcony door's curtains and refracted off the chandelier. On the balcony just outside, he could hear the soft cooing of rock doves.

A new and strange sensation gripped him as he realized he was not only in Cameron's room, but in their bed with them. He was unsure whether he was embarrassed or sick from the stress of it all. He looked to his side to see them lying seemingly asleep. It was strange seeing them in the daylight. They had the slightest hint of pink in their skin. Though the jaundiced, sunken look had not left their eyes, they at least looked alive, if maybe a bit ill. Although their rose-gold hair fell around them in perfect air-dried ringlets, they still had a noticeable halo of frizz. They looked angelic in this state.

The events of the night prior began to funnel back into Monty's head. Part of him hoped it had all just been one of his nightmares. It would have been easier for him to believe it was a bad dream if he had woken up literary anywhere else than in this bed. The pulsating pain in his head and wrist confirmed that his memory had not failed him. No matter how much he wished he'd been wrong, he could not convince himself of anything other than the truth. Cameron was far from any angle.

They *had* killed Dr. Giovanni. But he now also knew the truth about his old professor. The woman he had known was nothing more than a mask. His stomach twisted thinking back to how she was so proud of her "personal research," and now he knew that what she was proud of was torture.

*Of course Cameron snapped.*

But there was also the nagging reality of their situation. They needed the life of others to sustain their own. Monty had the understanding of what a vampire was in concept, but his exposure to them was all superstition and Hollywood, not a livable reality. He had so many questions now about what was fact and what was fiction. He wondered if the reason Cameron had been so animated about him staying out of the woods was because that was where their victims ended up. He wondered if he'd been right about that missing guy all along. He tried to shake the image from his mind. No matter what he thought, he *did* fear them, but that fear was greatly outweighed by a blooming fondness that emanated from deep in his chest.

He lay there just looking at them for a while. He watched them stir and twitch in their sleep, realizing they were crying. Tears trailed from their fluttering pink eyelashes and down their face to stain the pillowcase dark. They let out a gasp, and their eyes snapped open. Monty startled as they did so. They screwed up their face in an unpleasant expression and rolled over, coughing. He watched as the clumsily fished a handkerchief from the inside of their pillowcase to wipe their face. They sat up with a shaky sigh.

"Good morning." Their voice was nae a whisper, prompting

them to clear their throat.

"Nightmare?" Monty asked with his own groggy voice.

"Yeah," they cleared their throat again, "yeah, it's—you have them to right? It's so real, I feel like she's truly there, and it always ends the same way. No matter what I do, I kill you," they said so slow and quiet it sounded as if it was taking all their will to speak.

"I wonder if we're having the same dreams," Monty paused, trying to grasp more of his dream.

"It felt so real," they whisper again, choking back more tears. Though they did not say it aloud, there was a knowing understanding that they'd both been dreaming of Dr. Giovanni's spirit. Monty felt a growing headache throbbing behind his eyes and down his back.

"Maybe we did have the same dream," he hummed while rubbing his hand over his stubble.

"I think she wants you dead," they mumbled, flipping their locket over in their hands. "I just don't understand. Why is she haunting you? Ever sine I first suspected you were seeing her spirit, I've been confused. She's been haunting me since the day she died. I thought she was my guilty consciousness in truth. That was until you started acting weird too. When you informed me you were seeing her… I was relieved to know I wasn't insane but… confused," they explained.

"Can I level with you?" Monty asked as he willed his aching body to sit up.

"Please tell me what's on your mind."

"I came here to specifically *because* I knew your mother. I know now it was a different side of her, but she was like a mentor to me back in school. She'd taken a liking to me as a freshman, and she ended up tutoring me through most of the program. I thought I knew her better. I really did. You were right. She was like a completely different person to me. She offered me guidance and kept me on track in the absence of my own parents," he paused as a stick feeling clawed at the back of his throat. "Her death fucked me up so bad that I had to drop out of school. I couldn't let it rest... I felt like her soul was in distress or something. I suspected foul play, and I *had* to know what actually happened. So when I saw your add, I saw mostly the chance to find out what actually happed," Monty explained.

"Your thesis was correct, there was 'foul play,' and now I would think you've gotten the answers you were looking for," Cameron sounded very somber as they paused, "but Monty, I need you to try to understand me. I didn't kill her for money or this crumbling tomb of an estate. I don't actually know what you found in that tower, but that's where my old room was. That's where I spent most of my life, in that horrible room at the top of the tower. I was a caged animal, nothing more, being slowly poisoned and tormented for reason beyond my comprehension. I still don't know why. I chalked it up to cruel scientific indifference, or —"

"Cam," he cut them off, "I *literary* let you *drink my blood*. Like genuinely, what more do I have to do to show you I'm on your side in this?" He felt both frustrated and ridiculous in this moment.

"Right," their face softened, "right, I'm sorry, thank you. I won't lie. I expected a very different outcome of all this."

They muttered "Cam" to themself under their breath, hiding their mouth with their fingers, pretending to be lost in thought. The faint flush in their cheeks betrayed them.

After a long pause, Monty spoke again. "I went through her journal," he admitted. "The stuff that woman thought and did... I can't blame you."

"There's a part of me that deeply regrets it, you know? That's why I was so quick to just assume it was guilt starting to drive me mad." They were quiet for a moment. "Could you live with yourself if you were in my shoes?" they asked him with a burning gaze.

"Could I live with myself?" he stifled a sarcastic laugh. "I'm disowned, remember?" Monty huffed, "I haven't spoken to my family since I was seventeen. I couldn't care less whether they live or die. I don't know if I could *kill* my father... but the desire to has crossed my mind." He closed his eyes. It had more than just crossed his mind. He fantasized in his earlier years the way in which he would do it.

"What did he do to you?" they asked him. Monty took a deep breath. It still hurt to think about.

"We never really got along. He had a bad temper, but I swear he hated me the most out of my sibling. He hit me a lot over stupid shit, yelled all the time too. He's probably why I'm so jumpy..."

"I was a varsity linebacker with some pretty promising scholarships dangling in front of me like shiny keys. All I had to do was not fuck up. But I was a stupid kid, and I couldn't keep my hands to myself. Me and a teammate got caught making out under the bleachers. I didn't know being gay could get you expelled from public school, but it turns out they can totally do that if they make you out as a 'danger to yourself and others.'"

"'We won't have you spreading AIDS to the whole school,' I'm pretty sure is the quote I remember from the principal. Boy, you should have seen my father's face when he finally showed up to get me. When we got home, he beat me within an inch of my life," he explained, the memory causing him to go somewhere far away, "with his bare hands." He mimed a strangling motion in front of himself.

He remembered desperately trying to dig his fingers into his father's eyes as the man cut off the air from his windpipe while slamming his head against the living room floor. He could still feel his mother and sisters looking on quietly in fear and disgust, as his father snapped his nose with the hardest punch head ever taken. He'd blacked out and woke up with a work boot kicking his side in. He could still see the hate behind his father's eyes when he physically threw him out the front door of his childhood home, right down onto the mud-soaked lawn. He remembered his backpack colliding with his bashed-in skull just moments after. He could still feel the burning shame of showing up on Mina's front doorstep, soaked with rain and blood, barely able to move. Mina briefly fluttered in his thoughts, causing his mood to turn even more sour.

"He broke this ugly mug of mine pretty bad. I mean, my nose didn't start out this crooked. I think he snapped something in here too. But I never went to the hospital, so who knows?" He tried to laugh himself out of the memory. "Funny that even after all that, I didn't want him to get in trouble for what he did. I was worried about my mother and my sisters... maybe I get how you feel in a weird way. It's not the same, but—" Cameron interrupted his train of thought as they wiped a tear from his cheek.

"You don't have to explain more. I think I understand you. Even if I don't fully know what all the things you're talking about are," Cameron said with a weary look. Monty touched his own tears with a bit of shock. He did not realize he'd started crying.

"Right, you have no idea what high school varsity football is," he laughed, feeling a little stupid for even mentioning his past. It was only fair he offered some of himself up after everything.

"No, but I don't need to, to know what you mean," they sighed with a weary smile, "thank you." Cameron's attention flicked to his lips and back to his eyes as if silently asking for permission. Wordlessly, he leaned in to the magnetic pull he often felt towards them. Their lips locked, and for a moment he wondered if they'd gotten up for a cigarette in the middle of the night, as they tasted of bitter smoke.

The quiet song of mourning doves outside was abruptly disturbed by the ear-splitting ring of the phone, causing them both to startle and break their kiss. The bell was set loud enough to jolt a corpse from the grave. Cameron hastily scrambled across the bed to pick it up.

"H-hello?" they nervously cleared their throat. They quickly changed their demeanor and sat at attention on the edge of the bed, a fake cheeriness washing over them.

"*Ciao! Buongiorno, Zizi! Si, no, si. Mi hai detto che stavi venendo oggi. Si...*" Monty could not understand what they were saying to the other person on the line. He was so tired from the previous night it took him a moment to realize Cameron was speaking Italian.

"*Scusa, dimenticavo, si...*" they uncomfortably shifted as they pushed their hair from their face.

Though their tone was cheery, their body grew rigid and tenes as they conversed with the other person. It was someone familiar, respected, or possibly feared. Monty reflexively checked his watch for the time only to remember it was on the bathroom counter.

"*Ti voglio bene anch'io... Presto,*" and with that Cameron hung up the old rotary phone. They stared into the middle distance for a moment, their cheery demeanor melting away instantly.

"*Cazzo,*" the whispered under their breath.

"Who was that?" Monty asked. They flinched at his words, coming back into their body.

"My aunt... Arianna." They let out a shaky breath, running a hand through their hair. "I forgot she was supposed to arrive today. I've been so consumed with myself I haven't been keeping track of the passage of time," they continued.

"I hopped I'd be dead before she got here," they mumbled to themself before they turned to him. There was palpable fear etched on their long feature. "You cannot be here when she arrives!"

"You want me to leave?" Monty balked. Cameron looked as serious as the grave and a little frustrated.

"I don't want you to get hurt! Arianna, she's... how do I explain this?"

"She's like you, right?"

"Yes, she's a vampire. It's her blood that was used to turn me. Even if it wasn't by her, or her choice, she still takes responsibility for me," they explained, "but her views of the world, of people... She's so much older than me. I can't see her being okay with me having you here. It might be bad if she knows I let a human live and get away, but I'll take the brunt of that discipline. I fear what she'd do to you... I don't know if I could keep you safe."

"Well, shit," Monty let out a defeated nervous laugh.

"You could go into town for a bit? Is there somewhere you can stay?" they asked. Mina came back to mind. He'd left in such a bad mood he feared going back to her and explaining the truth. God forbid she found out she was right, that Leah was right. Could he even tell her the truth? There was something almost more appealing about risking death by vampire than trying to explain this to anyone. Another cold weight sank in his chest as he remembered something else important that had been nagging at him.

"Even if the answer to that was 'yes,' my engine blew last week," he realized, "I'm not good with cars. I think it was coolant leaking into the engine? Maybe? But I have no idea how to fix that. My van is basically totaled right now." Cameron gripped one of their arms nervously.

"Can you drive sick?"

"I think so, why?"

"My car, you can take mine," they said. His stomach churned at the idea of driving their mother's old car.

"Are you sure, won't that raise suspicion more?" he asked.

"My aunt is already suspicious. That's why she's coming here in the first place. Don't worry about me. Let's just focus on getting you out of here. How much time do we have?" They opened the drawer in their nightstand and rummaged around until they pulled a golden pocket watch emblazoned with the family crest. They popped the watch open and visibly tensed up.

"It's almost six!?" they exclaimed. They jumped up from their bed, nearly face-planting as they tripped over themself.

"She must have called from the airport? It's only a few hours' drive from JFK. I suspect she might wait until sunset, but that's not long!" They stumbled off to their closest.

He was shocked at how long they'd slept. He was still in agony and very tired as he groggily moved his aching body to sit on the edge of the bed. He watched Cameron throw things around their closet. He wasn't ready to put jeans back on yet.

"Give me a moment and then I'll grab some stuff and split," he yawned. "I slept for so long, and I'm still somehow tired." It felt like he'd not gotten even a lick of sleep.

"I haven't had decent rest either," they said from the depths of their closet.

"Vampires need sleep?"

"*I* need sleep, or rest at least," they explained. Monty was too tired to integrate their physiology further, not when he had to rack his brain to remember if he actually could drive a stick shift. Cameron came out of their closet dressed in tights and a little slip, with a corset loosely thrown around their waist. They were struggling with the laces.

"You need a hand?" Monty asked.

"Yes, actually, can you help me tighten this?" they said hastily, turning their back to him. He couldn't help but blush as they moved their hair away from the laces. "You pull the loops in the middle. It's too big, so just pull them until it's closed all the way," they instructed.

He nervously took the fine laces into his rough hands and gave them a pull. It was much easier to tighten than he expected, and Cameron did not seem to be in any distress, unlike the way people acted in the films he'd seen.

"Good?" he asked as he pulled until he felt slight resistance.

"You could honestly go a little tighter unless the panels are touching in the back?" They asked over their shoulder.

"I'll try to not raise suspicion, Arianna only stays for about a week at a time at most, so hopefully you won't have to be gone too long. When you come back, I'll answer more of your questions, I pro —*ahh!*" Monty had yanked the lace a little harder than he meant, causing Cameron to let out a breathy moan, quickly covering their mouth with a hand in embarrassment.

"Sorry, that's closed all the way," he apologized, nervously patting the back panel. They snatched the laces from him and tied them around to the front.

"T-thank you," they mumbled before swiftly walking back to their closet. "It's much faster with help, but you don't have to pull so tight next time. These things are expensive," they said, clearly flustered.

"Sorry, I've only ever seen those in films where they're trying to absolutely crush the life out of young girls," Monty mimed pulling the strings.

"It's fine."

"But yeah, I have a lot of questions. I think maybe more than when I first arrived," he watched them idly as they put on an elaborate black dress that reminded him of old photographs.

*They look like they come with this damn haunted Victorian dollhouse.* He thought to himself, watching them dress in black velvet and lace.

"I promise I'll be more open now, but first you need to get dressed and pack up," they fussed. Monty begrudgingly got up and dressed in his very crusty clothing from the night before.

"How will I know when to come back?" He asked while trying to find where his boots had ended up. Would he actually come back? Would Mina let him?

"You have a cellphone, don't you?"

"Right, duh," Monty laughed at himself. He was so tired that it was hard for him to form coherent thoughts.

# CHAPTER NINETEEN

IT was warm and damp outside in the uniquely gorse end of summer way. The humidity was so dense that one might have assumed they were actually inside one of the gray clouds that hung low in the sky. The rain had been far too much, drenching the lawn and sludging it with mud. It all hit Montague the moment he stepped out the front door, causing him to instantly start sweating. Cameron loomed behind him as they walked to his cabin, looking around nervously as if some beast would swoop down from the sky and carry him off like a stray rabbit.

Monty had not yet called Mina, or given her a text, or even opened his phone. It would be useless to try to contact her until he was most of the way off the property, anyway. As it was, he did not want to talk with her, not now. He was sure she'd let him crash at her place, although letting him return to the manor would be a different challenge. He couldn't focus on that right now.

Cameron handed over the keys to the old black Cadillac. They stood in the roundabout, looking down the driveway with an uneasy expression. Monty hopped into the old car and stuck the keys into the ignition. It sputtered, the transmission revving and revving but failing to start. He checked that the gearshift was in neutral and that he had the clutch all the way down, and tried again. Another stammering sputter.

"Come on!" he grunted to the dash as if the car could sense his frustration. He tried to turn the key again to start the blasted engine, wondering if he was doing something wrong.

Something inside screeched. There was a horrible sound from within the engine. Black smoke fumed from the hood. He could hear Cameron shout outside. More and more smoke poured from the hood, blacker than the faded paint job of the hood. He didn't know much about cars, but he did remember that black smoke meant one thing—*KABOOM!*

Monty jumped out of the car. He one arm tackled Cameron, pulling them several feet back from the vehicle mere seconds before the engine exploded into searing-hot flames.

"Goddammit," Monty spat, looking at the growing fire.

"What happened!?"

"I don't know! I swear nothing I did would make it *explode!*" He wanted to speculate, but there was now a growing fire very close to, thankfully very wet, woodland. He scrambled for the hose, showering the growing toxic flames with water. It did very little more than cause the blaze to sputter more erratically as the vehicle burst further into flames, the smell of burning tires mingling with wet ozone. Cameron looked on, stupefied by the the horrific heat emanating from the old Cadillac.

After a good while of noxious fuming fury, the car began to smoke and smolder. They both stood in silence for a moment, breathing in the toxic smoke under a humid, dimming gray sky. Monty's heart rate never fully slowed as the severity of the situation he'd landed himself in fully dawned on him.

"So... I guess I should change into something more presentable if I'm stuck meeting the family then?" He half-joked, finally breaking the silence between the two of them.

"I'm so sorry I've gotten you into this," Cameron murmured.

"Let's not kid ourselves. I got myself into this," he sighed.

"I'm still sorry." They looked ill.

"Well, it'll be okay… or it won't," Monty shrugged as apathy began to numb the buzz of his nerves. He was both frightened and slightly electrified now. He secretly wanted to meet Arianna, if not just because she was a figure that loomed over the estate. He wanted answers, did he not?

"I'll make sure the fire goes all the way out. You should go change," Cameron sighed.

"A good idea." He turned to make for his cabin, unsure show much time they still had before Arianna showed.

"Monty?"

"Yeah?"

"That holy symbol of yours—"

"My hamsa?"

"Yes, that. Please don't forget to wear it. If it can keep you from falling under my hypnosis… it *should* keep you safe from my aunt too," they said. He nodded.

☽ ✧ ☾

He didn't dawdle, as being alone gave him more nauseating anxiety than Arianna's impending arrival. He knew in his gut that it must have been Dr. Giovanni who had sabotaged the engine. He now realized she could have been the culprit in both vehicle's destruction. She had to be, right? It could not have been just pure bad luck? He'd had his chance. He'd pieced together Arianna must have been the woman she referred to as "sister" in the doctor's notebooks. He realized that if she was much older, and likely immoral, she could not have been Dr. Giovanni's biological sister. Although he assumed they might still be distantly blood-related.

He had two different realities tied to this unknown woman. According to Dr. Giovanni, it had been Arianna's idea to use her blood on Cameron, at least that's how he understood what he'd read, assuming this was the same woman. This woman too was supposedly more severe in her discipline. She clearly demanded fear from those who spoke of her. But Cameron also believed it was she who saved them from their mother's senseless torment. Once again he found that the more answers he got, the more questions swam in his head. Yes, he was tingling with anxiety, but his curiosity was now peaked. He wanted to see the full picture, even if was the last thing he did.

Even if he left now, he could not unlearn all that he'd uncovered here. He knew if he tried to explain any of this to anyone, he would be running the risk of being treated like a nutcase. He might accidentally reopen an investigation too, and the idea of sending people to a vampire den felt cruel and treacherous at the same time. As it was, the life he was risking was not much to him. He was a college dropout who would be met with a shitty job after shitty job to just keep a roof over his head. The miserable prospect of a dull life in dead-end jobs and little to show for his efforts did not fill him with any joy.

He forced himself to eat something as his stomach growled in protest at having breakfast at 7 pm. He saw little specks of white in the haze of his vision from the pain in his now mangled wrist as he re-bandaged it. Even after cleaning the puncture wounds Cameron had left, they were still red and angry with infection. He wondered if this would become an issue, and if his lingering ache was worsened by whatever poison was in their saliva.

He was unsure why, but he felt compelled to attempt to look at least presentable. He took the time to shave his goatee into the right shape and clean up his face. He felt ridiculous trying to dig out any kind of nice clothing. He located a black button-down shirt and a plain reddish-brown sports coat that had been crumpled in the back of a drawer. He was still a mess by all accounts, but he was a bit more put together than his usual self.

He downed two ibuprofen and said a prayer to no one in particular as he put his hamsa on.

☽ ✧ ☾

He was less than enthused to trot back up to the dilapidated Victorian, dreading what was to come. Still, he slowly trudged his scuffed boots through the damp lawn up to the manor as the sky began to dim to night. He could no longer see smoke from the Giovanni's burned-out car. He did not see Cameron out front either. All that remand was a melted heap of steel. The smell of burnt tires and fuel made his throat sore. He walked past the wreck to stare at his own rust-eaten '92 Dodge Caravan.

Despite his resignation, there was still something tugging at him. Something nagging in the pit of his stomach that made him want to try. Perhaps it was the last shred of his survival instinct. He looked over his shoulder at the mansion, as if he was anticipating getting caught.

He stumbled into his old minivan and jammed the key in the ignition. It too sputtered and refused to start. The way its engine clunked filled him with anxiety, and he took the keys out of the ignition as a sweet, chemical scent met his nose. He sighed and pressed his forehead against his hands on the steering wheel. It was worth a shot, but no luck. He was stuck. He slammed his door shut than he meant to.

"You know what's coming, don't you? She really is the woman you were so afraid of in journals, isn't she?" he growled to his car door. He was met with nothing but the sound of wind blowing through the now yellowing leaves. He ran a hand over his face, tugging on his growing eye bags, "I'm fucking losing it. I'm talking to myself now. I'm really fucking losing it." He turned and walked back up to the mansion, letting the old Victorian swallow him whole.

# CHAPTER TWENTY

MONTY found Cameron in the drawing room, making quick work of getting the fireplace started. The gloomy mansion was already cooling with the evening. He perched himself awkwardly on the couch, not sure what else to do. He stared up at the portrait of the woman with dark hair. Her stony, yet oddly familiar expression made his stomach twist with nerves.

"That's her, right?" he asked, pointing up at the painting. Cameron nodded.

"Please be careful what you say to her." They looked like they had more to add, but their train of thought was interrupted by the unmistakable sound of a car pulling into the roundabout.

"I'll greet her outside." They looked incredibly uneasy, "and I'll try to explain our situation if I can."

"I'll be here," Monty jokingly patted the dusty couch next to himself. Cameron gave him a weary smile before vanishing through the foyer.

He squirmed in his skin, a clammy, too-hot sensation overcooked his body as he tried not to dwell too much on expectations. He could hear them approaching the house, both speaking in Italian to each other. Arianna had a warm voice that sounded smooth and sweet like syrup as she spoke slowly and methodically. As he heard the front door swing open, he jumped up to greet them under the precarious dust-caked chandelier.

He was startled by the appearance of Arianna Giovanni, despite already having an idea of what she looked like. She was tall, almost the same height as Cameron in her stiletto heels. She had jet-black hair that was tightly pulled back into a large bun stuck high on her head with a long golden hairpin, a few wavy wisps falling on her face. Like Cameron, she had a long oval face with downturned lavender-blue eyes and a long sharp nose.

She wore a long fur coat over a tight black dress that exaggerated her hourglass figure. Her hands were laboriously laden with many golden rings set with large amethysts, and sported dagger-sharp nails painted aubergine. One hand clutched firmly around a golden serpent-handled walking cane. Her face had only the slightest hint of laugh lines. She looked no older than thirty-five.

"Zizi, this is my friend Montague that I mentioned," Cameron said, waving a hand in his direction.

"A pleasure," she said smoothly, lifting her free hand to him. He hesitated for a moment before sheepishly taking it and kissing it with a bow of his head, praying this was the correct response. When he looked up, his blood flooded with ice, as she gave the same exact unnerving half-smile that Cameron did. A smile that just barely concealed her fangs.

"Lovely to meet you," he said, trying his best to keep his words from catching in his throat. Her beauty was unsettling, like a painting pretending to be a human. She moved like a woman who knew the world was at her feet, the kind of person who could lift a finger and have whatever it was she desired. Despite never once in his memory desiring a woman, he found her uncomfortably irresistible. He could barely think straight in her gaze. He'd be on his knees in seconds if she demanded it. That very urge frightened him.

"Dear," she turned to Cameron, whose expression had once again become inscrutable in her presence, "would you be so kind as to bring up my luggage to my room?"

"*Si Zizi*," they nodded but made no motion to follow through.

"And then, I would love a drink," as she spoke her eyes flicked to Monty, "it's been a long trip and I simply could die for a glass of wine."

"I'll be just a moment," Cameron said. There was an edge of something in their voice Monty was unsure of. It was a warning of some kind, but to whom, he couldn't tell.

"Well, let's not dawdle here," Arianna said with a cheerful expression. "Come young man, I am oh so curious about you."

She turned him by the shoulder firmly, but not forcefully, in the direction of the drawing room. "I am pleasantly surprised to see a fresh face. It may shock you, but Cameron does not often have company," she said in a taunting tone. Monty could feel himself sweating in her presence. Her very aura made the hair on his neck prickle.

"So, Montague, am I correct?" she asked as they walked into the drawing room. The only light in here was coming from the crackling fireplace. Her eyes had the reflective glint of a cat's in the dark.

"Yes. You can call me Monty if you want." He forced a smile.

"Ah, Monty then, how did you become so well acquainted with my lovely nephew?" She asked as she sat down on the left couch under her portrait. The painting paled in comparison to the way she looked in the firelight. There was something wrong about the way she looked, like a memory, unreal and too perfect.

"Well... I came here originally to fill the groundskeeper position," he hated how unsure he sounded as he sat across from Arianna. A fleeting smirk crossed her face.

"Interesting,"

"We just sort of got along, I guess?" he nervously rubbed the back of his head. There was still a lump there from Cameron mistakenly throwing him against the footboard of their bed. This entire conversation felt surreal to him.

"What were you doing before this?" she asked

"I was in the undergrad biochem program at SUNY," he said vaguely. She lazily raised an eyebrow.

"Biochemistry, you say? Were you by chance in the hematology program? Possibly one of my sister's students?" she asked.

"Yes. I actually knew her pretty well. I was in her lab the semester, um, well, you know," he hesitated. Just the mention of Dr. Giovanni made him antsy.

"Ah, a shame. You must have been quite upset then, after my little sister's *accident*," she said, narrowing her eyes. He was unsure how to respond.

"I'm sorry for the family's loss." His words were virtually a whisper. This was not the right thing to say. He knew she was privy to the truth of the enter ordeal, possibly more than anyone else.

"Don't be. Better off without that brat," she scoffed. It was apparent to him that none of the Giovannis cared for each other very much.

He could feel Dr. Giovanni's portrait staring down at him, as though it could feel him thinking about her. The woman across from him was quiet for a moment as she pulled an art déco cigarette case and long cigarette holder from her snakeskin purse. She slowly lit it on the golden serpent table lighter and took a long drag before continuing the conversation.

"I am assuming Cameron has not told you much about the family?" She crossed her legs and propped her free hand under her elbow. He shook his head, unsure of what she was getting at.

"I mean..." he searched his mind for a satisfactory answer. Arianna could see she was not going to get more information from him with her first question.

"Where are you from, Monty?" She interrupted his train of thought, changing the subject. Smoke poured from her mouth and nose like a dragon as she spoke.

"I was born and raised here," he admitted. Her eyes lingered on his necklace, which had rustled its way out from under his wrinkled shirt collar.

"No, dear, I mean your family. No Frenchman looks, well, like that," she gestured vaguely in his direction, making him feel indignant. She narrowed her eyes. "Not trying to rob my poor nephew of his fortune, are we, gypsy boy?" Monty was taken aback.

"E-excuse me?" he coughed, "I'm not–"

"I'm merely joking." She waved a hand as if to dismiss his reaction. Much to Monty's relief, he heard the clanking of glass coming down the hall, signaling Cameron's return. They were scowling as they stumbled into the room, their large hands overburdened with three bottles and glasses.

"That took you long enough," she scoffed as she shot more smoke from her nose.

"I had a hard time making up my mind," they set down the bottles. One was a normal bottle of an Italian red. The other two had handwritten labels, *Jessica, 1995*, and *Timon, 1992*. Arianna raised an eyebrow upon looking at the selection they had brought up, mainly fixating on the red wine. Cameron hastily opened the bottles.

"Does he *know*?" She asked them with an air of shock. Monty felt a lump form in his throat at the tone in her voice.

"Yes," Cameron replied blankly, not even looking at her as they poured the wine. They froze for a second before deciding to sit next to Monty.

"And here I thought you were joking, darling," she let out with a curt laugh, extending an arm towards them. "So he really is not dinner. What a shame he looks like he'd taste sweet," she teased. Cameron looked less than amused. It took everything in Monty's willpower to hold still. Yet, to his dismay, his one knee bounced uncontrollably as his anxiety continued to mount. He wondered if he did taste sweet.

*Cam would know*, he thought.

"I told you, he is my friend. He knows of our um, unique, condition," they said more firmly. Monty tried to give a smile, but he felt a grimace come over him.

Cameron fidgeted with the little golden locket around their neck as they shifted, struggling to get comfortable. Neither of them was doing a good job of hiding how nervous they were. They both reached for their glass at the same time, earning a smirk from the woman across from them.

Arianna took her glass and lifted it lazily in a *"salute"* motion, which they both mimicked. She took a long swig of the thick red liquid, leaving behind a purple lipstick stain on her glass. She clicked her tongue. The blood in her sharp teeth made her look wicked.

"Well then, the silly formalities can be overlooked," she said with a breath of relief. Black smoke emanated from her entire body in a sigh.

"I truly thought you were being sarcastic, my child. I must say I have some questions to ask. I think things would go much smoother between us all if I had a better idea of..." she trailed off making a low, disapproving hum, "what exactly is going on here?" Though Arianna's tone was lazy, there was an underlying air of parental disappointment.

"What do you mean?" Cameron asked nervously.

"*Non mi piace che tu vada a letto con i cani,*" she huffed. Cameron scowled at her.

"You know, dear, I would very much like to know what happened to my lesson about playing with your food?" She spoke with a slow poison that felt like a dagger cutting through Monty. He hated how she spoke as though he weren't sitting right in front of her.

*"Cani"... doesn't that mean dog?*

"Do not speak about my *friend* that way. Mind some of the manners you have hammered into me," Cameron spat. Arianna flashed a murderous look before relaxing, letting out a sharp sound of discontent and leaning back in her seat.

"Well then, if he is not dinner, and not a thrall, do you then intend to turn him?" she asked. The room was deadly quiet for a moment, the only sound, the crackling fireplace.

"That wouldn't matter, right? I'm fine as is," Monty nervously laughed. The cold look the older woman shot Cameron told him she was not at all happy with that proposition.

"I'm not a stupid woman," she huffed. "Keeping a human alive, unenthralled, it's unheard of! Let to live, I've found you mortals can be, how you say, problematic for our kind. It would be far too easy for you to kill poor Cameron here all by his lonesome," she paused to run her tongue along her bloodstained fangs before continuing.

"You must forgive me, young man, but I do not fully trust you and your *deliciously* warm blood. It's quite lucky I've decided to come when I did," she said to him before turning her attention back to her charge.

"This *ragazzo* has been a bad influence on you, Cameron. Just look at you, dear! You're skin and bone. I've not seen you this slim since—"

"It's not his fault," they cut her off. She looked a bit taken aback that they would dare speak over her. "Monty has done nothing to harm me, quite the opposite actually."

"Watch your tone, child. I know a bleeding heart when I see one. *Avere un debole per i vivi è una ricetta per la morte,*" Arianna scoffed. Cameron grew flustered.

"You don't understand," they furrowed their pale brows. She shot a stream of cigarette smoke from her nose and took a deep breath.

"Perhaps I don't," she said as she poured herself another glass of *Jessica 1995.*

"I'm like this because of *her,* not Monty. Mother's still here, in the walls of this wretched place," they said, causing their aunt to freeze in her tracks.

"Darling, I know you have a lot of grief, but I thought we've taken care of that little... *problem,*" she said with a concerned tone, her eyes flicking to Monty repeatedly, as if accusing him for the cause of this behavior.

"I did what you told me to, but she's *still* here," they doubled down. "She is lingering in the woodwork, in my head, taunting me, tormenting me. I've been having hallucinations that morph into waking nightmares." There was a slight look of worry on Arianna's face.

"If I can interject here, I have also been seeing her," Monty said slowly, carefully. "She showed me visions of her death... she's also dragged me into the same waking nightmares. Cameron's not crazy. This place is haunted."

"She's been relentless," Cameron added. Arianna looked concerned, her thoughts moving around visibly behind her eyes.

"How long has this been going on?" she asked.

"She's been looming over me since the day she died. Like you had said, I originally believed her to be a manifestation of guilt. But the intensity of her presence has only been increasing since Monty got here. She's not let me get a moment's rest ever since that first night I failed to kill him," Cameron explained. They cringed as the words came from their mouth.

"You tried killing him?" Arianna asked with a tone of surprise.

"I tried. For a full month, I tried to do it. I'm not an idiot!" They made an effort to relax, "but I don't want to hurt him, and she knows that. Every time I try to fight her, fight myself, I feel like she grows more persistent. She wants Monty gone. I think she wants us both dead." Arianna just looked at the two of them for a good long while.

"I should have known she would stick around like a thorn in my side; even in death," Arianna huffed to herself, and then with a laugh said, "I find it ironic that she should be angered by the very same *thing* as me. Perhaps she and I still do see eye to eye."

"What do you mean by that?" Cameron asked. There was a dangerous edge in their voice.

"Do you know why I am here?"

"I assumed you were worried," they replied as they nervously gripped one arm, staring off in the distance like a scolded child.

"The last letter I received from you was an incomprehensible garbled mess. Either you're forgetting your mother tongue, or your handwriting has degraded to the point I am misreading your meaning. You sounded as though you wished to follow in your mother's footsteps? I had assumed you had forgotten how to hunt, and by the looks of it I am correct. That, or you've lost the will. In my rightful worry, I come to check on you, and I'm immediately greeted by an abandoned car wreck and a starving child with a human in tow, both blathering on about ghosts!" she chided them. Monty felt uncomfortable witnessing this exchange. He tried to make himself as small as he possibly could, wishing he could evaporate from this room without either of them noticing.

"You must forget that this is my estate and you are my responsibility. It is bad enough your mother let this place fall into utter disrepair. I will not tolerate insubordination from you, child. You forget you would be but a pile of ash if it were not for my interference," Arianna's words were sharp and parental. Cameron looked like a small child under her gaze.

"I am sorry," apologized in a whisper.

"I believe you are being haunted by that wretched woman, or you would not have been so quick to assume I'm here to cause you harm. It is in my best interest you live, and live well. You would do well to rememberer who's side I'm on." She spoke with bitter authority. There was a tinge of exhaustion in her words. Monty realized this was not the first time they'd had a conversation like this.

"Yes, ma'am, I'm sorry," Cameron whimpered in response.

"Straighten up, my dear," she clicked her tongue, and Cameron obeyed, pulling their shoulders back, still looking very much chastised.

"Well then," she sat her glass and purse down on the coffee table and abruptly hoisted herself up on her cane, "I grow bored of this chatter. Perhaps you could show me the composition you've been working on? I need something to lighten my mood, and I can tell this spat has upset your *cucciolo*," her eyes flicked to Monty as she spoke.

"Don't call him—" Arianna shot Cameron a searing look with such intensity that they instantly clenched their mouth shut so tight Monty could see the muscle in their jaw flex. They hesitated for a moment more before getting up to follow her lead, slowly holding an arm for her to lean on.

"You, boy, come with us. I don't want you running amuck unsupervised. Up, up, I won't bite," she shot a mocking grin that bared her fangs.

"Yeah, I'm sure," Monty groaned as he stood to follow them. "I'm not an easy meal," he joked, wondering why he had said such a thing. Something about his reply made her smile wider, more genuine. It left him with a deep sense of unease.

# CHAPTER TWENTY-ONE

MONTAGUE was sure in his gut that if he tried to run now, Arianna would drain his life before he'd even gotten two feet away from her. Still, it felt like she was willing to tolerate him for now, for Cameron's sake, if anything. There was no illusion in his mind; he was a prisoner at this moment.

"I see you've taken my advice. Though, I would not have chosen such a dark burgundy myself. Still, I'm glad to see that wallpaper gone," Arianna said upon reaching the freshly painted third story.

"Well, you didn't exactly make an effort to weigh in on color preferences," Cameron huffed, as though they were mad she hadn't given them paint swatches.

"Monty has been fixing the place, you know," they said after a moment, "I would not have been able to do most of this without him."

"Do remind me to give you a lesson about how to hire proper help at some point, won't you? Copying your mother's technique of keeping one man in the shed, who's sole job it is to keep the town from condemning this place, is not what I meant when I told you to 'fix this place up,'" Arianna hummed disapprovingly. Cameron looked genuinely embarrassed. They looked to Monty for a moment with a worried expression, as though they were checking if he was still there.

Arianna released their arm and lazily opened the huge double-doors to the ballroom. She was momentarily backlit by the doors to the balcony as her heels clacked on the marbled tiles, echoing through the cavernous room. Her silhouette against the paned glass looked like a black widow in her web.

The dusty chandelier above buzzed to life with the flip of a switch. At night, the grandiose room being lit by dull electric light felt wrong. Despite the room being utterly massive, a fabulous space to dance and entertain at least one hundred guests, it felt small with the darkness swallowing the far corners.

Monty looked at his exhausted reflection in the black marble of the chessboard tiles as he paced around aimlessly. He felt watched and ignored simultaneously. He was the only living soul here, and it was painfully isolating feeling the way he lingered, not wanted but not allowed to leave either. He was confused by how miserable that sensation made him feel.

"Darling, why don't you play me what you have been working on?" Arianna waved to the white grand piano that sat eagerly in the corner. Cameron hesitated for a moment before walking over to the piano, awkwardly moving their long skirt out of the way to sit on the bench.

"I will be truthful in that I haven't been practicing as much these past few months," they nervously admitted as they shuffled through the sheet music on the piano.

"Writing new work? Or have you been *giocare con il tuo cane esotico*, hmm?" Their aunt teased. Monty could see Cameron physically restraining their temper. There was a flash of red behind their eyes before they took a deep breath. "I know the skill is there. I won't penalize you for playing a piece I've already heard. Just entertain us, dear," Arianna said in a motherly tone.

Cameron's somber melody filled the ballroom, reverberating off the tile. Even as they played rather quietly, the tune filled every corner of darkness with something other than stale air. Before Monty could enjoy the beautifully performed waltz, Arianna demanded his attention.

"You," she snapped, moving her index finger in a "come here" motion. He warily crossed the dance floor over to her before his reflexes were tested. She tossed one of the golden fencing swords at him, which he somehow managed to miraculously snatch from the air. She herself pulled a long double-edged sword from her cane, flipping it with ease in her hands. The cane was merely for show. Monty's stomach dropped.

*What is she doing!?*

"Do you know how to fence?" she asked.

"No," he replied nervously as he turned the sword in his hands. The relief of realizing she was not about to cut his head off was short-lived. He felt a flutter of anxiety bubble up as he looked at the handle of the rapier.

'M.G.' was emblazoned on the gaurd, *Maria Giovanni's sword.*

He could hear the faint buzz of flies in his head as he saw his distorted face in the handle. Arianna slipped off her stilettos and carelessly tossed them to the side, a good five inches shorter now.

"Then pay attention," she taunted as she lunged forward, left-handed. Despite her tight dress, she was incredibly agile, her stockinged feet slipping across the marble frighteningly fast.

Monty sloppily blocked her blade from slashing his face, his form poor as he could only emulate the little swordplay he'd seen. It was harder for him to block her as they were mismatched hands, her left catching the blade in all the blind spots of his right. Cameron stumbled over their hands as they took a moment to watch what was happening.

"Oh, come now, you can do better than that!" She snapped her fingers. "Right foot forward, bend your knees." He tried his best to mirror her movements. He had no reason to believe she wouldn't maim him in this moment, so he headed her instructions.

"Stand like this, *en guard.*" She demonstrated a beginner position.

She lunged forward again to attack. "Lunge, attack, parry me!" She punctuated her instructions with a SNAP SNAP. He tried his best to do as she said, horrified she'd slice him if he took a moment to disobey.

"I don't know what parrying is!" he huffed out as he jumped out of the way of her blade.

"Lunge towards me," she ordered. He sprang forward to the best of his ability. Arianna whipped her blade around his so fast, he nearly dropped his sword.

"Please slow down," he panted, feeling his heart beginning to race. She merely nodded and motioned for him to come toward her. Cameron's playing began to sound mildly out of time and erratic as they tried to watch and play at the same time. He wondered if they were waiting to see if they would need to stop whatever was going on here. He wondered if they would be fast enough to stop Arianna from cutting him to ribbons.

Monty lunged again towards the dark-haired woman. This time, she moved in slow motion to show him what she was doing.

"You see now?"

"Yes."

"Good boy, let's try again then." And with that, she lunged toward him again. His ears burned at her praise. This time he was able to throw her blade off course with a bit more tact. They continued to spar, going back and forth with the eager clatter of metal. He was not agile, nor did he have good form, but he had a decent rhythm. He soon realized this was more of a dance than a fight. The snap of her free hand that kept him in time served as a tell when to parry. With every movement of his feet and clank of the metal sabers, he saw Arianna grin with a glint of excitement in her strange-colored eyes. She was clearly having fun toying with him.

"You're a faster learner than Cameron," she remarked. "Not the best I've seen, but you do have some natural talent. Quite amusing, I can see why he keeps you. I'm pleased," she complimented as they continued to spar.

"T-thank you?" He stammered, flustered by the backhanded compliment. He realized she was treating him like a pet, making him do tricks. That's what this sparring match was to her, the equivalent of getting him to spin and play dead. He was sweating through his sports coat by this point, but he felt he could not ask for a moment to stop.

He was thrown off his guard very suddenly by Cameron smashing their hands into several keys at once. They ceased playing in the middle of the song. In that same moment, Arianna disarmed him, sending the saber in his hands flying.

He expected it to clatter to the ground. However, it was caught quite firmly in Dr. Giovanni's floating dismembered hand. He stumbled back in terror, but Arianna merely rested her blade on her shoulder and moved some loose black hair from her face. She stared mildly bemused at her sister's interruption. The lights in the ballroom began to flicker, the chandelier swinging dangerously, crystals clattering heavily against themselves.

*Very funny!*

Dr. Giovanni's voice sneered as the rest of her body began to form from a swarm of flies. In the flickering light, she barely looked as if she were being held together by anything at all anymore. Her jaw was askew, empty-eyed, skin turned shades of green and blue with oxidizing purple veins visible across her loose flesh like streaks of lightning.

"How pleasant," Arianna said blankly, seemingly unbothered by the desecrated visage of her own sister. The darkness of the room began to swell and grow, the walls closing in around the dance floor. The rotting smell of the putrefying corpse of Dr. Giovanni overwhelmed his senses. Cameron was frozen as stone, their hands still gripped onto the piano. He could swear he heard their teeth chattering.

*Taunting me?*

Dr. Giovanni's voice gurgled, waving her saber about. There was a palpable buzzing sound of the electricity, straining against her will.

"Funny, it appears I happened to grab your blade off the wall," Arianna jeered. "Why are you lingering, sister? Your job here has been long finished. You aren't needed or wanted." Monty could feel the hatred of each other seeping from the Giovanni sisters like a noxious gas.

*Get out of my house!*

"Get out," buzzed over and over from the walls. Maria's practically unrecognizable face contorted with rage, and she flung her sword across the dance floor at her sister. Arianna ducked out of the way effortlessly, sending the sword at Cameron, who was not as fast as their aunt. They crossed their arms across their face, crying out as the blade slashed across their arms at a frightening speed before clattering to the floor behind them.

"Your house!? Dear sister, this is my estate, my money, my clan. You were merely borrowing what I had to offer. Look what you've done to repay me. You drove the very essence of this family into the ground. Not even the bastard child is truly yours!" Arianna scoffed.

*Vecchia!*

Dr. Giovanni's demented voice rattled through the closing walls and the flickering lights.

"You are not going to scare me off with parlor tricks, *bambina*," Arianna spoke with a stern tone. She appeared not to notice the walls of the ballroom closing in on them. It felt as though they had a heartbeat, warm flesh coming to enclose them, to devour them. Monty backed away from the two sisters and crouched down next to Cameron, who was gripping their bleeding arm. He gently placed a hand on their lap in hope of consolation.

"You know little to—" Arianna's contused taunting was cut off abruptly.

*GET OUT!*

Dr. Giovanni's voice seeped like poison from every haunted wall with an ear-shattering shriek.

*GET OUT!!*

Monty reflexively covered his ears as fast as he could, but the bloodied cries of Dr. Giovanni still sent shards of glass through his brain.

*GET OUT!!!*

Cameron doubled over, practically slamming their head against the piano as they covered their ears. Even Arianna's hands clasped against the sides of her head as her sword dropped to the floor.

Then the spirit was gone. The lights steadied, and the ballroom expanded with a sigh, returning to normal. Cameron quietly shuddered as they took their hands away from the side of their head. Arianna slowly released her own ears and stood back to her full height with a frustrated huff. It was quiet for a moment.

"I see, she truly *has* become a vengeful spirit," she admitted tiredly to Cameron, who was still pale as a sheet.

Monty removed his coat and fanned himself. His eyes lingered upon the saber on the ground, shining with a small tinge of Cameron's blood. Arianna looked pensively at her own sword as she placed it back in its sheath and picked up her shoes.

"*Fantasma,*" she mumbled to herself.

"I told you, I am not mad," Cameron said softly.

"In all my many years, I've not seen a specter of this strength. Her death was quite violent, but I never expected this," she pondered to herself for a moment. Her eyes lingered on Monty and pointed a ring-clad hand in his direction. "*Voi!*"

"Me!?" he asked, pointing to himself as he spoke, "what've I done here?"

"Nothing," Cameron piped up, cutting their aunt off before she could even start. "My mother wants me contained. She knows what she did, creating me. She knows whatever she did made me a worse version of what you are, Zizi. Monty has nothing to do with any of this." They looked down at their bloodied hand. Arianna looked up at the chandelier in thought.

"I would not consider your condition to be a 'worse' form of mine, quite the contrary, I would say. I do not think she understands fully the extent of her work. I don't care for Maria for many reasons, but," she nodded in Monty's direction, "I do agree that perhaps he is a problem. You are weaker since I last saw you. You are thin as a rake and painfully slow. You're clearly lacking in your studies and artwork. You are making stupid mistakes." There was palpable disgust in her words. "You don't need 'friends,' you need discipline."

"Isolation is not discipline," they grumbled as they crossed their arms across their body.

"Don't twist my words. I don't want you isolated, but," her face softened a little, "darling, please, what do you gain from keeping *un cane esotico?*"

"Can you stop talking about me like I can't hear you!?" Monty spat, finally losing a bit of his temper. He was now certain she was calling him a dog, or something worse.

"What's your point, Arianna? Because it seems to me you are simply here to make sure Cam stays fucking miserable in your 'sister's' absence." He stood up to confront her. "Quit treating me like I'm an animal and them like a damn child!"

He only made it a few strides before he felt his head rush. His vision flashed blank, as if he were fainting. He felt like a hand was pushing on the back of his head, forcing him to kneel. His legs buckled underneath him, and he fell on all fours to the tile floor. He was still conscious, but the world around him was relentlessly spinning like he was being consumed by vertigo. He felt like an invisible force had effortlessly stitched his limbs to the floor. It tried to push him all the way down, but he was able to resist.

"Don't you dare speak to me like that you foul mutt!" Arianna's words pour into Monty's ears directly through his brain.

"Stop it!" Cameron hissed. Their voice sounded far away to him, like his head was being shoved underwater. The illusion of protection his hamsa gave him was broken in that instant. It might have been keeping Arianna from outright killing him, but she very much could take control of his body. She had been playing nice out of her own desires after all. He felt nauseated by how fast his pulse raced in his paralyzed body.

Cameron slammed the piano shut, causing it to let out a loud drone in protest. In a flash of smoke, they were looming over the older woman.

"I said stop!" From the little Monty could see, Cameron's eyes had turned a scalding red, and they looked as if they were about to tear Arianna to pieces.

"Release him this instant or I swear I'll—"

WHACK!

Arianna hit them across the face swiftly with the handle of her sword-cane. Monty could almost feel the cold brass against his own face.

"Don't you *dare* raise your voice at me," she hissed like a cobra rearing to strike. "Stop being hysterical. You need to mind your temper. Do you want to prove your mother right? That she created a stupid, bloodthirsty beast that needs a switch and a cage? Are you going to kill me too?" She glared at them. Some blood trickled down the side of their face. The force of her blow had split their cheek.

"*Non, lo pensavo.* Don't forget I am the one who saved you from starving to death. Don't forget I saved your skin after *murdering* my kin. I fully intend to help you, but I demand some respect from you and your *cane!* You have more problems than you realize, *sangu misto.* Either kill him or turn him. I cannot proceed with your training while you are distracted by keeping a little *pet,*" she spat the last bit out.

Monty felt panic wash through his chest as she spoke. Arianna flicked her wrist, and very suddenly reality slammed back into focus for him, the room holding still abruptly. Despite knowing he had not been moving, he felt a nauseating inertia as his head stopped spinning.

"I'm not your enemy, but I will discipline you when your actions are going to get you killed! Have some sense," she said as she pulled the golden pin from her bun, causing her long black hair to fall down around her waist.

"Now, I must rest as I am thoroughly exhausted by all of this. I had hoped for a meal I am clearly not getting tonight. We will continue this conversation on the morrow." She paused for a moment as her eyes narrowed. "*Se lo lasci scappare moriremo tutti.* You let him run, and I'll see to his end myself. That is a promise." She then disappeared in a cloud of black smoke.

The room was quiet, just the whistling of wind that rattled the drafty balcony doors. Cameron quickly materialized next to Monty and helped him stand up, his bones aching as they did so.

"Are you okay?" they asked.

"I think so, but," he groaned and rubbed his sore head, "kill me or turn me?"

Cameron hung their head, hair falling to obscure their face. After a moment they whispered, "I'm so sorry."

"I'm honestly amazed she didn't just make that choice for you right now," he said.

"She's trying to make an example out of you," they paused. "We should leave. I hate this room."

"I agree. I'd love to never set foot in here again," Monty said as he picked up and replaced Dr. Giovanni's sword on the wall, not bothering to remove Cameron's dark blood from it.

# CHAPTER TWENTY-TWO

CAMERON locked them in their room with a feverish air of anxiety. They checked the locks twice with trembling hands, then turned and pressed their back to one of the carved wooden panels, letting out a long, exhausted sigh. After a moment of silence, they walked over to their stereo cabinet and quietly put on a record to fill the room with something other than the sounds of exhausted breathing. Monty hung his suit jacket on the back of the desk chair and wondered how well a locked door would keep Arianna out.

"I'm sorry I've gotten you entangled so deeply in this mess," Cameron apologized, not looking at him as they began to take their bodice off. They huffed miserably as they wiggled two long fingers through the gash in the fabric. "I loved this dress."

"I mean, you did warn me like a thousand times." Monty let out a long, frustrated groan and ran his hands through his hair. "I just wished you'd been upfront with me from the jump."

"I'm sorry, I know," they apologized as they wiped a bit of dried blood off their arm, "but Monty, what would you have actually done if I had told you the truth when you first asked me? Would you have even believed me?"

"Ugh, no, no, I know. It's just... fuck man, I don't know what I expected, but I didn't anticipate *this*," he said to himself with a panicked laugh.

"I should have insisted you leave when you first said you were considering quitting," Cameron sighed as they rubbed their cheek, which was rapidly going through the stages of bruising.

"Even if I listened to you, there's also the whole thing with your mother's spirit. She was drawing me to the answers I was looking for. You know, the more I've thought about it, the more I genuinely think she was hoping I'd avenge her death. It could have been her spirit keeping me here... or my own stubbornness." Monty felt his body shaking from a combination of nerves and exhaustion as he sat on the edge of the bed. He managed to kick his boots off, unintentionally sending them halfway across the room.

"Right," Cameron said to themself softly, leaning on the doorjamb of their closet.

"The point is that it doesn't matter, I'm stuck here now," Monty paused for a moment, "so kill me or turn me is the ultimatum? Turning me means what exactly? That's death too, right? So my options are die or die?"

"It's not quite the same thing, but it's still a grim prospect."

"I'm positive your aunt rather you just regular kill me. I don't think she want's someone like me mixing in with your kind."

"What do you mean?" they asked. Monty tensed, a bit confused by their response.

"I don't think me being a human is the only reason why she was so quick to call me a dog," he continued in a measured tone.

"You understand Italian?" They looked surprised and confused.

"No, but I mean, she was *treating* me like a dog. She called me a *gypsy* for fuck's sake," he added a little exasperated, "just, I can tell when someone's being racist." Cameron made a face as if two of the neurons connected for the first time as they let out a soft "*oh*."

"So, you know, I have to ask then, why even bother turning me at all?" he asked to the floor.

"I don't know... I don't even know if I *can* turn you. I was not created the 'normal' way, so I don't really know if you drinking my blood would even work. Not to mention it's likely I wouldn't be able to stop myself before fully killing you in the process. I don't think she knows if I'm able to do it either," they speculated as they squirmed out of their long layered skirt. They fished their cigarette case from the pocket before tossing the garment carelessly onto a black pile of clothing on the floor of their walk-in closet.

"How do you turn someone... the 'normal' way?" Monty felt uneasy thinking about the whole ordeal. He could feel his hands sweating as he clumsily removed his belt. Cameron fumbled as they hastily lit a thin pink-filtered cigarette with a golden lighter they pulled from the end table drawer. They took a long drag and stared mournfully at the lighter in their hand.

"I would have to infect you with my venom, but I would also have drain most of your blood, or at least get you to the very edge of death," they explained, smoke pouring from their mouth as they spoke, just like their aunt. "I then would have to force you to drink my blood. You need substantial exposure to both infected blood and venom for vampirism to manifest, and there's no guarantee your body will handle the change. I've been told most people just die in the process, even if their sire doesn't drain them dry."

"Great, yeah, okay, I don't like the sound of that one bit," Monty shuddered.

"Even if I knew it could work, and I wouldn't just kill you in the process, I don't think I could make myself do it. I could not in good conscience consign you to *this* for eternity," they gestured vaguely to themself. They were both silent for a while, listening to the end of the first side of *Black Celebration*.

"What's it like?" Monty asked as Cameron flipped the record. He could see them thinking, their thoughts rolling around behind their eyes. They tapped their cigarette in the ashtray on the end table and sat down next to him on the bed. They were now just in their underthings; the silk of their slip dress was distorted by their tight corset.

"It's painful, freeing, but something I don't know how to compare. My experience as a human gets blurry around when I hit puberty, eleven I think, since that's when the infusions started. I originally thought I was sick, and that fiction worked until I was fifteen, since that's when I started transforming. It was slow, painful, and I kept aging until I must have been twenty or so," they paused, looking far away into the dark room.

"Everything inside me aches in a bone-weary way. Light hurts my eyes. Loud sounds split my ears. I can smell your blood in your veins and the fear in your sweat. I can hear the thrum of your heart pushing your pulse," they explained. There was a hungry look in their eyes as they lingered on Monty's throat. He swallowed hard, realizing how painfully close to him they were now. They continued despite the fact that they certainly could hear his heartbeat quickening.

"I can see through night as though it were midday. The shadows bend to my will, and I can twist my body like the darkness itself into the illusions of greater beasts. I can use that power to force others to obey my will from inside their own heads. It's as if I were the space between itself, the liquid that makes up the veil between death and life. I cast no shadow and appear in no reflections, because all that's left of me is that... *space between*." They absentmindedly handed Monty the cigarette; his hand lingered for a moment before accepting the gesture. He took a shallow puff, his chest protesting but his nerves instantly untangling a little. He silently handed it back to them, their hands brushing. Monty was listening intently, soaking in every word as Cameron *finally* freely offered him some insight into their reality.

"None of that bothers me as much as the *hunger*. I have this hollow, starving ache in me that I can only satisfy with the life force of others. The less I have, the more the emptiness aches, the more intense the need to fill the void grows. It bleeds into a heavy bloodlust that, at times, feels insatiable. It's like no matter how much I take, I'll never be full and whole, forever starving. I don't know if it's a quirk of how I was made, but even when I should be sated, I find myself wanting more," they concluded.

"Do people ever willingly chose to become vampires? I mean you said it's both painful *and* freeing," he asked, the smell of sweet cigarette smoke wafting over him. It seemed to him Arianna relished her power, and he wondered if she would have chosen this life willingly. Cameron hummed as they savored another drag before answering his question.

"Yes, I can imagine some people see this curse as a blessing. They want strength, power, and some semblance of eternal youth enough to sacrifice their soul for it. That's what you give up for this life; your mortal soul is destroyed. I can't pretend to understand those who want this. I suppose some people are so scared of the unknown that knowable eternal emptiness feels like a better reality," they admitted, examining their cigarette and reflexively rubbing some of the more aggressive scars on their arm. Monty just nodded, not sure what else to say.

"You're basically immortal then, right?" he asked.

"Yes and no," they shrugged. "As you know, I can starve to death, which is the most painful thing to experience for my kind."

"Can anything *kill* you?"

"Yes, it just takes more... work," they paused for a moment, their face turning rather severe.

"If you stabbed a stake of wood or pure silver though my heart I would not wake again," they pressed a bony finger against the left side of their chest, "if then you were to cut off my head and burn my body to ash, it would be the end of me for certain. Honestly, just fire itself would do me in. I've been told some of us can perish in the sunlight, but the sun is mostly a discomfort for me."

"I'm surprised you'd actually tell me how to do it."

"You're in danger, Monty! I don't need to tell you that again. You *need* to know how to kill us. I trust you won't use this knowledge against me, and if you do, I'm willing to accept my fate. I know you don't think I'm a bloodthirsty monster, but I am yet to convince myself of that," they explained sternly as they put their cigarette out in the ashtray.

"I'm a good bit stronger than my aunt, physically at least. I think I could hold her off long enough for you to get in a final blow, or keep her here as this place burned down. If it comes to it, I'd rather you kill us both and save yourself..." they trailed off. There was a grim look on their delicate features as they stared at their shaking hands. They shook their head with a shiver.

"Are you saying I should try to kill Arianna?" Monty asked, very carefully choosing his words.

"If you have another idea of how you make it out of here alive, I am all ears, but..." they failed to complete their thought and once again stared off into the middle distance. They took a deep breath in an effort to calm their trembling body. "I've killed a lot of people Monty, and I will continue to have to kill in order to survive. Arianna is the same. This is a soulless, empty existence, sublimated by pure parasitism."

"Cam, can you quit talking like you're doomed? I'm pretty sure I can come up with a way for you to live without killing like everything in your path. You know people donate blood all the time, right? There's other ways to keep you alive." Monty gently brushed a hand across their face, rubbing his thumb along the healing skin on their cheek.

"Perhaps you're right. But still, what do we do about my aunt? As long as she's around, you are in serious danger. She won't just let you go. Even if you could get off the property, she'll hunt you down," they spoke softly, as if they were worried they might be overheard. Monty found it was difficult for him to formulate any sort of solid plan in the moment.

"We don't have to find an answer right this second," he said. They were so very close now. Desire and fear swirled around in his stomach. He softly closed the gap between them. Lavender, blood, smoke, and jasmine filled his nose as he pressed his chapped lips into theirs. Cameron pulled back faster than he expected, though their face lingered close for just a moment before they leaned back and looked away.

"Sorry," Monty mumbled, realizing this was not the right response to the situation at hand.

"No, no, it's okay. I'm just worried."

"I know. I'll figure out—"

"It's not just that," they cut him off. They looked nervous, fidgeting with the front busk of their corset as they spoke. "That emptiness is… aching worse than usual. The fear in you makes it all the more tempting."

"And?" Monty was painfully aware of his plus as he gently trailed a hand along their leg, feeling his calluses catch on the silk fabric of their stockings. Even in the dark red light of their room, he could tell they were flustered by his gesture.

"I know you trust me, and I've shown it's possible to control my thirst… but I don't know if I can repeat that trick. Not when I feel like this," they spoke in a near whisper.

Monty was getting the sense this might be the last night he was alone with them, the last time they'd spend time together this intimately. He had an impending sense of doom broiling under his flushed skin. He could feel his words becoming tangled in his mind as longing started to flood him.

"I can hear it rushing from your eager heart, I see it flowing in your veins, and smell it boiling in you. I want it so badly… if I had just the slightest taste right now, I don't know if I could get myself to stop." As Cameron spoke they very slowly crawled to straddle Monty's lap. His heart leaped into his throat as he looked up at their lustful gaze, their beautiful eyes half-lidded and chest heaving.

"Then don't stop," Monty managed to say as he gripped their waist, "just fucking kiss me already." They grabbed the collar of his shirt and pulled him in for a sloppy and starved kiss. His hot breath fogged against their cold lips.

They kept their blood stained mouth close to his as they pushed him back onto the silk sheets. Darkness slowly began to creep into his mind, his head going fuzzy.

They trailed their lips and tongue over his jaw and down to his neck. He could feel his frighteningly quick pulses taunting them. They playfully nipped at the crook of his neck as light bloomed behind his darkened vision. He let out a soft sound at the feeling of their lips on his neck, a sound he'd never made before.

He felt the hair on the back of his neck picked at the feeling of Cameron's lips against his main artery. He grew more and more excited at the thought that in this very moment he could be drained, killed in the blink of an eye. That risk made everything feel all the sweeter. Captured prey. He wanted them to take what they wanted from him. They could take every last drop of blood if they desired. They dug their nails into his shoulders, their breath labored against his throbbing vein. He felt their sharp fangs gently graze his warm neck, lingering as they panted hard against their constrictive clothing.

*Please, just do it.*

"Bite me," he whimpered, to his surprise, out loud.

"Monty," they let out a breath against his neck, fingers lingering under the chain of his necklace. They abruptly went rigid.

"*Dio!* What the *fuck* am I doing!?" Cameron snapped out of the trance. They ripped themself from his grasp. He was simultaneously relieved and disappointed.

"What?" he asked. They merely shook their head and backed away from the bed.

"I don't know what I'm doing letting myself entertain this," they swallowed. He propped himself up on his elbow.

"What's the worst you'd do?" he asked coyly. He knew full well what they were capable of. He was playing with death. He needed them, and he could see now as they stood in front of him, that they were just as excited, their arousal visible under silken fabric.

"You already know the answer to that. *Dio,* when you touch me, my prey drive goes wild! I could tear you to shreds!" Their voice was trembling.

"Then tear me to shreds, why don't you?" Monty got up and slowly closed the gap between them. Cameron backed up towards the wall until they were caged within his arms. Despite knowing full well the consequences of their losing control, his tight dress pants demanded attention more than any sane thought in Monty's mind.

"I know what you're really asking from me and... I won't be able to stop myself... if I let us... um..." They were unable to finish their sentence though labored breathing.

"Have you ever...?" The question lingered heavily between them. Cameron looked everywhere else other than Monty's face.

"Ah well, a good deal actually... but only with people I've..." They looked nervous.

"Killed?" He finished their sentence for them. They nodded.

"It's how it works. We use seduction and hypnosis to lure in prey, and then when you're at the most vulnerable we strike," they explained.

"Cameron, *please*, you're not helping me want you less when you describe it like that," he ran a hand through their hair, trailing down the side of their face and down their neck before lingering his wandering fingers under the fine chain of their little golden locket.

"You're hungry, right?" he asked. They were trembling as they nodded.

"Monty... I... what if I actually hurt you?" they asked, softly placing a hand on his chest.

"Then hurt me! Please, I can't take it anymore. You're all I can think about at night when I'm alone. Please... I need you," he begged. He moved closer, their bodies practically touching. He was surprised at his own neediness. "I'm willing to take the risk. I don't know if we will get another chance before one of us is toast. So, hurt me, break me, do whatever the hell you want to me! Just please, god Cameron, fuck me!" he pleaded. His begging worked. He could see the confidence return to Cameron's features as their eyes glazed with arousal. They knew he was right; it was now or never.

# CHAPTER TWENTY-THREE

"OH, Monty," Cameron sighed darkly. He could see them weighing things in their mind, their pupils dilating as they searched his face for something. He closed the gap between the two of them again. Their skin burned to the touch, flesh icy compared to his flushed face.

After a moment, they slipped their hands between them and pushed Monty back away, hard into the bed. The wood groaned under the sudden dip of his weight. It excited him that it took so little of their effort to move him around like a rag doll. He propped himself up again on his elbows to see them better.

They loomed over him now with a ravenous look in their eyes. "How am I ever supposed to resist when you plead with me like that?"

Darkness began to entangle Montague's mind as his heart pounded in his ears. The shadows pooling around him paralyzed his muscles in place. The room grew out of focus until all he could see was Cameron's ghostly visage. The twisting butterflies in his stomach made him shake under their gaze. They hooked their fingers into the waistband of his pants and pulled him closer to the edge of the bed, causing him to lose his balance and fall supine. He felt himself twitch with excitement as their hand brushed the tent in his pants.

"What exactly does a big guy like you think of alone at night then? Do you dream of dominating me?" they asked in his ear, barely audible. It sent a chill through him as the image of them squirming under him flashed in his mind.

*No, that's not what I want.* Embarrassment flooded him.

"Actually," his voice caught in his throat, "I've never been with someone who can manhandle me like you so, I, um…" A twisted and delighted smile spread across Cameron's face, sharp fangs glinting in the crimson light.

"You *enjoy* being prey?" they asked with a whisper and coy grin. Monty nodded as he averted his gaze.

"Ah, I've thought about this quite a bit, *dolcezza*. I should have realized you were a masochist sooner," they teased.

"I thought it was obvious," Monty laughed a little.

"I just suppose I didn't want to assume," Cameron hummed softly. The look of lust in their eyes was unsettling. They rubbed their hand along his member through his pants, causing him to shudder violently. He let out a whimper as they teased him. It felt like his tongue had been twisted into a knot and every word he could possibly speak had been drained from his mind.

Cameron pulled away for a moment, fumbling with their slip and corset before tossing them away. They were left in just their garters, stockings, and a lacy black pair of briefs that very barely hid their excitement. They leaned over him and tore his sweat-soaked shirt from his body with such force that the fabric audibly tore.

"So selfless to give yourself to me like this. But you truly have no sense of self-preservation," they mused in a low tone directly in his ears. Their voice made the darkness holding him down pulsate with electricity.

"I can't actually do what you want with this on," they said. A slim hand pulled his necklace off and delicately placed it on the end table. There was the slightest sense of actual panic as they removed his hamsa, parting him from the only thing keeping him from being fully engulfed in them. The panicked sensation was numbed as quickly as it overcame him.

Cameron took a painfully long time to slip off his pants. The cold air against his skin caused goose bumps to form across his body. Once he was left trembling in his boxers, his captor slipped off into the darkness of their room.

With very little warning, he felt tendrils of dark smoke yank his body all the way onto the bed, propping his excited and shaking figure against the soft pillows. Even though the dim red light still illuminated the room, it felt impossibly dark.

He could practically taste his heart as he felt that familiar feeling of being stalked by a hungry coyote. It felt as if many delicate hands were holding him down, Cameron's hands, pinning his arms and legs into the soft silk pillows. There was an intoxicating heaviness in his mind. All he could focus on was his excitement as his body became entangled in their web.

Monty's head span as the smell of expensive cigarettes, metallic blood, heavy musk, and sweet jasmine filled his senses, *Cameron*. Their scent was everywhere around him, and it made his mouth water. He gave a deep sigh in a vain attempt to control his labored breathing.

All the hair on his neck stood up, and a chill ran down his spine. His nervous system was waiting to be torn limb from limb. Even if he wanted to run now, it would have been impossible. It felt like his body was being stitched down to the bed with invisible threads of silk. He could feel his will draining. Why would he even want to run? This was all he could ever possibly desire.

In a cloud dark as night itself, Cameron materialized over him. They moved as though they were floating, a gentle long hand lingered on his chest, their fingers combing through his sweat-soaked chest hair. Gentle hands trailed up to his neck. He could hear his heart rushing in his ears as slim fingers wrapped around his throat, pressing gently on his jugular veins just below his jaw. He could feel his breath hitch as little bits of white light gently popped behind his eyes. Cameron forcibly, though gently, turned his head to face them. Their eyes were half-lidded, surveying him like a fine cut of meat.

They teasingly leaned in for a kiss, but moved back as their lips brushed, causing Monty to groan in protest. Their hand loosened around his neck and trailed down his body, removing his sweat-drenched boxers. He sighed with relief as his strained member was finally greeted with fresh cool air.

"*Relax*, Monty, you're shaking," they cooed in his ear. Sparks shot through his body as they teased his cock with a maddeningly gentle touch. He writhed under their ministrations, being held forcibly in place as he moaned.

"Oh, you sound so much sweeter when you're actually melting in my hands," Cameron's voice flooded into his ears, coming from inside his very mind. They crawled on top of him, their weight barely registering to him as they perched themselves on his pelvis.

One of their hands slid up the base of his skull and grabbed a fistful of his thick damp hair. They pulled him into a dizzying kiss, their scent creeping through every pore, their tongue slipping into his hot mouth, filling him further with their intoxicating aroma. Their taste and smell made him forget everything. He forgot who he was, what he was doing here, everything other than Cameron. They growled hungrily into his pliant mouth. He could feel them shaking, panting, drooling with bloodlust. He could practically feel his blood trying to burst from his veins, teasing his vicious captor. They pulled away, their beautiful face hovering over him, framed in golden curls.

They slowly kissed down the length of his jaw, down his pulsating neck, across his heaving chest and down his soft fluttering stomach, until they were positioned between his strong trembling thighs.

Cameron let a small laugh escape their lips before they leaned down and took the majority of his length into their mouth. The icy tingle of their saliva was shockingly cool, though not unpleasant. Monty felt shocks of lightning bolt through him, going through his chest, his stomach, and every single one of his joints. He felt himself grip onto the silken sheets as he tried to hold in his sounds of ecstasy under their touch. His vision was pulled into the darkness, and his body felt like it was floating.

He could think of nothing other than *Cam, oh God,*

*Cameron,*

*Cameron!*

Monty did not realize he was practically screaming their name as he writhed under them, his body twitching. He could barely hold out much longer as sweat pooled around him. He whined with disappointment as they pulled away from him.

"Oh, you are so gorgeous," their voice crooned in his brain. They leaned forward over him, and he realized they were fingering themself. They planted a sloppy kiss against his lips, moaning softly into his mouth. Their soft whimpers made them sound like a whining hound.

Cameron ground against him teasingly before they positioned themself over his throbbing cock. They teased him slowly. He could faint from how fast his breath escaped him. He couldn't wait any longer. Without warning, he bucked his hips and slid into them with shocking ease. They let out a long moan that sounded like the howl of a coyote as they lowered themself all the way onto him, nails digging into his shoulders. Their sound of ecstasy was so familiar it caused him a moment of pause.

Their bodies were shaking as they both got used to each other, sitting there for a moment, breathing heavily. Some cold sweat dripped down from Cameron's quaking body. Their strawberry blond hair was wet, simultaneously dripping and stuck to them. They sat back suddenly, sinking deeper, causing Monty to let out a long groan.

"Please," they painted, their voice still in his head, "move." He realized he could move his body again. Without further hesitation, he began thrusting into them, every jolt filling him even more with ecstasy and lust.

Cameron's head fell against his neck, their lips panting into the crook of his neck as they rode him. He wished they could pull him closer, deeper, to the point their bones would collide together. He needed more. He could feel their lips lingering against his frantic pulse. He could sense the familiar prickle of excitement as fangs hesitated against super-heated flesh. They were panting like a dog in heat against his pulse point.

"Please," his voice was but a breath, "stop holding back."

In a flash of white-hot pain and ecstasy, Monty felt sharp fangs dig deep into his trapezius muscle. He threw his head back and let out a long guttural cry of ecstasy, as the sudden agony of burning venom coursing through his body caused him to release. Explosive light bloomed through his darkened vision as he felt himself pump hot seed deep into the Cameron.

He felt their teeth tear through his flesh. The pain slowly numbed as they gulped desperately needy mouthfuls of his blood. They snarled and moaned against his skin, ice-cold tongue lapping against torn flesh and body writhing with ecstasy. If he had been in a different state of mind, he might have panicked at how lightheaded he was becoming as his blood was drained.

He felt a new kind of pleasure as a shivering darkness took over his consciousness. Cameron released a guttural, animalistic groan as they gulped more and more of his blood. He could hear his flesh rip in their jaws, but he was powerless to do much of anything to stop them from completely draining him. The pain was beautifully distracted by the eclectic buzz of hot venom, willing his heart to keep pumping sweet blood through his arteries. His eyes roiled with blissful delight as his jaw hung open and slack. Nothing in his life had ever felt this delectable. He felt the seductive power of unconsciousness calling him. He yearned to give in to the ultimate bliss of submitting himself to the void.

Deep in his animal mind, he was glad he was subdued, the fear of dying blissfully numbed to a pleasant afterthought. But then, as he felt something more vital break in Cameron's powerful jaws, his survival instinct finally, *finally*, awoke for the very first time. Monty mustered all his strength and managed to grip a fistful of damp golden hair and tear the hungry vampire from his neck with great effort. He felt their fangs tear out of his flesh with a burning squelch.

Cameron cried out as they drew back, splattering them both in hot blood. Monty shivered as the shadows holding him down slowly receded. He could feel the trickle of his blood flowing from his wound, soaking the sheet under him. He was delirious as he pressed a hand to the gored spot in his neck, his panic starting to bring him back to reality.

Cameron's face was drenched with blood, their eyes rolling still as they tried to come back to themself. Monty pushed them fully off him onto the bed, which was now soaked with far too manly bodily fluids to feel pleasant.

"Fuck," Monty huffed as pain was starting to overtake him. He felt simultaneously fantastic and moments from death. Cameron's body shuddered, and their face very quickly transformed from pleasure to panic. They put a hand to their mouth and shot upright and shrieked a string of incomprehensible profanities.

"Guh, help me out, this—ugh, this BURNS!" Monty huffed as the lingering sublimation of their venom turned to fiery poison. It spread with frightening speed down through the entirety of his body from his gored neck. "Bandages, antiseptic, please," he pleaded.

He had seen them move impossibly fast before, but if the bed had not shaken with their movements, he'd have assumed they had manifested the bandages from thin air.

"Oh no, no, I knew I wouldn't be able to stop myself. I'm sorry! I'm sorry! *Cazzo!* I knew I would hurt you. I'm so sorry." They shook violently as they gently removed Monty's hand from his wound.

"How bad is it?"

"I'm not sure how you're still conscious," they said very softly.

They were crying, tears washing clean trails through the blood drenching their face.

"Adrenaline finally decided to kick in for once," he joked before all thought was replaced with searing agony. He was deaf to his own screaming as the sharp sensation of antiseptic caused his vision to bleach white.

"Don't move, please. I'm sorry, *dio* I'm so, so sorry. I shouldn't have entertained this," Cameron's apology fell from their lips in a flurry. Monty couldn't reply as he was too focused on breathing through the pain. He could tell he was still bleeding. Though he couldn't see the injury, he could feel Cameron press his flesh back together as they bandaged where his neck met his shoulder. As they continued to wind gauze around him with shaky hands, the pain dulled to an aching throb.

"I should not have done this. Oh, Monty, I'm so sorry. I wish I could find a way to stitch you up. I nearly tore a chunk clean out of you." They were visibly far more shaken than Monty.

"Is it *that* bad?"

"Monty," their expression was grave.

"You know that was pretty damn pleasant up until you almost killed me," Monty half joked.

"Monty, please, if you didn't push me off when you did, I *would* have killed you just now!"

"But ya' didn't," he pointed out. He could tell he was a little delirious. There was a slightly pleasant and happy sensation lingering in his foggy mind. He felt like giggling and screaming in terror simultaneously. Cameron pressed him gently into the sheets.

"Please don't try to move," they instructed. "You need to rest."

"Sure, sure," he hummed, closing his eyes.

"*Dio*, I-I cannot believe I lost myself that easily," Cameron's voice trembled.

"How do you feel?" Monty asked.

"What, me!?"

"Do you feel less distracted by hunger?"

"I…" they paused and shifted. Even with his eyes closed, he could tell their energy changed. Then, very quietly they said, "I feel amazing. I haven't felt this spry or been this clear of mind in months."

"Then that will come in handy when we have to fight the real threat here," Monty huffed, satisfied with himself.

"You… don't tell me you let me do that because—?"

"Nah, I did just really wanna have sex, but you being stronger is a good side effect."

"But what about you!?"

"I'll be fine, I'm a big guy after all," he smiled to himself, loopy from blood loss. "You are right, though. I need rest. Make sure one of your crazy relatives don't kill me in my sleep, will ya' beautiful?" he slurred some of his words as he closed his eyes.

"I'll keep you safe. Just sleep," they said, combing a hand through his sweat-sodden hair, and then quietly to themself they whispered, "Oh *dio* what *have* I done?"

# CHAPTER TWENTY-FOUR

MONTAGUE stumbled through nothingness. His eyes were wide open, and yet, all that stood before him was a pure expanse of darkness. He could feel the musty hallway carpet beneath his feet and peeling paper under his fingertips as he stumbled forwards. He was being drawn along by a force beyond him. He ached, but marched on all the same, as if there was something at the end of this hall he *had* to reach.

There was a faint buzzing in his ears, a single fly fizzing around his head. He swatted at nothing in the darkens. More flies began to encircle his head, some landing on his sweat-soaked face. He continued to brush them off with mild irritation.

He was suddenly acutely aware he was not alone in the darkness. Though he could not see through the black, he felt the presence of someone familiar, just to his left. The droning hum of flies swarming her figure, mingling with the smell of damp sweet putrefaction, was enough for him to know just who was next to him. He could taste her rot in his mouth as she shambled alongside him down the hall, two stiff and ruined bodies moving towards nothingness.

*How much more of this can you take, Montague?* Dr. Giovanni asked.

She sounded concerned.

"What?"

*They will not let you leave here alive.*

He tried to reply, but his vocal cords felt like sandpaper, and no air flowed from his lungs.

*Avenge me and save yourself, Montague. Don't make my same mistake. Don't think you can control them.*

His body burned as more insects landed on him. They crawled over his skin and bit into him with sharp little stings. He could feel them crawling over every part of his sweat-drenched skin. He reeled as he felt them bite and crawl into the sharply torn flesh of his neck. They were devouring him alive as though he himself were a rotten carcass.

He wanted to scream and flee from the sensation consuming his body, but no matter how much he swatted at himself, his skin continued to crawl. There was nowhere to run. He could not peel his meat from his bone, no matter how much he desired to do so. The swarm growing around him felt like dirt pouring over his head, blurred alive in a hellish buzzing grave. He felt a strange fear that was not wholly his as he fell through the impossibly deep soil.

☽ ✧ ☾

Monty's eyes shot open with a ragged gasp. As his vision drew focus, he could feel the pain come creeping back into his body. It was a dull, stinging ache across every limb, emanating from the bite in his left shoulder. In addition to the pain, he felt the warm heat of exhaustion deep in his bones. He was tempted to go back to sleep as he lay in soft silk sheets, but his mind was awake now.

There was a golden hue to the sunlight that danced around the dusty ruby crystals of the chandeliers. Those impressive fixtures hung heavy from the ceiling, glinting like two huge red eyes set in the skull of a grand beast. They felt impossibly high to him as he watched the dust molts float around every ornate carving of old wood overhead. It was hard to see these little details in the elaborate architecture in the dark of night, but now they were quite evident to him. Little serpents warped around high beams, their presence etched into every part of this dusty manor. He realized the sun was likely setting now, as the shadows were already stretching long through the room.

"You're finally awake?" Cameron asked softy.

"I am alive, yes," Monty's voice was raw. He tried to clear his throat. He sat up with a wince. "Did you rest at all?" he asked.

"No. I did not feel the need... I took a lot of your blood last night. I was too anxious to rest until you woke again."

"You look better," Monty said. There was something very different in the air about them. They were pink and bright, a glow in their eyes he'd not seen the entire time he'd known them. Their face was softer, healthier, with a new youth that made them appear barely twenty. It was the first time they truly looked fully alive.

"I think if I had taken that much from anyone else, I would have killed them. I'm astonished that you're not only alive, but seem fairly stable," Cameron's tone was both shocked and relieved.

"I'll be honest with you, my body hurts, but I think that's from whatever's in your spit, rather than the blood loss itself. I mostly feel like I have a killer hangover," Monty grunted, his head swimming just a little as he moved around.

"Do you think you'll be okay?"

"Oh yeah, I'll be fine," he half lied as pain-induced floaters bloomed in his vision, "maybe some ibuprofen though first."

He gently brushed a hand over the bandages. Even the faintest bit of pressure made him feel queasy. He was too preoccupied with his wounds to even realize Cameron had managed to bring him a glass of water and a little bottle of pain medicine.

"Oh, perfect," he sighed with relief, chugging the water like he'd been on a deserted island for the past forty-eight hours.

They were quiet for some time, listening to the coo of rock doves perched out on the balcony railing. Their little *"woo-ooh-hoos"* soothed even the weariest of souls.

"So... how am I getting out of here?" Monty asked after some time. "You don't happen to have any camping equipment lying around?"

"What?"

"Tent stakes?" Monty replied, miming a stabbing motion in his chest.

"Oh, no, I don't keep things like that lying around. I assume, though, there might be something helpful in the gardening shed?"

"I mean I could probably make some if I had a little time," Monty said, thinking to himself. There was surely something in the shed that he could use to whittle some wooden stakes. There might be other things in there that would prove helpful, but his brain hurt from trying to remember its contents.

"Are you sure this is the best idea? Like what happens if we succeed, other than me getting to walk away alive, ya' know?" he asked after a moment of thought. This whole ordeal felt dreadful.

"I'd be free from my sire technically, meaning no one would hold any power over me. I suppose the rest of the estate would be mine too," Cameron said after some thought.

"Is this dusty tomb worth killing your aunt?"

"Monty, this plot of land is a tiny fraction of the family assets."

"Right, but, sorry if I'm being presumptuous, she's the last of your family, no?" he asked. Cameron let out a long sigh.

"Yes. I don't want to kill her... But I won't pretend I don't resent her a bit. What happened to me was not inevitable. If she never gave my mother her blood to experiment with, none of this would have ever happened. I know she technically saved me from certain death, but she was the one who told me to kill my mother. She only showed up when it was nearly too late. If she had intervened sooner, when it was clear something was wrong, I might have been able to be saved."

"It's not like I even really wanted any of this. Arianna entrusted this land to me under the condition I fixed the decay my mother let fester. Everything I'm meant to do is in service of the family name, and I know if there were more of us left, I would mean nothing to her," Cameron explained. There was a whoosh of dove wings outside, something scaring them off the balcony.

"All I know is this: she is like me, starved for blood to the bitter end. Killing her would keep a lot of innocent people out of shallow graves, but—"

Cameron's train of thought was interrupted by a loud, impatient knock on one of the bedroom doors. A wash of terror came over their soft face.

"*Cazzo*–one moment!" Their voice cracked as they stumbled out of the bed, nearly falling to the floor. They frantically looked around for something.

"Do you think sh—?"

"Shh," they hushed Monty frantically. Unpleasant ice sank into his veins. Another, less patient knock.

"*UNO MOMENTO!*" Cameron shouted. They finally found their long red smoking robe, hastily tying it on as they ran to the door and fumbled with the lock. They opened it to reveal Arianna.

"Good afternoon." Her tone was as warm as a January morning. She was dressed in royal purple and adorned with a huge golden serpent necklace. It had two little ruby eyes, and if it had not shimmered so, it might have been mistaken for a real living thing.

"G-good afternoon, Zizi," Cameron stammered. Arianna's nose crinkled with disgust as she looked over her kin. They reflexively closed the robe tighter over their bare chest under their aunt's disapproving glare.

"It's nearly sundown," she said, peering over their shoulder to see Montague. Her expression quickly shifted from mild annoyance to shocked contempt.

"I'm sorry, I didn't think to set an alarm," Cameron admitted, partly closing the door as if to shield Monty from her line of sight.

"I thought you *killed* that whelp last night!"

Monty could see Cameron's body go rigid. Arianna's lavender eyes scanned over them again. She crossed her arms and let out a hiss of dark smoke that emanated from her very countenance.

"W-why would you think that?"

"You're flushed, the room reeks of blood," she clicked her tongue disapprovingly, "nor was he a very quiet victim... Well I suppose not a *victim*, since he appears to be still very much alive, to my chagrin."

"Ah, I'm s—"

"Get dressed. I have plans for you today," she interrupted them without missing a beat.

"Tell your *cane*," she pointed to Monty with her chin, "to go back to his duties. If you're going to keep a pet, he might as well make himself useful. He's not to leave the property under any condition. As it is, I'd rather not have to worry about him running around town off his leash. Do I make myself clear?"

Cameron stood impossibly still for a moment. Though Monty could not see their face there was a palpable sense of distaste as they chewed their words around in their mouth.

"Don't refer to *Montague* like that," they said firmly. Arianna raised an eyebrow, but her listless eyes did not change emotion.

"Why should I not now?" she asked in a measured tone, a flame of rage somewhere carefully hidden in her beautiful features.

"He's not just some servant or dog you can order around," Cameron said, standing up a bit straighter.

"Oh? Is he not the groundskeeper of *my* estate?" She shot back in a nasty tone.

"He's not *your* servant, he's *my* friend," they said, their temper slowly boiling.

"More than friend, based on the *disgusting* murderous racket you two were making last night. You sound like a child affectionately referring to a stray he's brought in—"

"Stop talking about him like that!" Cameron barked, cutting her off. Arianna looked mildly shocked.

"What have I told you about speaking to me like that, *ragazzo*?" Her eyes narrowed with a dangerous venom. "Have your brains gone soft from playing with your food? Look at you, boy! You're so disgustingly thin you might as well be a mummy. Have you been savoring the same one meal for weeks at a time like this? Is this why you are so pathetic?"

"Please stop."

"Sympathy for your little human is going to kill you," she scolded. Cameron went to speak, but she held up her hand. "I won't tolerate your harming yourself like this. You are making a mess of things just like your mother and I won't stand for it. Not after all the hard work I've put into this family. Now go put on some clothing... and perhaps some perfume. I'll expect you out front in no more than half an hour. I realize now you need to be taught quite a few lessons again." She went to turn away but stopped for a moment. Cameron looked like they were going to say something, but Arianna continued.

"It would be in your best interest to tell your little friend, *Montague*, to not get any smart ideas while we're gone, *capisci*?" Then she stormed off in a cloud of black vapor before even letting them exhale a response.

Cameron was quiet for a moment as they hung their head in the doorway.

"*Sì, capisci*," they finally uttered in a quiet, defeated tone to the floor before closing the door. They pressed their back up against it as if afraid she was going to try to barge back into the room. Monty awkwardly rubbed the back of his head, cold sweat coating his aching body.

"This is going to be harder than I thought," they finally said, rubbing the heel of their palm across their distressed face.

"Do you think she overhead us?" Monty asked his original question with a nervous laugh.

"I don't know. I hope she just meant not letting you run off,"

Cameron whined, stress clearly beginning to bubble up inside them again. "You need to be careful. If you actually do try to run while we're gone... I know she can track you. You won't get far," they said very seriously.

"Remember," they mimed stabbing themself in the chest.

"Do you think I'm going to be able to—"

"At this point, you've got to try. Look, Monty," they began as they sat down next to him on the bed. They looked like they were listening for something for a moment. The continued in a very hushed tone, "I'll do what I can to convince her you're not a threat, nothing to worry about, and that we should just let you go on your merry way. Maybe I'll convince her I've enthralled you? I don't know, but us being gone will give you some time to get things together. If I can distract her long enough, we could catch her while she's weak in the morning light. I'll be weaker to but.... I'm feeling a lot more myself after last night. If all else fails, you can still burn the mansion down."

"I understand, but... Fuck man, I hate this," Monty let out a long groan and ran his hands through his hair. It felt like his blood had been replaced with liquid lead.

"I do too," Cameron sighed, rubbing their tired face again. "I just don't know what else to do at this point."

# CHAPTER TWENTY-FIVE

MONTAGUE went back to his cabin to collect himself as twilight fell. His joints groaned as he stepped into the shower. Water poured over him, and migraine-like spots of glowing voids swam in his vision like stars. He watched blood drip from his wound, across his chest and down the shower drain. The warm water felt heavenly on his tense muscles, but made the bite on his shoulder sting as though it were full of fig wasps. Every bone in his body was pulsating with the dull ache of exhaustion.

He gave a sigh as he then found himself staring in the bathroom mirror. He could now see just how bad the wound really was. Instead of two little puncture wounds like on his wrist, it was a ring of savage tooth marks in his flesh. There were sliced trenches where Cameron's fangs had been forcibly torn out of muscle tissue. He needed stitches, but butterfly bandages and a healthy among of gauze were going to have to do for now.

The past night had the very opposite effect on his appearance as it did on Cameron. He was haggard and exhausted. The dark circles around his black eyes aged him several years. Not quite as much as the flash of white he noticed when he went to detangle his hair. He'd been aware of it, sure, but this was the first time he saw truly just how far it had spread. It was a shocking streak of white in his jet hair.

He thought about Cameron. They would never be surprised by a new flash of gray like this. They were destined to be forever young, frozen in time like a photograph of someone who once was. No longer human, no longer aging flesh and bone, they were something else entirely. No matter how Monty thought about it, he was their prey. Nothing could change that fact.

Perhaps it was his blood loss and fear-addled mind, but for a moment he considered it. The idea of eternal life tempted him now that he had to face his own mortality. That "escape" from the threat of death would come at a great price, however, and it was one he was not mentally prepared to pay. Not any more than being ready to lay down and die.

It wasn't the pain that scared him; he had no way of knowing how the agony measured between life and undeath. No, that was not the issue; it was more the prospect of losing his humanity. He was not really a spiritual person. Most of his seemingly spiritual gestures were a force of habit left over from his upbringing. Still, the promise of damnation through eternal life felt more blasphemous than his soul could bear. Perhaps he was really truly afraid of the unknown?

Still, he considered it.

Monty dried himself off and changed into more comfortable clothing. The cooling night air lingered in his cabin, and it froze his sore body. He dressed hastily, carelessly throwing on cargo pants, a white long-sleeve shirt, and his trusted denim jacket. His feet ached in protest as he crammed them back into his boots. He wanted to rest so badly, but he had work to do and didn't have long to do it.

The night was dark and cool, the moon's light becoming nothing but a sliver in the sky, a taunting smile of perfect white teeth. The stairs shone far brighter now with little light interference from the moon. Only a few wisps of clouds rolled by in the sky, and Monty could swear that in that moment he could see the Milky Way overhead. The breeze sent a chill down his spine as it rustled the drying leaves.

Summer had finally died, leaving fall heavy in its absence. The smell of the autumn night air was a pleasant respite from the dust of the manor, despite the nose-tickling perfume of autumn mildew beginning to blossom. As he stood in the yard, looked up at the night sky, the thoughts of the impending new moon made him ponder the coming darkness.

*I'm feeling the fear of oblivion, aren't I?*

Now that he was alone, he finally let the gravity of his reality sink in. The thoughts of death loomed heavy over his head like the pendulum of a grandfather clock as the rising moon ticked every minute by. He was strangely calm. Part of him thought he would wake up any moment and discover this whole thing was some oddly vivid dream. He'd never once given himself the grace to consider an afterlife. He hoped it was more than just the empty expanse of space. Maybe he'd open his eyes in a new life, born to a family that loved him just a little more.

He shook his head. He had to push this out of his mind if he was going to keep himself alive. Brooding now wouldn't do him any good, yet still his stomach churned with terror even as he turned his focus to the dreadful thing he had to do.

Monty tore the rusty doors of the shed open and clumsily plugged in the string of bare bulbs to illuminate the gardening tool graveyard. As the lights flickered on, they sparkled off the blade of the scythe, and an idea lit up along with it.

*Now that's a blade I bet I could take a head off with*, he thought to himself.

As he scrounged around for tools to fashion his other weapon, he began to cook a plan in his mind of just how to end a vampire. He eventually found a serviceable pull saw and a rather old looking gardening knife. Despite its age, the blade was still well aligned and sharpened easily. He serviced the scythe as well, sharpening it until its blade made him nervous. He then tied a rope to it with a rusted wrench on the other side as a counterweight.

He was shaking as he walked just past the overgrown threshold of the woods behind his cabin. He now knew that the coyote that had been stalking him through these woods was Cameron. Despite this, he still felt the dread of encountering something hidden in the foliage as he began to saw limbs off a nearby cherry tree.

It was silent as he worked. No bugs or frogs hummed rhythmically, nor was there any sound from small creatures scurrying in the leaf litter. All he could hear was the sound of his labored breathing as he tried to saw through wet autumn tree limbs. It was hard to force his body to move swiftly.

*I'd probably feel better if I'd been hit by a bus*, he grumbled to himself as he took the bundle of branches into the shed to whittle them down. He'd had about three that felt like they were the right size and weight. Cameron had neglected to tell him how exactly to make an effective stake, so he based his calculation on something he'd used to hold down a tarp. He could barely hold the wood as he trembled.

He felt his stomach growl in protest and realized he was shaking from hunger of all things. He gathered up his clumsily whittled stakes and the scythe and stumbled back to his cabin to make himself something to eat. He put the two best stakes he'd made in the inside pocket of his denim jacket.

As he reluctantly ate the terribly dry sandwich he had cobbled together, his eyes caught the silver plastic case of his cellphone on the coffee table. It dawned on him that he had not checked his phone in maybe a week now. He looked over its plain display, no bars, no service as he flipped it open. He dreaded the impending influx of messages from Mina that would likely bombard him when he moved back into service range. Even when they'd had a spat, they'd never gone this long without talking. Mina felt painfully distant to him in that moment, like someone in a far-off land he used to know.

He tossed on his jacket and decided to take himself and his flimsy little phone down to the gate where he knew he got decent cell service. But first, he took a moment to stop under Cameron's balcony. He gripped the wrench, holding it like a football, and threw it as best he could, up onto the balcony. It clanked loudly and slipped around and through the railing, hooking the rope perfectly. Now he had a backup weapon he could easily get from a safe spot inside. He was pleased with his ingenuity.

He didn't linger to pat himself on the back, and instead half ran the rest of the way down the drive, past the rusted awful gate that sealed off the property. He flipped the phone open again and was met with an avalanche of missed calls and increasingly frantic text messages. He had to wait a moment as it buzzed and glitched with the onslaught of information that came through all at once. The most recent text having been sent only twenty minutes prior, timestamped at 1:51am. A hastily written message from Mina begging him to call her lingered on his screen.

A panic washed over him realizing he had no idea what he was going to tell her as he dialed her number. It only rang thrice before she picked up.

"MONTAGUE L. VARON YOU BETTER BE FUCKING DEAD!" Mina's high voice shrieked on the other end.

"Hi Mina," Monty cringed, holding the receiver away from his face.

"You better start explaining yourself! I thought you drove off the side of the mountain, or WORSE!" she shouted.

"I'm sorry! I was away from my phone," he explained.

"For a full week!?"

"I lost track of time..."

"Lost tra—LOST TRACK? I've been fucking trying to reach you for *a week*, Monty! I've been trying to apologize! I thought you were playing some kind of fucked-up joke to get back at me. I was about to report you fucking *missing*, dude!" Mina cursed.

"I'm sorry! I'm okay, seriously. I just had... a pretty intense few days. But like, I'm fine, I swear," he reassured her.

"You don't sound fine. Your voice is shaking. I'm sorry, but I really thought that twink fucking 'disappeared' you like those rumors Leah's been going on about," she ranted, the phone reception crackling.

"Oh, my God, Mina. Seriously, I'm—"

"What the hell have you been doing where you haven't even been able to send me a simple text back, man? Like just so I knew you were ALIVE?" she asked. He hesitated for a moment. He had no idea if she would even believe him if he attempted to tell the truth.

*God, is this going to be our last conversation?*

Panic washed over as he tried to keep his voice steady.

"I just got really caught up with work and, like, I think I've been very distracted. Cameron's aunt came to visit, so I've had my hands full, is all," he began his white lies.

He had not even told her yet about what had happened with Dr. Giovanni's ghost, that she was a ghost, how he discovered Cameron was a vampire, the fact Arianna basically had a gun to his head. His mind swarmed with panicked thoughts. There was too much he couldn't say. Mina was already doubtful about ghosts. He had no idea how he'd explain to her that he was trapped here with two vampires.

"It's really not like you to neglect your phone for that long, even when you've got 'a lot going on,'" she said after a long pause.

"Well, you know how awful cell service is here," he tried to laugh her off. They both were silent for a moment as he shifted his weight nervously, digging one of his boots into the gravel dirt of the drive. The connection crackled a little in the dead air.

"Okay, so, I already had a chat with my parents, and they've set up space for you, not on the living room floor this time. I'm gonna come up there and get you tomorrow," she huffed, the anger in her voice dampening to gentle resignation.

"WHAT!? Wait no, don't do that! You can't come here, Mina!" he panicked. There was no way he could let her get involved in this mess. Putting his own life at risk was one thing, but Mina was another story.

"Yo, what the hell? Why not?" she asked.

"You—um, you just can't," he said firmly. Anxiety began to spread through him like fire.

*If she comes here, Arianna will kill her too!*

"Okay… what the fuck are you not telling me, Montague?" she asked, "because I know when you're not giving me the whole picture."

*Would she even believe me?*

Monty touched the wound on his neck.

"You thought I was crazy when I told you about how I thought Dr. Giovanni was haunting the place," he began as his voice quivered. He debated trying to explain vampires to her. He started to pace where he stood.

"This again with the ghosts?" she shot. Before he could interject, she cut him off. "I really think the led in that old paint has to be getting to you."

"It's not lead paint. Come on, I'm serious. Cameron has seen her ghost too. This place is totally undeniably haunted!" he snapped.

*Ghosts and vampires… she can't come here.*

"Can you just trust me for once? I've got it under control, but I can't super leave right now. Theres some freaky shit going on here, but I've got it handled! I'll be *fine*. I just need you to trust me when I say you can't just show up here, not now, okay? I can explain everything to you later."

*If there will be a later…*

"Monty! Are you listening to yourself!? Imagine if I was acting like this after not hearing from me for over a week?" she snapped back. He was silent for a moment as his heart raced.

"Yeah, dude, exactly! Not going to lie to you, man, I don't super think Cameron is of sound mind either," Mina continued, phone crackling again a bit more aggressively this time. Monty tried to move around to improve his signal. "Like what the hell have they done to you, man?"

"I said I'm *FINE*! Cameron hasn't done anything bad to me,

jeez," he lied as firmly as he could muster through his blooming terror. He touched the bandage on his neck again and winced slightly. He was quiet for a moment as some more aggressive, buzzing static began to crackle over the phone line again.

"You suck at lying, Monty," she groaned as she began to break up. He couldn't hear what she said after that because the other end crackled too loudly. It sounded like there was an intense buzzing inside the phone, hundreds of little flies interrupting the phone call.

"Hello? Monty!? Are you listening to me?" Mina's voice came back clearly.

"I'm sorry, I just had some weird interference," he said, shaking his head a bit in an attempt to get the buzzing sound of the interference out of his brain. His whole body was pulsating with electricity.

"I said, I don't care if you think you're fine. You sound super not fine. I've never heard you so terrified, man. Did you find out the truth about Dr. Giovanni's death?" She paused for a moment. "Wait, oh fuck, was Leah right!?" Her words made every muscle in Monty's body tense.

"...No..."

"Okay, yeah, that was the world's least convincing 'no.' Shit! I knew that fucker was no good! Alright, I'm coming up there tomorrow first thing!" she repeated.

"Mina, seriously y—"

"No man, I'm not taking no for an answer. Pack your van and I'll see you tomorrow, alright? I'll try to get there as early as I can."

"Wait, Mina, no!"

"No arguing, we're getting you out of there. It's late, get some damn sleep."

"Mina, they are vam—"

"I love you, Monty. I'll see you tomorrow." She hung up on him.

He stood there for a moment, paralyzed as the other end of his phone buzzed its dial tone. He slammed his phone shut, ending the call. He cursed loudly to himself as he threw his phone as hard as he could down on the driveway. The antenna snapped clean off and went flying into the weeds somewhere.

He felt sick. Some tears welled up in the corner of his eyes. He could barely process his own mortal peril. Putting Mina in his shoes made him even more horrified. He ripped at his hair, fully melting down into tears of anguish. He let himself cry for the first time he could remember, kneeling on gravel, fully overwhelmed.

☽ ✦ ☾

After who knows how long, Monty finally took a deep breath and did his best to collect himself. He snatched up his now scuffed and practically useless cellphone and walked back up the drive. Some tears and snot still lingered on his face.

The dreadfully familiar feeling of being watched flooded over him as the hair on his neck stood on end. He stopped in the middle of the driveway to listen for movement. The only sound that met his ears were the chirps of crickets and drying leaves being gently rustled by a cool autumn breeze. Perhaps here in the dark of night his paranoia and terror was beginning to take over.

He had only walked a few steps more before freezing again, as he was sure he saw someone walking in the woods next to the driveway near the house. He knew that Cameron and Arianna could not have been back already. He would have seen them come up the drive. There was one other "person" he feared it could be. Though the figure he saw was not quite like any of the Giovannis. It was bigger, stockier, and had a heavy gait. He was certain no one else had been on the property but himself. He sped up the driveway towards the figure.

*Why don't you run?*

He heard a voice whisper past his ear, taunting him. It was so soft that it felt more like a breath on the wind than a true spoken voice. He was not even sure if he had heard those words at all, or if he was hallucinating things in the night breeze. His blood ran cold as his heartbeat began to tighten his already stressed chest.

*Why do you stay?*

Dr. Giovanni's voice buzzed in his ear with the chorus of rancid flies. She was somewhere behind him in the woods. He couldn't pinpoint exactly where she actually was. He said nothing back to her, biting his tongue in fear. He continued to walk slowly up the drive.

*Are you prepared to die, Montague?*

Her voice hummed out of the night air.

"Are you trying to herd me into a trap or something!?" he spat into the darkness. His voice sounded horribly loud in the night air. He cursed to himself and turned his head to look in the direction of the rustling leaves.

His eyes met a shining pair of yellow ones, something that rather belonged more to a beast than a man. He stared unblinkingly at them for a moment. They glinted eerily the way that a cat's might in the dark, like the way that Cameron's caught even the slightest bit of light in the dark of night. A horrific image seemed to make its way to his mind as he stared into those eyes, realizing it was something like a reflection. Despite knowing there was no mirror there, he knew the eyes he stared deeply into were his own.

In a sudden revelation, sight adjusting in the night to make out a shapeless mass, Montague saw the creature before him. It was himself. Rotten and wrong in the exact same way as Dr. Giovanni was. He had a halo of swarming flies, his dark eyes turned a shade of gold with the fog of death heavily pulled over them. His neck was an open, bloodied wound that smelled no more pleasant than the doctor herself. Awful stale blood and maggots burbled out of his rotting gore. He reflexively touched the bandage over his real neck. It was dry.

*Your time is up!*

Dr. Giovanni's voice gurgled from his horrible mirror, a bit of black bile pouring from his prone lips. He was physically unable to remove his gaze from his own horrible visage.

# CHAPTER TWENTY-SIX

THE burst of headlights coming up the drive snapped Montague out of his waking nightmare. He panicked and dove directly into the woods where his horrible mirror had been standing just moments before. He crouched down, doing his best to keep himself hidden. He waited for Arianna's rental sedan to pass up the driveway before he stumbled through the dark trees to make his way to the back of the house. He'd have to sneak back into the mansion somehow.

Every inch of his body was trembling and heavy as he moved. He feared what Arianna might do to him if she suspected he had been trying to make a run for it. He had no idea what she and Cameron had been up to all night, but they were back sooner than he had expected. He checked the cracked screen of his phone. It was just about three in the morning, still a long way until sunrise.

As he approached the house, he could see the two Giovannis struggling with each other. Arianna practically dragged Cameron from the passenger side of the car. He could just barely make out them bickering with each other in Italian. The sound of the splashing fountain drowned out most of their words as they conversed, though it looked like they were both very agitated. He could only see the back of Cameron's head, so he couldn't tell their emotion, but their body was tense.

Monty's heart stopped pounding and his breath froze in his throat as he noticed Arianna looked directly at him, over Cameron's shoulder and straight into the dark woods. Her gaze was fleeting and fell from him as quickly as it landed. He was not fully sure she had actually seen him or just merely thought she'd heard something. He waited with bated breath.

Arianna rather forcefully pushed Cameron towards the mansion and made a motion to her car in the coach house. They sighed, nodded, and went inside. She watched them enter the old Victorian before she turned to the coach house. All Monty could hear now was his heart, crickets, and the burbling of the fountain. The vampire appeared to be staring at his dead van, almost confused. He watched her then puncture all four of its tires with her sword.

*Oh, come on! That's overkill*, he thought to himself.

In that moment, he somehow managed to lose track of her. The gentle chirp of crickets and the light fall breeze calmed him. He assumed she must have been satisfied with her handiwork and decided to go inside. He let out a sigh and stood back to his full height.

WHACK!

Something cold and hard collided with the back of his skull, causing him to see stars and stumble over. A strong, slim arm wrapped around his neck and pulled him into a headlock. It felt like the night itself was seeping into his mind, choking his every fiber of oxygen. The sickeningly sweet smell of roses and copper flooded his lungs. He could barely breathe as he clawed at the arm around his neck.

"Well, well, what happened to my warnings, *cagnolino*?" Arianna whispered with a grin in his ear. Pure panic washed over him after the initial shock of being caught passed, realizing what was happening. He felt a force beyond his own mind trying to make him yield, stop struggling, *don't resist me!*

"It's like you're trying to make things harder for your poor master. We really aught to get you a collar and leash," she laughed deviously. She ran her hand over his torso, sending sparks of acid through his muscles. Her hand froze over the lump in his jacket pocket. She pulled out one of the whittled stakes with an air of amusement.

"Hah! I knew it! Clever, but not clever enough, *cagnolino*," she hummed, replacing it in his pocket with a little pat, as if to brag she was unphased by his vain efforts to arm himself.

"*Andiamo ragazzino*, I'm not waiting around for you to kill us in our sleep." She dragged him through the woods back up to the old Victorian. He struggled against her grasp and the force inside his mind, making his legs move against his will. Her control was far more efficient and forceful than Cameron's, issuing quick commands of his body rather than soft coercions.

"Please! Let me go!" he choked out, trying to pry her arm around his neck loose, the blackness tugging around his eyes as little pricks of light danced in his vision.

"I won't–AHK–I won't run, I promise!" he panicked as he could feel himself starting to lose consciousness. His legs felt loose under him as he fought tooth and nail to keep his vision.

Arianna roughly released her arm from around his neck. He did not have a sure footing, and his face collided hard with the porch steps. He let out a groan of pain. He narrowly avoided breaking his long nose. However, the impact caused some blood to dribble down his face, staining his shirt.

Before he could even get the stars out of his eyes, Arianna grabbed the scruff of his denim jacket and hoisted him up to his feet. He was still weak and confused. He stumbled like a drunk, unable to control his movements. Arianna snatched his arm hard, as if to keep him from bolting. She eyed the blood pouring from his face for a moment. Her eyes wandered over the bandage on his neck.

"Please, I didn't —"

"*Silencio*," she hissed, opening the front door and throwing him into the hallway entrance. He stumbled over his own feet, his entire body shaking from the smell of blood in his nose. He tried to grab the stake from his jacket, but his body would not obey him. His arms would not move, nor would his legs let him run.

*You do what I say!*

Arianna closed the door behind her, locking it tight and tossing her keys into her cleavage. She grabbed him again by the arm, this time twisting it around behind his back. The force caused him to let out a cry of protest as his bite wound throbbed. It burned worse than he thought possible.

"Gah! Stop, please!" he pleaded as his breath caught in his chest from the pain. He knew this was not necessary, she already had full control of his body. He could feel her between his teeth and the fascia of his joints puppeting his usless body.

"I said quiet!" she hissed, pushing his arm behind further, threatening to tear his shoulder out of the socket. He was panting and crying from the blinding shocks of venom ripping through his ruined body. The terror of realizing he was at the end of the road washed over him like a storm. Arianna's threads of shadow pulled him further into his head. It felt like his mind was being pulled apart and his psyche was struggling not to self-destruct. He could barely keep his eyes open against a strangely asphyxiating void. The air in his chest felt like he was gagging on chimney smoke.

Arianna pushed him through the pitch-dark mansion, down a corridor on the first floor he'd not gone into before. He could feel bile building up in his throat as tears and blood fell from his face.

"Cam~er~on," she called with a singsong gloat as she dragged Montague into the drafty atrium, "I told you your *cagnolino* would try to run off, did I not?"

The room was far more akin to a forlorn greenhouse than a normal sunroom or atrium. The plants inside were no better kept than any of the exterior and yet seemed even more furiously overgrown and excessively sprawling. Most of the non-windowed walls were engulfed with cancerous ivy that climbed up and out of a shattered glass windowpane in the ceiling. Every potted plant was gnarled and sprawling, some even taking root through their pots and into the floorboards, worming down into the disrupted earth under the mansion. Sat in the center of the room was a little fountain with another awful, larger-than-life cherub sculpture. Water barely spurted out of its clogged mouth into the pool below.

Cameron sat at the edge of the fountain. To Monty's horror, he now could see that their face had been caged in a silver muzzle. Though most of their skin was covered by a long black dress, there were still visible rapidly healing bruises around their neck. Terror spread wide across their face as they looked up from the water of the fountain.

"Monty!?" they gasped.

"I caught your *cagnolino* sneaking about in the woods," Arianna pulled Montague's arm, forcing him closer to her body with a whimper of pain, "or perhaps plotting something, hmm?" She hummed. Her voice ripped through his body like the zing of electrocution.

"I was trying to get cell service!" His voice quivered no less than his knees. He could barely see the dark atrium past the light blooming in his eyes. Most of his energy was being spent on resisting the urge to scream from whatever Arianna was doing to his sanity.

"Let him go!" Cameron demanded. Arianna shook her head and pulled out one of the crudely whittled stakes from Monty's pocket and waved it tauntingly.

"I don't suppose you need these to use the telephone?" Arianna jeered, her voice coming from inside the folds of his brain. Cameron's face somehow managed to lose more color as they eyed the piece of wood.

"I told you he would try something like this if you let him roam free. Your little *cane* has been plotting to *kill* us!" she hissed. Monty tried to get out of her grasp, pulling against everything in his body and soul. Despite his best effort, he couldn't fight against her, his entire body feeling as if it was spreading with hot paralyzing fire. His ears rang loudly, and head began to spin, the floor slipping out from underneath his feet. He couldn't breathe.

"I said, let him go!" Cameron's voice roared over the high-pitched din in his head.

Very suddenly Monty felt himself collide with the dirty atrium floor in a daze, his vision blurry, but coming back to him. He drew air back into his overtaxed lungs as he tried to scramble back a bit into the overgrown potted plants. His body still felt heavy, tied down to the floorboard by threads of shadow. Cameron was standing between him and their aunt, shaking. Their fangs were bared underneath the silver bars of their muzzle, and their eyes were blazing a scalding red.

"You bastard child, *sangu misto*, why are you defending him!? Your pet is plotting to kill us!?" Arianna barked, her features beginning to contort with anger.

"I am the one who told him to arm himself," Cameron's voice faltered, shaking with barely restrained fury.

"Have you *impazzito!? Pazzo!? Folle!?* Gone completely out of your mind!?" Arianna spat in disbelief. The little color she'd had in her greenish-pale skin had fully drained. Her face then twisted with rage. They both truly looked like the monsters they were, all their subterfuge of beauty now dissipated by unmasked hatred.

"I'm tired of you treating me like this. I'm not some stupid child like you think I am. I knew you'd try to kill him the second you could justify it." Cameron approached her slowly.

"Oh please, do you hear yourself? Do you really think a splinter of wood in the hands of a little human would do much of anything?" Arianna scoffed. "You've half killed him already, boy. I don't understand why you suddenly care so much about his life now."

"Shut up!" Cameron barked. Arianna raised her hand to hit them, but they were faster, gripping her wrist and throwing her down. She turned to mist before hitting the ground and re-materialized in front of them. She hooked the golden serpent hilt of her sword-cane in their muzzle and pulled them to their knees.

"*Marmocchio!*" Arianna spat. "You cannot hurt me. I am your blood mother, your sire. The blood that flows in your veins is *mine!* Now and forever! You may be a strong fledgling, but you are still *mine.* Have you not learned anything tonight!?" Cameron's gaze snapped up to her, their enter body freezing.

"You were given a gift, and this is how you treat me? I gave everything to make you better and stronger than your forebears, and all I get in return is insubordination! What a mistake it was to create my masterpiece from that girl's ungrateful bastard!" She continued. Cameron tilted their head the way they did when pieces of the puzzle finally started to click.

"You…" their voice was soft, "there really never was a plan to find a cure… My mother was telling the truth. You didn't save me… you *used* me."

"Finally, you prove you're not as dull as you act. Oh, don't look so shocked. Why would Maria lie to you? You know she hoped you'd side with her. That's why I had to get rid of her in the end. I truly expected better from you. After all, you did the job for me so beautifully. You killed your mother of your own free will after all," she gloated. It was clear to Monty, who had been silently witnessing this interaction from the shadows, that she was taking some sort of perverted joy in the way her words made Cameron writhe.

"You… told me to kill her, but it's you who I should have killed that night," Cameron's voice was frighteningly calm. In one fluid motion, they grabbed the discarded stake from the floor and lunged at their aunt. Before they had even closed half the distance, Arianna's body broke apart into a plume of smoke. Without seeming to exert any energy, she hooked her cane around their midsection and tore them down to the ground, sending the little splinter of wood flying into the overgrown plants.

"Murder is all you know! You truly are nothing more than a bloodthirsty beast!" she hissed. From the floor, Cameron transformed in a breath of dark vapor into a huge, mangy coyote.

Their muzzle speed into the bars of the silver cage strapped to them. The smell of burning hair and flesh filled the air as the grate dug into their gnashing maw.

"Of cores I am, look at the one who sired me!" Cameron retorted. They made a move to lunge at her, but she was far faster, causing them to clumsily collide with the rotting floor. With one clawed hand, Arianna gripped the scruff of Cameron's mangy neck. They hung limp like a puppy as she effortlessly tossed them into the fountain. There was a wet snapping sound, and they let out a yowl of pain.

"Yet you are weak and distracted. You should be able to tear me asunder! But look at you. You are nothing more than a pathetic *bambino*. Your deference to your plaything has crippled you. I will not have you squandering our powers anymore!"

Her attention turned to Monty, who was trying to scramble further into the foliage for cover. Her glistening red eyes caused him to freeze. He physically felt his mind stop, his body being pulled down by hundreds of monstrous hands. Monty knew exactly what the look in her hungry eyes meant.

As she lurched at him, Cameron leapt from the fountain and threw themself on top of Monty. They were limping, with their back leg lifted and twisted oddly.

"Don't you dare touch him!" they growled.

"You are both feral animals! You need to start behaving, boy, or I will have to put you both down!" Arianna snapped.

"Shut up! Get away from us!" they snarled. "I'm done listening to your bullshit! I was a fool to think you were trying to remedy my mother's mistakes. Get away from me before prove to you just how much of a monster I've become!"

"Get out of my way! If you do not move and let me dispose of this vile creature you've brought in, I'll unmake you with him!" Arianna drew her sword.

"Do it! Run me through like you've been threatening to all night! Beat me to a pulp like you love to do," Cameron snarled and lowered their body to better protect Monty. "You'll have to render me ash before I let you lay another finger on him!"

"What a waste of blood you are!" Arianna raised her sword high and froze as the call of a house sparrow interrupted her snarling.

There was the slightest light-blue hint of daylight coming through the atrium windows. The sky was washed with the faintest hue of sunrise approaching. Arianna looked up through the shattered skylight of the greenhouse at the dissipating stairs overhead.

"You are lucky to have been given this gift in the way you have, child. You will never know fear of the sun. One day you will thank me for what I have done for you. I hope you grow out of this phase soon. You exhaust me," she said.

Without another word, Arianna disappeared in a cloud of black smog. The oppressive insanity that had been battering Monty's mind vanished as fast as she did.

# CHAPTER TWENTY-SEVEN

THE calm early morning air was punctuated by the faint song of bird calls and the weak burble of the greenhouse fountain. Cameron transformed back into their humanoid form. Their arms shook, and they collapsed onto Monty with a pained groan.

"Sorry," they mumbled and rolled off him to lay on the dirty floor. He let out a sore grunt as he finally moved his body up to sit.

"S' okay, thanks for not letting me get obliterated," Monty coughed. The burning sensation from his neck spread like fire through the whole of his chest, making his lungs hurt like he'd been coughing on chimney smoke. Cameron forced themself to sit up next to him. There was an audible snapping sound as their leg straightened back into its correct position. Arianna had been rough enough to break bone in the struggle without seeming to break a sweat herself.

"Are you okay?" they asked as they rubbed their calf.

"I'll be fine," Monty grunted, unsure of that fact, "you?"

"I don't know," Cameron mumbled, looking very tired and small. Monty looked out the glass of the atrium at the slowly growing morning light.

*So much for getting a stake into Arianna at sunrise.*

"I wasn't expecting her to be so scared of the sun," Monty remarked as he watched the sky turn from a blue night to a greenish yellow.

"I've seen her up during the day... but never out in actual sunlight. I imagine her weakness is far worse than mine. I think she might actually burn in the sun."

"It would make things a lot easier if all we have to do is force her to go for a morning walk," Monty groaned sarcastically. He had seen Cameron in many states of awful, but they looked far more miserable than he could have fathomed.

"My mother was telling the truth the whole time," they whispered quietly, they were running a thumb over the engraving on their golden locket. "The entire time, she never lied... even through all that horrible torment... but why?" They looked on the edge of tears. Monty was unsure what to say.

"I know you feel bad about the whole... you know," he sighed and gesticulated vaguely, "but genuinely, she never *had* to do any of this to you."

"I hated her so much for it all. I don't think my anger was completely misplaced, but I venerate Arianna like she was a saint. She deserves more of that anger. I suppose she will get it now," they said.

"I hope you don't take this the wrong way, Cam, but while I get killing the people who have hurt you, don't you worry about the consequence at all? Like legally?" Monty asked, shifting slightly.

"Why would I care? Unless they knew to make handcuff out of silver, I could just vanish. Human laws mean nothing when you can outlive everyone involved."

"Touché."

"Money helps too. Most humans will look the other way with a wad of cash in hand," Cameron pointed out.

"Right..." Monty said, remembering how he got himself into this mess in the first place.

"Just because I can get away with it doesn't mean I don't feel remorse," they added, noticing his visibly uncomfortable expression.

"I mean, if I could have cracked my old man's skull and known the only thing I'd have to live with after was the guilt... well, I would have done it."

"I can always return the favor for helping me kill my aunt."

"Cam!"

"Sorry, I'm joking," they lied, holding their hands up in defense. Their expression darkened again with a deep sigh.

"You know, I often wonder if my father had suck around, if things would have played out this way. I wish I knew anything about the kind of man he was. All I know is he had to have had the most annoying hair in the world," they pulled on a wild golden lock with a frustrated cry-laugh.

"I-I always assumed that my life was not much more than a lab rat's... now I realize it's more like I've been punished for the simple crime of being born!" Their face twisted into violent tears.

"Oh, Cam." Monty's chest felt tight watching them cry. They pulled him into a tight hug as they sobbed, the cold metal of the muzzle digging into his tired flesh. He wrapped his arms around them and held them tightly, running his hand to smooth over their hair.

"I'm so tired of this," they hiccuped through tears, "I want to be rid of this curse!"

"Here, why don't we start with ridding you of this," Monty said, moving to take the muzzle off. Cameron pulled away quickly.

"No!" Their eyes were red with tears, but there was also a palpable fear on their face.

"What?"

"No, just... let me keep it on for your sake," they said, hand hovering over the claps. "I don't want to hurt you any more than I already have. I don't know if you have looked in the mirror, but you are not well. I hurt you horribly. I am still sorry for it."

"Are you serious? I don't feel great, but I'm alive, and I know you're not a monster. I can tell this hurts you. Let me take it off."

"Please, Monty, you might trust me, but I don't, not right now," they doubled down. Monty sighed.

"Okay… still, why does this burn when you touch it but my hamsa doesn't?"

"This is pure silver, the cager and clasps at least. I imagine your necklace must be an alloy, sterling? Speaking of, where is your necklace?"

"I think it's still in your room."

"You should have it. Maybe it doesn't do much of anything, I don't know, but we need every bit of protection we can get at this point," they said softly.

"Oh, it helps! I'm sure of it after this encounter. I felt like my brain was being flayed by whatever weird mind control your aunt was trying to use on me," he shuddered. The sensation of shadowiness in his gray matter lingered. It felt like Arianna had been trying to break him from the inside.

"Then all the more reason to wear it," Cameron nodded solemnly.

The both of them were quiet for a bit as they watched the sun come up through the dingy windows of the greenhouse. The blues of night slowly blossomed into verdant greens and the mesmerizing wash of burgundy clouds.

"So, what's our plan here?" Monty asked once he could see the sun peeking up in the sky.

"We end this bloodline for good," they said firmly, more so to themself than Monty, "we stake her while she's resting. Then we cut her head off and burn what remains in the fireplace… And then when that's all done, you do the same to me."

"What!? Cam, no I'm not killing you!" Monty balked.

"This bloodline has to end. That includes me," they reiterated firmly. "Even if there was a way for me to live without causing insurmountable death and pain to my fellow man, this clan is clearly cursed," they got very quiet, their eyes were wet with tears. "Please, I don't want to haunt this world for eternity in this soulless half-life."

"Cam, you can't ask that of me. I barely have the stones to end Arianna. You can't seriously ask me to kill someone I care so much about."

Cameron wiped some of the tears from their face.

"There's a world beyond this house, one you can live in without fear. Also, like you won't be alone, not for a good while. I'm not gonna to just drop you the moment things are safe. Let's burn this place down and go somewhere far as hell away?" he pleaded with them. He saw them thinking, though tears obscured their expression.

"I'm pretty embroiled in a murder or two now, so it would probably be in my best interest to go missing after all this," he half joked. Then, more sternly, he added, "I want to stay with you and explore the world beyond this stupid little town... with you."

"You're serious?"

"Dead serious," he said. Cameron laughed through their tears.

# CHAPTER TWENTY-EIGHT

MONTAGUE found his necklace on the end table in Cameron's room. It felt a bit unpleasant rubbing against his bandages around his neck. In that moment he caught his reflection in Cameron's huge semi-shattered mirror. He looked utterly wrecked, sporting a swollen, crooked nose that still had the remnants of a nosebleed, and deep circles below his dark eyes. He could see that some blood had started to soak through the gauze on his neck. He wondered how long he could weather this wound before he needed real medical attention. He would have to worry about infection later.

"I don't know if I could take a head off with this," Cameron brandished their golden fencing saber, "but it won't hurt to have." The glint of the blade sparked a memory in Monty's mind.

"No, that super won't do the job," he said, making his way out to the balcony.

"Where are you going?" Cameron asked, bewildered. The cool morning air hit Monty in the face as he stepped out onto the balcony. The sky was already blazing with daytime sunlight. He took a deep breath of morning air, the smell of dew still strong on the wind. The breeze rustled his hair as he found the end of the rope he'd slung up the night prior.

"This could probably do the trick," he said to himself as he pulled the scythe up onto the balcony. Cameron's lavender eyes went wide as they scanned over the blade.

"There had to have been an easier way to bring that inside," they shook their head.

"This house is huge. Doing this saved me valuable time last night," Monty shrugged. He took a good long look at Cameron standing there in their bedroom. They looked like part of the old home, beautiful and ornate, but ultimately left to fall apart in the absence of care.

"Are you sure you wanna do this?" Monty asked, detangling the rope from the handle of his gardening tool.

"No, I'm not sure, but I don't know what else to do. I don't think anyone will be free until my aunt is gone. I think... we need to get rid of this whole place, to be honest. What's been done here cannot be undone. Do you understand what I mean?" they said as they pondered the ceiling.

"I'm just your accessory to murder at this point, Cam." Monty jokingly pat them on the shoulder. Then, more seriously, he added, "I don't need to fully understand. Sure, I'm not stoked about all this, but I'm trusting you and your judgment."

"Thank you," they mumbled. His hand wandered up from their shoulder to brush the strap across their face. His eyes lingered on their caged mouth.

"I really wish you'd take this off, just so I could kiss you," he hummed, fidgeting with one of the silver buckles.

"I'm sorry," they said softly. "I don't think you could take any more of my venom, not without serious consequence. I'm scared to just nick you with a fang right now."

"When this awfulness is done, can you promise me at least one kiss?"

"When this is over, and you are healed, I will promise you much more," they said with starry eyes, leaning into Monty's touch.

"Then let's go kill your sire, shall we?" he grinned, breaking away from them and hoisting the scythe over his good side. He double-checked his pocket and, sure enough, a roughly whittled stake was still in there.

They walked out into the hallway. It was uncomfortably quiet and gloomy in the dusty bowels of the mansion. The light pouring in from the huge stained glass that backlit the steps was tinged with streaks of gold and red. Monty's mind was running through exactly how he was going to get this stake through Arianna's heart.

Cameron held up a hand, a profound look of confusion strewn across their face.

"*Che cosa?* Do you hear that?" they asked in a hushed tone.

"Hear what?" he asked curiously, straining his ears. It took him a moment, but the sound finally registered. He heard the unmistakable rumble of a motorcycle. All the remaining blood drained from his body.

"Fuck, Mina!" he exclaimed under his breath.

"Mina!? Your friend?" They also look panicked, their eyes darting over their shoulder down the hall in the direction of presumably Arianna's room.

"Oh no, oh no," Monty shook his head. His mind was racing what the best course of action even was. He heard the bike pull up to the front and the engine kick off.

"Why on earth is she here? She's in serious danger," Cameron looked wide-eyed at him. "Did you tell her about—does she *know*?"

"No! I didn't get to tell her anything useful. I tried to talk to her last night, but I couldn't explain. She insisted on coming here to bring me home, and then she hung up on me. I have no idea if she will believe us if we tell her the truth," he explained, running a hand through his hair wildly.

There was a firm knock on the front door.

"Monty!" Mina's voice called through the front as her fist pounded on the wood, the brass knuckles of her motorbike gloves echoing through the dark house. Cameron and Monty stared at each other, neither sure what to do. Another knock, a bit more forceful this time.

"Montague!"

"She's going to draw out my aunt, if she hasn't already. At least try to tell her to get out of here!" Cameron finally whispered frantically, beginning to descend the steps. Monty ran down past them and yanked open one of the huge oak doors. Mina practically punched him in the gut as he slipped outside.

"Holy crap! There you are, Christ, you look horrible! What happened to your neck, and why are you carrying a scythe!? I've been trying to call you nonstop and getting nothing but voicemail!" She bombarded him with questions, her baby-pink motorcycle helmet under one arm. To his shock, she had her father's hunting rifle strapped to her back.

"Mina, what are you doing here!? I told you not to come up," he pressed in a hushed tone. He tried to gently push the smaller woman backwards off the porch.

"Get off me," she wriggled out of his grasp. "I told you, dude, I was coming to get you in the morning!" she reminded him.

"Mina, you have to leave! I can explain later, but you really gotta get the hell out of here, like right now! You're in danger!"

"Danger? I knew something sketchy was going on here. If I'm in danger, that means you are too, and I'm not leaving you to get your ass killed, man!" She hunger her helmet on the railing post and removed the rifle from her back. She then forced her way past him and into the house. Cameron looked stupefied as she entered.

"There you are! What did you *do* to him? Huh? Holding my best friend hostage or something!? It looks like you've drained the life out of the man. You've driven him completely crazy!" Mina spat as she advanced on Cameron. She pointed the gun at them, but her fingers were far from the trigger. They put their free hand up and backed away from her. Monty grabbed her by the back of her pink motorcycle jacket.

"Mina, don't!" he pleaded.

"Why not? They've clearly hurt you!? You're fucking covered in bloody bandages and your face is half smashed in, Monty," she added, trying to wriggle out of his grasp.

"I-I—please, keep your voice down," Cameron stammered.

"Why should I? And what's with the sword? Why do you have a goddamn muzzle on? What's *wrong* with you!?" Mina interrogated Cameron.

"Mina, there is a lot going on right now. Please, you gotta get out of here. It's not safe, and Cam is *not* who you need to be worried about," Monty pleaded.

"What do you mean?" She asked, lowering the aim of the gun slightly.

"Monty, just tell her the truth," Cameron sighed.

"Mina, I'm gonna need you to get really open-minded for five seconds. Like way more than you have been with what I've told you."

"Alright, fine, I'm suspending my disbelief," she said, lowering her gun fully, still visibly on edge. Monty let go of her jacket.

"Cameron is a vampire."

You could hear a pin drop. She slowly turned to Monty, a bizarre look of giddy disbelief on her round face.

"What?" She spoke softly. "You're joking. You mean like Blade? Dracula 'I vant to suck your blood' vampire or... is that some kind of innuendo?"

Cameron opened their mouth as wide as they could in their muzzle and showed her their fangs. Her dark eyes widened.

"No, no joke, or innuendo," they said nervously.

"No fucking way, you're serious!? Is that why you've got the—?" She motioned to her lower face.

Neither one knew how to respond to her. Her eyes flicked to the bloodied bandages on Monty's neck. "Wait, they didn't—"

"No," he and Cameron both responded in unison. Mina let out a sigh of relief.

"Okay so, what happed to this place being haunted? Or was I

right about the carbon monoxide leak?" Mina asked.

"Oh, it's still haunted. Dr. Giovanni's spirit never left the property. Cam can back me up on that," Monty clarified. Cameron looked ill at the mere mention of their mother.

"This is true," they nodded.

"Holy shit," Mina said softly to herself. He could very much tell she was trying to process this new and very strange information.

"Wait, so, *shit,* Leah was actually right about what happened to Dr. Giovanni?" There was a rattling in the dusty crystals of the chandelier overhead.

"Yes, but you need to understand it was, um, would you say, self defenses?" Monty's uncertainty was very audible as he looked to Cameron with a slight grimace.

"We can call it what it was. I killed my mother as an act of vengeance," Cameron admitted, looking down at their saber, "you can think what you want—"

"But you trust me, right? When I say it was warranted, that woman made my dad look like a saint," Monty interrupted. He could see there was an understanding behind Mina's eyes.

"Cool, cool, cool," Mina nodded, anxiety palpable on her round face. "Ghosts *and* vampires, great. So then if Cameron is not the one I should be worried about... what kind of exorcism were you two planning with those tools?" Mina tried to gain clarification.

"No, so, you see, the thing is that Cameron's not the only vampire here. Their sire has been keeping me here like a caged animal... amongst other things. Right before you showed up, we were getting ready to... *handle* the situation," Monty explained, waving his unruly gardening tool for emphasis.

"So I wasn't wrong when I said some Blade shit," she joked, "you guys were seriously about to go vampire hunting."

"It's a little late now, but this is what I've been trying to explain. Honestly, at this point, you are probably going to have to join us. Unless you leave like, *right now,*" Monty added.

"Well, I'm here now. I was hoping I didn't have to actually use this thing, but I have a whole box worth of buckshot in my pockets," Mina patted her jacket, "and I'll tell you it's not pleasant to ride with your leather packed with live rounds."

"I'm glad you planned ahead because I think we're going to—"

Monty's words were cut off by the front door slammed shut.

Faster than perceptibly possible, Arianna had materialized from thin air. She swiftly grabbed Mina, pressing the sheathed body of her sword-cane against the smaller woman's throat, choking her. Mina's rifle slipped from her leather-clad hands as she struggled again the vampire's grasp. In the same instant, Cameron drew their sword to Arianna's neck. Likewise, Monty attempted to take some kind of threatening stance, scythe held out in front of himself clumsily.

*This was not the best weapon choice…*

"Gah! What the—" Mina protested as Arianna wrangled her, forcing her jaw upwards and exposing her heavily tattooed neck.

"*In nome di dio, cosa sta succedendo qui!?* Who is this *ragazzina?*" Arianna hissed with venom. She eyed Mina's ink-covered throat with a look of disgust.

"Let her go… NOW!" Cameron demanded.

"*Zittire!* Are you trying to build a zoo here!? Is one pet not enough for you?" Arianna spat. There were waves of malicious dark smog emanating from her long black locks. She was not putting much effort into looking whole or human.

"You hurt her, and I will make you regret not killing me when you had the chance," Monty growled, moving closer and trying to see if it was possible to swing at her without hitting Mina. Arianna let out a ringing laugh.

"Oh please, are you going to slice me up with your gardening tools, *cucciolo?*" She laughed and addressed Cameron, ignoring the tip of their sword at her throat. "Really, you pretend I'm so stupid to not know what you beast are up to? Why should I not I drain the life from both of your pets this very second?" She bared her fangs against Mina's neck.

"I have people waiting for me. They know where I am! And! And the police—*detectives*—are coming for me if I'm not back by noon! The people in this town *know* what goes on here! You might have paid off the police once, but you really think they will keep putting up with this nonsense?" Mina was resisting whatever the vampire was trying to do to her, managing to talk a mile a minute.

"You expect me to believe you, *ragazzina?* They won't find you or your stupid *motocicletta* if they do! How are you this resistant!? *Inginocchiarsi! Sottomettiti! Silencio!*" Arianna hissed, pulling Mina by her ponytail as she struggled. She licked a line up across Mina's jugular, causing her to shudder. Cameron pressed their saber into the skin at their aunt's throat.

The heavy crystal chandelier overhead rattled as though there'd been an earthquake.

"I'll slit your throat before you can even swallow a drop of her blood," they warned with a dangerous growl. Arianna furiously threw Mina down and spun to strike Cameron in their stomach, causing them to back away from her and lose their posture. Mina stumbled and dusted herself off and snatched her rifle off the ground.

"Only so many people can go missing before it's a real problem," Mina added with a venomous expression, cocking her rifle.

"*Proprio come pensavo, cazzo!* I should kill all three of you animals!"

"I'm just here to get Monty," Mina said firmly, "you let me leave here with him, and no one ever has to come up here again, and then you can just keep chucking bodies in the woods, or whatever, and hope nobody notices."

"Oh, I don't think you will be leaving here," Arianna scoffed. "Now, Cameron, behave for once in your *pitiful* life and help me clean up your mess!"

With an audible crack, the massive old chandelier that loomed above them snapped loose from its rusted chain. Monty reflexively grabbed Mina and pulled her out harm's way before it landed right where they'd all been standing, shattering in an impressive explosion of glass shards on the floor below.

The room was deathly silent.

Monty felt blood trickling down his face as he lay panting on the floor. He'd been nicked across his brow by a flying shard of glass. Arianna was standing stupefied just inches away from the chandelier. Its steel centerpiece should have landed squarely on her head, but she'd been faster than it. Cameron had fallen back on the steps, the hem of their skirt shredded by shattered glass. Mina groaned and rolled over.

*Do it!*

Dr. Giovanni's voice whispered through the air, lingering on the still settling glass.

*Kill her!*

Monty wasted no time in pulling the wooden stake from his pocket. His muscles sprang into action as he lunged up from the floor and rushed Arianna. He was blind to his body's motions as his adrenaline spiked. With all his force, he shoved the piece of wood deep through the vampire's chest. It miraculously pierced her flesh with just his brute strength, sallow skin parting to ooze tar-like blood. Her face shifted from shock to mild amusement as he released the stake and stumbled back. He was shocked she appeared utterly unaffected.

"You still really think a little splinter can hurt me, *cucciolo*?" She laughed in his face. Moving imperceptibly fast, she drew her sword from its sheath and sliced right across Monty's abdomen.

"MONTY!" Cameron shrieked. Blood bloomed from his wound faster than he could feel the searing pain of steel cutting through meat. Arianna moved to strike again.

In one fluid motion, Mina lined up her shot and pulled the trigger. With a thunderous crack of gunfire, Arianna's face was blown clean off in a messy spray of buckshot, splatting the curling wallpaper behind her. Gore misted Monty in the face, causing a nauseating sensation to rise up in his stomach as he groaned and fell to his knees. He could feel hot blood soaking his shirt as he gripped the gash in his stomach. He felt a copper tang and sting of bile in the back of his throat.

Arianna was still for a moment, as bits of her brain and bone slid down the wallpaper and sizzled into nothing. Dark smoke rose from her torn flesh as muscle instantaneously began to knit itself back together over her exposed skull. White bones and teeth restored, sinewy and tar-tinged muscle tissue flourisher across her face, and her eye bloomed like a violet back into its socket. She was laughing low and bitterly. She pulled the stake from her breast and threw it into the mess of shattered glass.

"How rude!" Her voice rose from the smoke pouring from her reconstructing throat. Though she was trembling, Mina pulled another round of ammunition from her baby-pink leathers and begin to reload the rifle.

Still recomposing herself, Arianna made to lunge at Mina. Cameron's saber parried the healing vampire's own just inches from Mina's throat. They slid between their aunt and the two humans. They were trembling. Their eyes had gone a horrible color, more crimson than the blood soaking Monty's shirt.

"I will make you regret every century you have walked this earth," Cameron snarled through their silver cage.

"Are we playing games this morning?" Arianna taunted, skin now stretching over the fat of her cheek.

"Fuck you," Cameron barked, taking a wild swing at her. They backed her up away from the other two with frightening speed. Arianna was able to parry them with ease. As the remainder of her face reformed to something recognizable, it was clear she was shocked by her charge's ferocity.

The mettle of their sabers rattled through the foyer as Cameron forced her to retreat up the steps. Their swords clattered and glinted with inhuman speed, slicing and praying with ringing force that echoed through the entire manor. It was impossible to tell who'd move next, or how. Cameron was faster than her, managing to nick her a few times, and having no issues parrying her odd-handed attacks. They tore an impressive slice through her thigh as they reached the second-story landing. She let out a shrieking gasp.

*"Piccolo bastardo ingrato, ne ho avuto abbastanza!"* she shouted and without warning grabbed Cameron by the muzzle. Her hand sizzled, the smell of burning flesh filling the hall. Cameron lost their balance and dropped their saber, sending it tumbling down the steps. She ignored her cooking skin and proceeded to pull her double-sided blade against their neck, digging it in under their jaw. She released the muzzle and with her now charred hand, gripped the end of her sword and pulled it deeper into Cameron's thin neck.

Despite the growing pain in his body, Monty snatched his scythe up from the pile of shattered glass. Adrenaline numbed his pain as he sprinted up the stairs, ignoring his throbbing heart and the cold sensation growing in his stomach.

"You are nothing more than a failed experiment!" Arianna hissed into Cameron's ear as she proceeded to cut through their throat.

"A messy!" She yanked on her blade against their skin.

"Useless!" She pulled harder, blood pouring from them.

"Failure!" She'd nearly sliced through the majority of their throat.

"Just like your mother!"

Before she could pull her blade all the way through their neck and fully decapitate them, Monty hooked the scythe around her grip on the sword handle. With one swift motion, and as much force as he could muster, he cut her hand clean off. She let out a horrible scream as her sword flew back against the window, sending cracks through the glass panels of the serpentine family crest.

Before any meaningful amount of Arianna's blood had made it to the dusty carpet, her body broke apart into a cloud of thick black fog. A nexus of dark energy and pure malice erupted from the very spot she stood. Flesh and bone rose from the storm as tendrils of night reformed into the body of a massive, horrible wyrm. Golden scales shimmered across her towering serpentine form as the darkness congealed into a beast. She opened her maw to flex her venoms laded fangs with a great murderous hiss.

Freed from her grasp, Cameron gripped their neck, choking and sputtering on their own blood as the wound healed in a hiss of smoke. They were trembling as their esophagus and vocal cords struggled to come back together.

Another splatter of buckshot flew over their heads from Mina at the bottom of the steps. The metal pellets tore some golden scales from Arianna's body, black tar oozing from where they'd been ripped off. With the sound of pure demonic rage, Arianna whipped her tail around and thrashed those nearest to her. Cameron was sent back, colliding against the railing. Monty fell back, cracking his skull against the hardwood so severely he was blinded by stars.

"I should have known you were trouble the moment I met you, *cucciolo*! You have been nothing but a horrible influence. I should have known you were one of my little sister's pawns. How dare you turn my own blood against me, you *fitly animal*!" Arianna's voice boomed from her monstrous form.

Familiar gloom grew around Monty as shadow attempted to stitch him to the floor. Arianna grew increasingly frustrated as dark tangles of shadow tried to worm their way into his mind with little effect. He fought tooth and nail to free his body, ignoring the cacophonous force of *submit, submit, submit* pounding at the very back of his psyche. He felt like a struggling fly in a web in the most literal sense, his limbs feeling physically stuck in dark malicious threads.

She reared to strike him, fangs flared. Terror flooded his aching body as he braced for a deathblow. Time slowed to a crawl.

He saw Cameron's gleaming eyes filled with an unknowable fear and hatred. Their face was twisted in an expression of pure animalistic rage, their growls a gurgle of blood from their slit throat. They swung the scythe around the serpent. Sharpened blade collide with scales as Cameron mustered the full extent of their will, pulling Arianna back from Monty. The serpent was met with another crack of the shotgun. This time the shot shattered through one of her pale amethyst eyes in a spray of tar.

Monty fought through the pain ripping through him and rolled away towards the massive stained-glass window. His eyes caught golden light shining off the brass handle of Arianna's sword lying on the ground. He felt a chill fill his enter body. A buzzing sound and the smell of sweet rot overtook his senses. Crouched next to the blade, spectating the scene before her, sat Dr. Giovanni. Her visage was rotten beyond human recognition, and yet through blackened skin and shining bone, maggot and meat, Monty knew her. Her honey-amber eyes turned to him. She appeared more real to him now, as he felt himself slipping past the veil of life. The pain in his abdomen and the smell of his own blood in the air told him there was not much time left. He was desperate; he could feel his strength failing.

"Help," he choked out, "please help me end this."

She reached out a rot-whittled hand to him. He hesitantly grasped it with a strange understanding, like the feeling of being aware he was falling asleep. In that moment, she and Monty became one, her spectral form possessing his flesh. The sensation of decaying death from Dr. Giovanni's embrace was so overwhelming he could have gone mad in that moment.

*You know what to do.*

Her voice was calm in his ears, defining him to the world around him. He could feel her hands on his as she willed him to pick up the snake-handled sword by its blade. He ignored the cutting sensation in his palms as he swung the heavy brass handle against the window with the might of three men. The huge stained-glass windows shattered spectacularly in a rain of ruby and citrine shards.

At the same time, Cameron swung the scythe wildly, and with one final slice, they cut the serpent's head clean off, showering everything in a wash of shadow and viscous rotten blood.

As the severed head of the serpent hit the floor, a blinding burst of direct sunlight flooded the mansion. With an ear shatter shriek, Arianna's segmented body withered wildly as she blistered, boiled, and burned up in the morning light. An explosion of dark energy came from her corps. Each dark tendril burned up in the sun like tissue paper in a campfire. Searing horror shot through every fiber of the mansion with the vampire's death, like lightning burning through power lines. Her body was rendered to nothing more than fine ash and a scattering of gold jewelry on the carpet.

With a strange sense of satisfaction, Monty felt the writhing coldness in his body dissipate, and with it, the remainder of his strength. He dropped the sword from his mangled palms and clutched his abdomen, his shirt hot and sticky with his blood. He spat pure metallic copper into what had been Arianna Giovanni, and crumbled before the still smoldering pile of ash.

# CHAPTER TWENTY-NINE

COPPER! Everything tasted horribly like copper. Monty's eyes fluttered open. His head was resting in Cameron's blood-soaked lap. Their shaking hands were brushing his shaggy hair away from his face.

"Hey, stay with me, please," their voice shuddered. He could see Mina crouched nearby, covered in gunpowder and bloodstains.

"There you are! Shit, man, that does not look good. I'm going to call an ambulance!" She fumbled in her pocket and pulled out her cellphone, unused shotgun shells spilling out with it. Cameron shook their head.

"You're not going to get through. There's no service here. But Mina, I'm not sure he's going to make it that long," they explained with a level of chilling calm.

"H-hey, I'm not dead yet," Monty choked out. Talking hurt far more than he expected. He tried to gather his thoughts, the faces of those around him fading in and out. His heart was rushing in a feeble attempt to keep going, his pulse weakening with each beat. He felt lightheaded and strangely giddy.

"No, and you're not going to die either," Mina reaffirmed. She turned her attention to Cameron. "I have my bike here. I'm going to go get help. Can I trust you to keep him alive?"

"I can try, but he's already lost so much blood. It might be… too late by the time you get back," Cameron replied honestly.

Monty knew it too, he could feel it coming, death loomed over him, heavy and oddly freeing. He drew another ragged breath in, savoring the morning air as much as he could before the scythe of the reaper came down on him to ferry him off to oblivion.

"You're not gonna just let him die?" Mina shouted through tears.

"There's one thing I can think to do, but… I don't know if it would even work," they said, looking down at Monty.

"You mean turn me?" he asked, his mind racing at the sudden prospect of cheating the inevitable.

"Yes, but I don't know if I could go through with something like that. I—"

"I want you to. Please, don't let me die," Monty interrupted them. He didn't have time to grapple with consequence in his current state. All he saw was one last opportunity.

*"Some consider this a blessing."*

Cameron's words replayed in his head, and now he understood why someone would willingly choose undeath over the end. For him, it would be worth it, to have more time to live the life he hadn't.

"Let's not get hasty, yeah? I'll be back so fast you won't even realize I left. And then we'll get some real help," Mina gripped one of Monty's ruined hands.

"What if it's the only option?" he asked feebly, knowing he was standing very precariously at this precipice.

"It won't be," she said with tears in her eyes.

"I'm dying, I know I am, you know I am," he coughed again, letting out a groan of agony, practically gagging on his own blood. Cameron smoothed more of his hair away from his sweat-soaked face.

"It's a real possibility. If I don't attempt a turn soon, it will be too late," they said, placing their hands against his pulse. "I will do this if it's what you really want Monty, but you have to understand there's a chance it won't work and you will..." they had to choke back their tears, their calm facade beginning to crack like a porcelain mask. "You might still die."

"Then so be it," Monty sighed, closing his eyes.

"I'm not going to waste any more time," Mina said. "You keep him alive as long as possible." Cameron nodded, tears leaving clean streaks on their grime-covered face.

"You shouldn't come back here if I have to do it. I can't keep you or anyone else safe from a newborn's hunger. In this state, after losing so much of his own blood, I won't be able to stop him if instinct takes over. Do you understand?" Cameron explained to Mina. She was deathly quiet for a moment. She was clearly weighing something in her mind before responding.

"How will I know it's not safe to come back?"

"We still have to burn this place to the ground," Monty murmured into Cameron's lap.

"Right... If you see a blaze, it's too late. You won't find us here. You should report Monty missing... let them think I killed him too. There's been too many deaths on this property. Too many of them are my fault. We need to lie low. Maybe, just maybe, people will think I've died too," they told her. There were tears streaming down Mina's flushed face. She knew she wasn't coming back.

"Man, I told you, Monty, this is how you get disappeared," she joked with a tearful laugh.

"Once again, you're right." Monty's laugh turned to a choking, copper-tinged cough. "Mina," he paused, "I just want to say thank you. Thank you for everything," Mina crouched down and planted a kiss on his forehead.

"Always," she whispered.

"Goodbye."

Then, Mina sprung up to leave. There was a somber understanding knit into her brow as she gave the pair one last look and bounded down the stairs. The both of them sat quietly for a moment, knowing they wouldn't see her again. Not any time soon at least. They heard her rev her bike and tear out of the driveway at an unwise speed.

Monty took a ragged breath, trying to push back his tears. A wave of cold white light washed over him as he felt his lungs heave. He coughed out a chunk of something bloody and coagulated, rolling forwards with Cameron's help to expectorate his insides onto the carpet.

"Shit," he groaned, wiping the corner of his mouth with a shaky hand. The looming totality of death caused him to shudder. His whole body was going cold. He felt something calling to him, willing him to close his eyes and give in.

"I think... my window to stay alive is closing pretty fast. I think you have to do it *now*." He proceeded to pull his necklace off, the silver hamsa digging into the yawning wound of his palm as he did so.

"This isn't living, you know. It's a hollow half-life as a starving ghost image of your former self. I will destroy your mortal soul if I do this to you... If I don't turn you at least... at least you can die now with your soul attached," Cameron sobbed.

"Fuck my soul!" Monty used the last of his strength to yank the muzzle free from their face, sending it flying down the steps with impressive force.

"I've made up my mind. Soul or not, I'm still *me* if I change. I've barely gotten a chance to live. I'm not ready to die. I'm not ready to leave you..." he added weakly as he could feel his mind beginning to slip away from him.

"Please, can you do this for me?" He asked, pulling them even closer. Cameron swallowed their tears and wiped their face clean.

"What if I can't do it? What if my blood doesn't take?"

"I'm gonna die either way, please, at least try," Monty closed his eyes, a sense of relief washed over him as darkness began to creep into his mind. He had no energy left to argue. What happened now was out of his control. He submitted fully to the sensation creeping over him, urging him to relax. Another role of whiteness pulled him further away from his thoughts and worries, like he was floating away in a lazy river.

"*Dio*," Cameron softly cursed under their breath.

Monty felt his body being moved gingerly into a darker corner of the hallway, away from the morning light. He felt Cameron lean down and slowly remove the bandage from his neck. They press their mouth slowly to his weakened pulse.

"I'm so sorry for how much this is going to hurt," they whispered against his skin.

They hesitated for a moment.

"I love you."

Then two sharp, hot fangs sunk deep into Monty's jugular, pumping hot poison directly into his heart. He had so much already in his body that the fresh wash of venom felt almost refreshing. They shakily restrained themself from drinking any of his meager remaining blood stores.

He wheezed as they pulled away, the wasp-like sting beginning to overtake him. Cameron hastily bit into their own wrist to spring forth their own depleted crimson flow. They shakily pressed their cold wrist to his lips.

"Drink," they whispered. He hesitated for a moment before he parted his lips and let their infected blood fall into his mouth. It was metallic and sweet, like wine. Every bit that passed his lips made him thirstier. The more he drank, the more he felt he needed.

A strange ache, a throbbing, began in his head and slowly cycled through his body. Without realizing he had greedily clutched their arm, gulping down full mouthfuls of their ichor.

"I'm sorry, I can't give you more," they said, prying their wrist from his gasping lips. He groaned with aching need as the burning throb in his veins grew unbearable. It felt like every atom in his body was being pulled apart. The pain of his injuries paled in comparison. He let out a cry of tormented agony as he writhed, an insatiable fever tearing through him.

His skin was on fire, being consumed by a sharp hunger that permeated through every fiber of his nervous system. He could feel every joint in his body, as if his skeleton was grinding against itself, mutating with poison filling every bit of marrow. His blood ran through him with a toxic acidity.

His heart collapsed in on itself into a black hole as its frantic beating began to slow. A void in his chest was opened, a chasm of darkness which weighed heavily on his lungs. It felt like all the air had been siphoned out of the world and his organs had been pulled into the vacuum of outer space. All the oxygen in his body was being burned, turned into hot black smoke. He was so consumed by the agony he forgot everything other than the feeling of his flesh forging itself back together in the pit of grotesque smog. Every molecule became something different, new and strange.

Suddenly air drew back into his lungs, his mind coming back to him. As quickly as it overcame him, the torturous feeling of his body reforming came to an end. There was a burning and wretched feeling in his chest, a kind of starvation that pulsated through him like a migraine. Other than this aching, he was no longer brutalized or dizzy. He found his faculties coming back to him. He realized the searing sensation is his abdomen and palms had dissipated. The sting of infection in his neck had ceased, and his nose was no longer congested with blood. Though he had been pulled back from the void, his body was frigged, as if it had not fully come back with him from the other side.

He managed to sit up. There was a sore looseness in his gums. He ran his tongue over the discomfort and felt, to his horror, something come loose. He spat out two of his own teeth from his mouth. When he went to feel for where they'd gone missing, he realized two razor-sharp fangs were poking through his gums as they slid in with a CLICK. The sensation caused him to shudder with disgust.

His eyes burned as he looked toward the light coming in

through the shattered stained glass. Everything felt as though it was being illuminated by ten suns. He wondered if Cameron's strength had passed to him as he stared at the blinding light. He hesitantly put a hand towards the sunlight. He'd expected his skin to boil, but no, it just felt like the sting of sunburn. Cameron grabbed his hand and swiftly moved it out of the light.

"Don't do that!" they panicked.

"It's fine, see." He held up his unharmed hand. They visibly relaxed.

"How do you feel?" They asked. He sat for a moment unsure what to say. He didn't know how to describe how he felt. It was alien. He could smell everything, Cameron, the dusty carpets of the old mansion, the dirt and grass outside, the chlorine in the pool, the leaves on the trees, Arianna's disgusting perfume lingering in her ash, blood on practically everything. He felt the pain of starvation pulsate through his core again at the smell of his own blood smeared on the carpet.

"Hungry," he said bluntly to Cameron, who gave him an understanding nod. They looked wrecked, run fully ragged and exhausted. Despite this, he could not help but find them as lovely as ever. For the first time, they looked real, solid, and alive to him.

"I know it must be painful. Can you hold on?" they asked, looking him over.

"Yes, I'm okay," as he spoke he felt as though a knife was being pried under his rib cage, causing him to wince.

"It's going to take a little to adjust," they explained. "There's still some blood-wine in the cellar, to at least take some of the edge off before we can get you a *proper* meal."

"Right," he nodded, "we both will be needing that now." He sighed, not ready to fully face the consequence of what they had just done. He was shocked at how clear of mind he was in this moment. He took another long, quiet moment to let his senses adjust. He listened to the birds calling in the trees and basked in the feeling of the daytime breeze coming through the shattered window. He felt more alive in this moment than he had in years.

"Thank you," he said softly to Cameron. Without warning, they pulled him into an embrace, holding him as tight as they could. After a long while, they pulled back and held him at arm's length. A cocktail of emotions washed across their tired face.

"I really do love you," they said, looking him over.

"I love you too," he replied and gently pulled them in. He finally closed the gap between them, kissing their blood-soaked mouths together deeply. He savored the sweetness of their lips that he so desired, their blood mixing together in perfect harmony.

# ACKNOWLEDGMENTS

This book started by accident back in 2022. After a brush with death, I found myself in dire need of a way to cope with the world around me. What started off as a silly—very self-indulgent—short story, slowly grew legs and ran away from me. After many years in development, I've learned a lot about writing, including how much it means to me as an art form. The fact that this book is in your hands today is a testament to the love and dedication of many people in my life who have championed me and my work. I could not have completed anything of this magnitude without their support these past few years. Queer love may not solve everything horrible in the world, but it sure makes the horrors a lot more bearable.

Thank you to my editor Morgan Cunningham, who taught me a lot about how to properly craft a decent horror story. I am eternally grateful for her help, not just with this manuscript, but also with undertaking the monumental task of keeping my sickly self alive. This book would not have been possible, nor would I be where I am today, without her help.

Thank you to Teigan Lukes, who not only helped me through two beta reading periods but also took the time to teach me how to graphic design properly.

A massive thank you to all my beta readers—Ramsey Miller, Slug, Fish Rose, Viktor, Sam, Nathan Passey, R. Lyons—I could not have finished this without all their help and feedback. I am eternally grateful for you all coming on this journey with me!

Last but not least, thank you, my reader, for what is a book without the reader? I could write endlessly, but if no one ever saw it, what would be the point? You make this a real, tangible story that lives in the world. Thank you!

# CONTENT WARNINGS

- Graphic depictions of death, murder, blood, and gore (this is a horror story after all).
- Graphic descriptions of insects, animals, and animal death (e.g. spiders, flies, snakes, coyotes).
- Mentions of suicide.
- Physical descriptions that may be triggering for those with eating disorders.
- Mentions of disordered eating.
- Graphic depictions of child abuse (including medical torture) and familial abuse.
- Homophobia and misgendering of non-binary characters.
- Violent acts directed at cis women, non-binary people, and queer men.
- Racist behavior and slurs (Arab and Romani).
- Alcohol and tobacco use.
- Explicit depictions of alcoholism.
- Explicit depictions of sex (consensual).
- Depictions of erotic behavior under the influence of alcohol.